'What do yo
excitement?'

'Oh. . .I suppos...
very *romantic*, i...
would like there to be?' Alice stood up and
came to him. Tilting her head, she gave him a
half-smile. 'I can see you cannot understand at
all what I mean. However, you are Henry's
advocate; pray state your case.'

She was laughing at him, he knew, in that
irritating way she had of turning every discussion into a light-hearted game. It occurred to
him that if she had been any other girl in this
secluded place he would have kissed her. . .

Dear Reader

As our gardens show signs of life, so we have the green
shoots of excellent reading for you. Sylvia Andrew has
another marvellous Regency heroine in SERAFINA,
and Laura Cassidy explores the tribulations of civil
war in A REMEMBERED LOVE. Laurel Ames gives
us Bristol 1818 in CASTAWAY, an unusual setting
for a Regency, and in THE NAKED HUNTRESS, by
Shirley Parenteau, Lyris is blackmailed into marriage.
Enjoy!

The Editor

Laura Cassidy followed careers in both publishing and
advertising before becoming a freelance writer when
her first son was born. She has since had numerous
short stories and articles published, as well as four
novels. She began writing for Legacy of Love after
discovering sixteenth-century romantic poetry, and very
much enjoys the research involved in writing in the
historical genre. She lives with her husband, who is a
creative consultant, and their two teenaged sons, near
London.

Recent titles by the same author:

MAIDEN COURT
THE BLACK PEARL

A REMEMBERED LOVE

Laura Cassidy

MILLS & BOON and ROSE DEVICE are trademarks of the publisher.

First published in Great Britain 1994
by Mills & Boon Limited

© Laura Cassidy 1994

Philippine Copyright 1994
This edition 1994

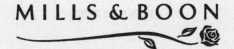

MILLS & BOON

MILLS & BOON LIMITED
ETON HOUSE, 18–24 PARADISE ROAD
RICHMOND, SURREY, TW9 1SR

MILLS & BOON, the Rose Device and LEGACY OF LOVE are trademarks of the publisher.

First published in Great Britain 1994 by Mills & Boon Limited

© Laura Cassidy 1994

Australian copyright 1994   Philippine copyright 1995 This edition 1995

ISBN 0 263 78992 6

Set in 10 on 11 pt Linotron Times 04-9502-94400

Typeset in Great Britain by Centracet, Cambridge Printed in Great Britain by BPC Paperbacks Ltd

CHAPTER ONE

IT WAS the summer of 1643 before the war between Royalist and Parliamentarian, which had engulfed England for more than a year, became personal to the three families who owned the estates which formed a three-pointed star around the village of Larkspur in the county of Kent.

The Carringtons, with their tradition of canny merchant-dealing, might have been expected to be in favour of the middle-class Oliver Cromwell's meteoric rise to prominence. The Rokesbys, with their ancient and silk-strong ties with the throne, might have been expected to support the King. But neither had declared themselves as yet, nor actively joined either cause. The third manor, owned by the gentle and unworldly couple Squire Richard and his lady Emma Ashley, was not seen to have a potential allegiance to either faction, unless it were to that which would be sure to protect the easy and pleasant life they were accustomed to.

There was a young person in each of the three manors: Henry Carrington of Fox Hall, Christopher Rokesby of Oaks, and Alice Ashley of Ashley Manor. The two boys were both eighteen in this year, Alice two years younger. All had been fast friends since early childhood, all had uncannily similar histories, for they had lost their natural parents in their young years and been brought up by elderly relatives, and all had good looks and distinctive personalities.

Walter Carrington, Henry's uncle, was a bluff choleric man, unimaginative and guileless. His nephew, tall and thin and blessed with the Carrington red hair but not the hot temper to match, was thoughtful and

5

cautious and slow-talking. Had blood ties not decided these affairs, both boys would have been happy to exchange their guardians. Then the mercurial Chris Rokesby, with his love of the land and instinctive understanding of all living creatures both animal and human, could have ridden the estate with jolly Walter—who had a soft spot for all wild young things—and Henry could have sat with Chris's elderly cousin, William Rokesby—who had been Cambridge-educated—and discussed dry intellectual matters; both in these roles would have been content. Unfortunately, life was never that orderly.

Alice Ashley would have fitted most comfortably into either of the households of her friends, for she was supremely adaptable. If necessary she could have been an excellent hostess to the Carringtons' undemanding, hard-riding, hard-drinking guests, excellent future mistress to their dutiful servants and kind mentor to their subdued tenant farmers. Equally, she could have satisfied Will Rokesby's demand that any relatives of his apply themselves to duty and learning, for she had an acutely intelligent mind and an unbecomingly masculine grasp of all matters financial. As it was, Alice was the mainstay of Ashley Manor, gently propping up her uncle's ineffectual pursuits.

On this perfect summer evening she had been sixteen years old for the whole of the hot golden day, and was in her room putting the final touches to her toilette before going down to receive her guests.

It was the custom in the three manors to gather together each year to celebrate the birthdays of their young people, and the Carringtons and the Rokesbys had been bidden to Ashley tonight for supper and Alice wished to appear her best for the occasion.

She washed in the rainwater that her maid had brought for her, then carefully put on the dress made especially for this evening. It was not entirely to her

taste, for fashion at the moment delcared that ladies'
gowns be depressingly plain. The Puritan influence
decreed that necklines were modestly high, sleeves
narrow and finished with only an inch of lace, and that
there be so little material in the skirts that ladies were
incapable of making the delightful shushing sound that
the feminine Alice so admired. The whole costume was
made from one of the new colours too—a subdued
cinnamon-brown.

'You look beautiful, Miss Alice,' her maid assured
her. The truth was that Betty Mote thought her mistress
beautiful in any dress. Even her mannishly cut velvet
riding habit, or an old print cotton dress, with its skirts
looped up over shapely ankles as she moved about the
stable-yard caring for her beloved horses. Betty had
been born in Bude in Cornwall, Alice's father's home, a
few years before her young mistress, and when Alice's
parents had been tragically taken by the summer sickness ten years earlier both little girls had held hands on
the bumpy ride to their new home in Kent. They had
been more friends than mistress and servant ever since.

'Thank you.' Alice looked thoughtfully into her glass.
Was she beautiful? Certainly there was little to be seen
of the exquisitely pretty subject of the tiny miniature she
had brought with her from Cornwall, and which now
hung from its gold chain on the wall of Uncle Richard's
study. That child had been rounded, pink and white of
face, with large blue eyes and a waterfall of dazzling fair
hair. The girl reflected tonight had a pale oval face, a
square and determined chin, a straight little nose, and
hair still luxuriant and glossy, but now of a very unusual
colour—in some lights a glinting brown, in others the
dark red seen in a newly husked horse-chestnut. Only
the eyes were the same: candid, and blue-grey as a
robin's egg.

'Are you lookin' to see if the extra year has added a
few lines?' Betty asked teasingly.

'No,' sighed Alice, 'I am looking to see if I have acquired a little more sense.'

Betty smiled and reached for the flask of gillyflower scent. She sprinkled a few drops on her palms and ran her fingers through Alice's hair, before drawing it back and fastening the circlet of pearls which allowed a fall of ringlets. Many ladies now wore the enveloping hood of stiff linen which hid most of their hair, but Alice refused to have anything to do with this hideous innovation. Betty stood back appraisingly.

'He'll ask you again tonight, you know.'

'I know.' Alice cupped her chin in one hand and sighed again. Henry Carrington had been asking her to marry him for a year now. Indeed, it was generally accepted among the three families that the marriage would certainly come about. Henry wanted it, his uncle wanted it, Alice's aunt and uncle were very much in favour of it, but still she could not make up her mind to make the situation formal.

'He has everything to make you happy,' Betty declared. 'The Carringtons are the richest folk in these parts and you have known the young man nearly all your life.'

'Perhaps that is the problem,' Alice said moodily. 'I *have* known him all my life. There is little excitement in that.'

'Excitement has no part in marriage,' Betty said sturdily. 'And, lovely though you are, and should have at least a hundred proposals to think on, there is a dear lack of young men around here.'

It was true. Henry Carrington and Christopher Rokesby were the only two elegible men for a twenty-mile span around Larkspur. It was, if the two girls having this conversation in the cosy room reflecting the last of the sun had but known it, the reason why the turmoil in England had hardly touched their lives.

All over England young men were choosing sides

now, breaking their mothers' hearts, making their
fathers alternately proud and fearful. The proud male
youth of England were riding off from their homes clad
in Cavalier silk and velvet, or the blood-red of Puritan
homespun. This war, as any other, was of the old men's
making, but it was the young who had to do the fighting,
had to die or limp away from the battlefields of Edgehill
or Newbury. It was their families who had to suffer the
loss of their sons, and the consequences of publicly
supporting King or Parliament.

'But what are you waiting for?' Betty frowned. 'I
can't see that it matters a whole lot if he asked you first
when you were fourteen. It only shows how steady he
is.'

'I know, I know.' Alice rose from her little cushioned
stool before the dressing-table. She smoothed her skirts.
Betty could not understand her hesitation, and that was
hardly surprising. And yet. . . The Carringtons were
very wealthy, Fox Hall was the grandest manor in this
part of Kent, and, even without his expected inheritance
from his Uncle Walter, Henry was rich in his own
right—or would be—for his father had been a merchant
with interests in the Americas and in the far Dutch West
Indies with their sought-after and costly harvest of
spices. Henry's gold was in trust for him, to be claimed
on his majority or upon his betrothal, and he was kind
and steady and handsome. And yet. . .

She said, 'Well, I suppose I must go down now.'

As she descended the stairs into the hall the porch
door swung open and the first guest arrived. Alice
looked down at Christopher Rokesby's black head with
affection and irritation mingled. He has made no effort
to dress for the occasion, she thought. Christopher wore
well-seasoned soft leather breeches, an old velvet coat,
several fashions departed, a linen shirt adorned with
torn ruffles of lace and muddy riding-boots. He crossed
the hall, looked up and saw her.

'Alice—you must forgive my unorthodox attire,' he said with his charming smile. 'I was well aware of this engagement tonight, but thought I just had time to visit one of the outlying farms. As I rode home it occurred to me that I could proceed to Oaks and change, but would then be lamentably late coming here. So I decided to waive the formalities and be first to wish you joy on your anniversary.' He took her hand and kissed it as she reached the bottom step. 'I also have no gift for you—it is still at home in my room.'

'Never mind, Chris,' Alice said cheerfully. 'The thought was there, I have no doubt. However, before anyone else arrives, I think you might like to make use of one of the guest chambers to—er—titivate a little.'

Chris ran a hand over his hair. He wore it long, in imitation of the King—as was still the fashion of the day, even though many men had lately submitted to the short cut favoured by government supporters. It was this style of hairdressing which had caused them to be termed 'Roundheads' by a laughing Queen, on viewing a section of government soldiers drilling. Chris Rokesby's hair was naturally curly and thick, and needed none of the artificial aids other gentlemen of his class employed. Nor would he have resorted to them if it did; he was almost perversely non-conformist, never following any set rule, and already had a reputation for speaking and doing the unexpected. 'Am I a little wild-looking?' he enquired in consternation. 'There is a brisk wind today, despite the heat, but I have no wish to shame the celebration.'

'You could never do that. . . Ah, Betty, please take Master Chris away, and——'

'Clean him up,' Betty supplied, with the familiarity of an old and trusted friend. As children she and Chris Rokesby had had many a battle—and not always only verbal—before they had grown up and taken their respective positions in life. There remained between them an affection which Chris seemed to inspire in any who spent time in his company. The two disappeared into the library behind the stairs, which Richard Ashley kept as his own special place for reading and writing and—mostly—just daydreaming.

Alice proceeded into the many-windowed hall with its comfortable settles and broad fire hearth—unlit tonight, but garnished with fresh flowers—to overlook the table. She walked slowly around it, noting the glittering silver and Florentine glassware, the dazzling napery and the blaze of wax candles in well-polished silver candlesticks. Richard Ashley had never been wealthy—he was a younger brother, and the older Ashley son, Alice's father, Robert, had inherited the family estate in the west and the Ashley fortune had been greatly diminished at the time of his death—but he had travelled extensively and brought home interesting treasures. Alice, who loved the delicate wall-hangings of silk brought from the Orient, the Italian wine goblets, the French rosewood tables and chairs, took enormous pride in keeping them, and the house, in perfect order.

On the highly glossed court cupboard she found good red wine and helped herself. Sipping it, she glanced over her shoulder out of the windows to see the three Carringtons riding up the drive. She watched Walter dismount heavily, Henry spring lightly from the saddle, the dying sun burnishing his coppery head, then both men carefully help Mary Carrington from her perch. Alice went to the door and opened it.

If Chris Rokesby's efforts on her special night had been less than pefect, the Carringtons did not disappoint her. Both men were clad in smooth, fine silk breeches and short coats, severe in cut but enhanced by a froth of Flemish lace at breast and cuff, sparkling white stockings and mirror-bright leather slippers. Mary wore a gown of sumptuous maroon satin, also plain in design, but she had not been able to resist enlivening it with all the jewels she possessed. Alice smiled radiantly and extended her hand to Walter.

'Dear Uncle Walter, how happy I am to see you.' She turned to Mary and planted a kiss on her flushed cheek, and then turned back into the hall, where she gave Mary over to a maid who bore her away to remove her cloak and help rearrange her complicated toilette. She gave each of the men a glass of wine, and Walter took his and sank into a chair by the hearth. He was not getting any younger and any ride, no matter how short, was rather an effort for him these days.

Henry laid a hand on Alice's arm to prevent her joining him. 'I wish you all joy on this day, Alice,' he said, putting down his untouched wine and sliding his hand down so he could grasp her wrist.

'Thank you, Henry.' As always she was a little uncomfortable when he touched her. Why this should be so, she could not have said, for she was by nature demonstrative in her affections, and she was so very fond of him. . .

He reached into his coat and took out a little leather box. 'Here is your gift.' He sprang the catch and the light from the candles immediately flared within the large stones of the ring.

Alice said, 'Henry! It is beautiful. . . But, for me?'

'Yes, indeed.' He removed the circlet of gold and rubies and, taking her left hand, began to slide it on to the third finger. Instinctively she doubled her fingers into her palm.

'It is very beautiful, but—it is the betrothal ring your mother wore, is it not? I remember your showing it to me once.'

'It is the same,' he agreed. 'And I offer it to you tonight for the same purpose.'

'Henry——' Alice glanced at Walter, who was gazing into his glass '—now is not the time—nor have we fully discussed the matter.'

Henry turned her around to face him. 'We have been discussing it for a year now, sweetheart. If you are refusing me, very well; I can accept that. But this dithering is no good for either of us.'

Alice looked reluctantly into his face. His eyes, dark brown and steady, held hers. 'I have asked you,' he went on, 'not once, but many times. Tonight you must give me your answer.'

'This is not fair,' she murmured. She could hear the sound of hooves on the drive; Chris's cousins were arriving. On the gallery above she could hear footsteps as her aunt and uncle came down to join the party.

'Answer me,' Henry insisted.

'I——'

Another moment and she would have allowed him to place the ring on her finger, but the library door opened and Chris came out and swiftly across the hall. He gave no sign that he understood the significance of the scene being played out between his two friends, nor did he acknowledge the glance that Alice flashed him—which might have been a plea for help—but he broke the spell by putting an affectionate arm around Henry and drawing him aside and over to the window, saying, 'Hal—I need your advice. Listen——'

If he had not come just then, Henry thought bitterly. If he had not been there—— But Chris was always there whenever he felt he had Alice on the point of acceptance—at least that was so just lately. Was it intentional? Henry studied his friend's strong profile in the last effort of the sinking sun. They had all three been friends for so long—in fact Henry could not remember a time when Chris and Alice had not been there to argue with him, care for him, support him.

At what point in time his friendship with Alice had changed into something else, something more compelling, he could not have said, but it had, and once the thought was there—as usual for him—it refused to be dislodged. For the first time he realised tonight that he had never discussed this new feeling with Chris, never mentioned the depth of his new emotion towards Alice. That was strange, he thought, puzzled, for no matter, small or large, had ever not been talked over between them.

Chris paused in what he was saying. 'What are you staring at?' he enquired. 'If it is my dress, I apologise to you, as I have to Alice, and will to her aunt—I simply did not have time to prink before my glass as you apparently did.' He flicked an irreverent finger under the bright fall of lace on his friend's breast.

Henry laughed. 'No, 'tis not your refusal to make yourself presentable; I am used to that. No, I was thinking on something else.'

'So? Tell me.'

Alice's gift from her aunt that morning had been a floppy-eared puppy, a so-called King Charles spaniel, very popular among ladies as lap-dogs. It had succeeded in losing itself beneath Aunt Mary's voluminous skirts and Alice, anxious to help but convulsed with laughter, knelt a moment and lifted the rich material to try to coax it out.

Henry said, 'I was asking Alice to be my wife when you interrupted us. It is not the first time, but I believe she was about to say yes.'

Chris considered this, his eyes on the laughing girl.

'What? You don't approve?' Henry asked.

'Why should you think that?'

'Well, do you, or don't you?'

'Is my approval necessary? Presumably you first applied to Richard Ashley.'

Henry fumbled with his watch-fob. The watch had been his father's and was rather ornate in design—not entirely fitting to Henry's new ideas of suitable decoration. 'No, I haven't done that yet.'

'Dear me, and you are usually so precise as to etiquette.'

'Please don't joke about this—it is too important to me. You and I both know that they—Richard and Emma—will agree to anything if Alice does. It might help her to make up her mind if you support me.'

Chris raised an eyebrow. 'I cannot remember any occasion when she has accepted advice from me.'

'Knowing you are for the match may tip the balance. So, I am asking you, are you?'

'No, I am not sure that I am.'

Colour rose in Henry's fair face. 'What do you mean, not sure? Don't you want her to be happy?'

'Of course I do! I also want you to be in that pleasant state.'

'But, man, I have always wanted her! I think before even I could identify what it was I felt.'

'Then let her decide without coercion—from anyone, including myself. To say she changes her mind as the wind changes course is to understate the case. But once that mind is made up, without pressure from outside, she will be constant as dye.' He paused, wondering why he should say all this, why he was so sure it was so, then went on, 'After all, what is the hurry in this? You are but eighteen, she fifteen.'

'Sixteen. . . There is more to it than just our marriage,' Henry muttered. 'You know—you have always known—that I obtain my majority on my wedding-day in terms of my inheritance. And before that, on my official betrothal, I have access to those monies left in trust for me.'

'You will have access in a year or so whatever. Why in such haste for it now?'

Henry was silent.

'You cannot ask for my help in this without telling me the whole story,' Chris pointed out. 'You have a

comfortable life, have you not? Your Uncle Walter is
generosity itself——'

'It is not the same as having one's own gold,' Henry
interrupted. 'Certainly Uncle Walter indulges me, but
only as he chooses. If I had my own money. . .'

'You would raise a private army and join Parliament's
ranks?' Chris enquired bluntly.

'You know it is my dearest wish. It is a cause worth
fighting for, and I am committed to it.'

Chris looked out over the darkening gardens. Alice
was a talented gardener—each bed had its riot of late
blooms and the climbing rose just below the open
windows gave off its heady scent. He did not reply.

'Which side are you committed to?' Henry asked
curiously. 'You have never actually said in all our
heated discussions.'

'I have not yet decided,' Chris said slowly. 'Like
Alice, I have not yet made up my mind.'

'Alice!' Henry smiled indulgently. 'She has no need
to disturb her mind over such issues—I have heard her
argue in turn for both factions.'

'Don't underestimate her,' Chris said quietly.

'You are the one who does that.' Henry smiled. 'You
taunt her constantly about her changeful ways.'

'Perhaps such taunting clears the way to constructive
thought,' Chris returned lightly. Yes, he had always
enjoyed teasing Alice Ashley. She was not like any of
the other young ladies he had met in civilised manor
halls, who simpered and tossed their hair and indicated
that any serious subject was only a matter for gentlemen. Alice said what she thought—always, even if what
she thought was different each time she spoke.

'Chris,' Henry said seriously. 'If what I wish comes
about and I can. . . If I do manage to raise that private
army you spoke of, I would greatly like you to be a part
of it.'

'Me?' Chris grinned. 'Me, in the ranks of such as

Cromwell, who I hear demands little short of sainthood from his troops? Do you think he would have me?'

'I would have you,' Henry said stolidly. 'You would be a good man to have on our side in a fight.' He meant it. Chris would never pick a fight, but nor would he walk away from one and, young males being as they were, had had plenty of scraps in the past, always regretted by whoever had begun them with young Rokesby.

Chris smiled wryly. He knew what Henry was thinking, and appreciated the compliment. He also thought that Henry had no idea of what he was talking about. *He* did. A little over a year ago his cousin Will had sent him with two horses to deliver to a farm on the far side of Canterbury. On the journey Chris had been unlucky enough to be set upon by two gypsies, intent on relieving him of the fine horseflesh. In the ensuing tussle Chris had killed one of them before making good his escape, and had regretted the incident ever since. He could still feel the hot anger he had felt on engagement, still feel the shock and horror when he had left another human being—little older than himself—on the road, his unseeing eyes open under the April skies. Killing was a desperate business, Chris thought, and killing one's fellow Englishmen even more desperate. 'If you ask me so particularly,' he said, after a moment's silence, 'I will talk with Alice about your proposal.'

'You have no feeling for her yourself?' Henry demanded suddenly, having watched the changeful expression on his friend's face. 'Other than friendship? If you do——'

'If I do, what?'

'I would take it amiss,' Henry said heavily. 'Your reputation in that area is growing, and you obtain it with no reputable lady.'

Chris laughed. 'Careful, my friend, your Puritan streak is growing wider by the day. You will fit well with the New Model Army, I believe.'

'I hope so,' Henry replied composedly. 'But, as to Alice?'

Chris rested his blue eyes thoughtfully on Alice, who had succeeded in retrieving the puppy from its hiding place and now allowed it to caress her face with an eager pink tongue. 'As to Alice? She is my friend. Should she suddenly become of interest to me in any other way, you will be the first to hear it from me. I promise.'

Later that night, when the party was pleasantly full with the excellent meal it had consumed, and agreeably tipsy on the free-flowing wine, Chris invited Alice to take a turn about the gardens. Anxious for a little fresh air—as it was an informal occasion all three older men had lit their pipes, and their smoke, mixed with the lingering savoury smells, made the atmosphere in the hall stale and heavy—she agreed.

Out in the cool night she showed Chris several new plants she had acquired. Two were doing well, having adapted themselves to alien soil in a country far from their birth, but the third drooped and wilted in its new home.

'What is it called?' Chris asked, touching the sad blooms with one forefinger.

''Tis mimosa. I admired it while visiting Kate Sidney at Penshurst last year, and she asked her steward to send me a cutting.' Alice frowned. 'It is from France, I believe, from the south, and was growing on one of the sunny walls at Penshurst—so pretty that it made me think of a waterfall of yellow. I have tried to duplicate its position but with little success.'

'Hmm.' Chris studied the poor specimen. More than anyone Alice knew Chris shared her love for growing things, both vegetable and human—there was no one more reliable than him for consulting on some malaise in the animals on the Ashley estate, no one who took more interest in the crops of field and orchard. 'Perhaps if it survives the winter it will do better in the spring.'

'I hope so. Shall you wish to go any further? It is cold after the heat of the hall.'

'No. . . At least, let us sit in the vinery for a moment.' He led the way into the covered wooden framework, where Alice and her head gardener were coaxing along the bounty of translucent green grapes which were a great favourite at Ashley. Enclosed, this area was a pleasant place to sit on cooler days and look at the view beyond the rose garden. Alice and Emma often passed the mornings here with their needlework.

Alice sat down on one of the wooden benches. It was not very dark in here, for the moon was full tonight and cast its light through the clusters of fruit, producing an oddly soothing green haze. Chris propped one shoulder against the vine trunk, which was as sturdy and thick as a man's thigh. 'I wanted,' he said, 'to have a talk with you, Alice.'

'How unusual,' she teased him. 'You usually say I talk far too much.'

'Yes, well, on this occasion I shall do the talking. About Hal.'

'Oh. . .' Unaccountably she was disappointed, and wondered why.

'He has told me of his proposal, and asked me to— to——'

'To extract an answer where he could not?'

'Hush. Let us not begin sparring immediately. I only wish to say that you could find no better man, no more steady and caring man, were you to wait forever. Also, he is wealthy, with expectations of greater wealth in the future.'

'I know all that. However, perhaps I do not look only for riches—there must be more than that, or so I feel.'

'There is more than that. As I have said, you could hope for no more worthy husband.'

'Worthy. . .' Alice plaited her fingers on her lap, admiring the way the milky light played over them. 'Does it seem to you, though, that when one is married one should feel a certain joy and—and excitement? Henry, dear though he is to me, does not inspire that feeling.'

Excitement? Chris looked more attentively at her. What he had said to Henry earlier, about giving Alice time to make up her mind, had been good advice, he thought. The Alice he knew was indeed changeable, and he wanted his friend to be sure he did not take a capricious child to wife. What she had just said added a new dimension to the girl he thought he knew. So she wanted excitement, did she? he thought, amused. With no idea at all of what that might mean between a man and a woman, Chris was sure. Alice always had her head in some book or other. Presumably she had picked up this notion from between the pages of one of these. Why, then, he puzzled, did her words bring an instant response from some secret place within him? It was no more than a flicker, akin to the darting flash of light silver fish made deep beneath the waters of the dark Medway, but he paused a moment to consider Alice afresh.

She was beautiful, yes, even so young and still with the bloom of childhood on her, and intelligent too, for years ago, during a plague of sickness in the area, Walter Carrington had thought it sensible to gather all three children together at Fox Hall for their lessons. Chris and Henry had been attending the local school for boys—and harsh and exacting it had been—Alice a sedate emporium for young ladies. Brought together in the library at Fox, with a thin young man as tutor, the three had vied with each other for position. At least, Chris and Alice had locked intellectual horns; Henry had sat back and attempted to keep the peace. But there were other qualities to Alice, Chris thought now.

Courage—what other slim young girl would have dared to mount and tame some of the unruly horses stabled at Ashley? Loyalty—oh, in abundance, for once she gave it to another she never reviewed that allegiance. Her loyalty was absolute in the case of the two neighbouring boys, as well as the rest of her few friends, her sweet and incompetent aunt and uncle, and a number of spirited horses and a quite vicious hound-dog that she was patiently sure would one day cease trying to savage every other creature in the universe.

Alice was like the little Russian toy Richard Ashley had acquired in his youthful travels: a wooden painted doll, containing another wooden painted doll, containing another—and so on, until one found the small, secret tiniest doll of all.

The silence had lengthened between them and Alice looked up enquiringly. 'What do you mean by excitement?' Chris asked.

'Oh. . . I suppose I mean romance. For 'tis not very *romantic*, is it? The arrangement Henry would like there to be?' She stood up and came to him. Tilting her head, she gave him a half-smile. 'I can see you cannot understand at all what I mean. However, you are Henry's advocate; pray state your case.'

She was laughing at him, he knew, in that irritating way she had of turning every discussion into a light-hearted game. It occurred to him that if she had been any other girl, in this secluded place and with the perfume she wore exciting his senses, he would have kissed her. . . He said stiffly, 'I am not his advocate, in fact I advised him to wait for you to grow up a little, for fear he would marry a woman and find he had acquired a child.'

She laughed. He had often thought that were he to hear that laugh in a crowd of a hundred strong he would know it for hers—it was distinctively joyous and unrestrained. 'And you don't like children, do you? At least the—er—ladies you spend your leisure with could not be described as anything but mature.'

Chris flushed. His latest mistress was Molly Judd, daughter of the landlord of the Evening Sun—several years his senior, but as warm and generous a companion as any man could wish for. He did not reply.

'Well,' Alice said, 'you won't speak of such affairs to a lady, I am sure.'

'No lady would have raised the matter in the first place!'

'Oh, come now, you did say we should not begin to argue tonight.'

'I did not begin the argument. . . But I resent your raising a subject which is obviously only my business.'

'Quite so. Now apply that thinking to yourself!'

He said impatiently, 'Hal asked me to.'

'And I ask you not to! When, or if, I want your advice—or anyone's—I shall ask for it.' She said the last very deliberately.

'Yes. . . Well. . . Of course, I accept that. But,' he added awkwardly, 'as to your comments about—romance, may I just say this? Such a feeling goes away, quite quickly, I think, and then one is left with whatever else there is that you have in common. It would seem prudent to be sure that there is a great deal of this other.' This interview had not gone in the way he had expected. He had thought to put Hal's suit sincerely—for he truly cared for his friend's future—but now he thought, 'Tis Alice's future too, and—and——

Alice was looking at him curiously. 'Are you speaking from experience?'

He hesitated, then, 'Yes. I am.'

'And it went away, what you felt for. . .her? At what point?'

At the point when she told me quite clearly that I was not rich enough for her, he thought bitterly. But thank God it had, for within a twelvemonth Chloe

Lammington had ruined the good man she had accepted, and now he could barely recall the hold she had had upon him. Certainly he felt no fondness for her, only a remembrance of the fever induced by the swing of her shining fair hair, the movement of her body, whose curves had not quite been hidden by her demure gowns.

'Chris?'

'Oh, there were difficulties.'

'How strange that I never knew of this,' she said reflectively. 'I thought I knew *all* about you.'

'No one knows all about any other person—or indeed all about themselves. However, you don't want my advice, but I have tried to my best for Hal. Let us go in now, before your uncle feels he must ask for my intentions.'

As they followed the path around to the back door of the manor Alice paused, and laid a hand on his arm. 'Chris, are you still sad about this lady?'

'No. I told you—it went quite quickly, whatever feeling I had.'

'And there has been no one else you cared for in that way?'

He took her hand and raised it to his lips. 'You can't have all my secrets, you know, Alice, even if it is your birthday. But just this once—no, there has been no one else. And I am glad enough for that, for it hurts, this romance you hanker after.'

He had shaved that morning, for he was one of the new breed of young men who did not favour a full beard or even the more fashionable moustache, but already she could feel the strong new growth above and below the smooth lips. 'I don't like to think of your being sad,' she said slowly.

'Well, you don't have to,' he replied lightly. He released her hand and took her back into the lighted house.

* * *

The rest of the evening progressed pleasantly enough. Alice was yawning by midnight, and longing for her bed when her uncle produced another bottle of port—for the journey, he said—and filled the glasses again. Alice watched the wine go round with irritation. She thought everyone had had quite enough, and it was her birthday after all and she wished to retire. She sat with the puppy asleep on her lap, its ruffled belly exposed, mouth wide open to reveal sharp white teeth, and willed the party to end.

'Hmm.' Walter put down his glass eventually and stretched. 'I think we must be going, m'dear.' His wife prepared to rise. Solidly put together beneath her gown, she found it an effort to get herself out of the comfortable chair. Before she could accomplish it, Walter said reflectively, 'I have had the commissar on my doorstep again, Will—he invited me to sell him horses, but his manner suggested that it would be in order for me to *give* the creatures to Parliament.'

'Jonas Spragg? Was that the man who called?'

'It was. Ridiculous name! Why do they all have such odd names?'

'One cannot help the name one is born with,' Henry put in.

Richard went around with the port bottle again. He said, 'He came to me as well, but it was men he wanted, not horses.'

Alice frowned. 'Why, Uncle Richard, you made no mention to me of this. What did you say to him?'

'I said that my tenants would decide for themselves if and when they committed themselves to leaving their families to go a-soldiering.'

'Well,' conceded Alice, 'that was the right thing to say.'

William said heavily, 'It was volunteers he came to Oaks for, too.'

'What answer did you give?' Henry enquired. His

manner was still casual but Alice sensed that he was suddenly very attentive to the turn the conversation had taken.

'I had no chance to say anything,' William said mildly. 'For Chris threw him and his three hobbledehoys out—and set the dogs on them for good measure.'

The party exclaimed. The older women looked worried, the older men doubtful.

'That was ill-considered, Chris,' Henry said.

'It probably was,' agreed Chris. He had taken a seat at the windows and the vivid crimson of the drapes accentuated his dark head. 'But it was an instinctive move. I'll have no one suborning my men and preaching treason.'

'Treason?' Henry turned in his chair to stare at him. 'Parliament is for the people—it *is* the people—a duly elected body which upholds the law of the land. How can what its representatives say be treason?'

'They oppose the King,' Chris said quietly. 'Treachery is the word for what Parliament has been about for these past two years, howsoever you dress it up in terms of keeping the law.'

'I think,' Alice said, 'that each should make up their own mind about this.'

'That is what you think, is it?' Chris turned on her. 'And how might men like Peter and Paul, my shepherds, who can neither read nor write, make up their minds whether to go forth and kill their brothers, John and Silas, my stockmen? Both pairs have listened to the different sides, been partially convinced, but not one of the four knows the whole argument.'

There was an uncomfortable silence. Walter Carrington broke it. 'Hrumph! I really think it is time we were leaving now. Mary, Henry——'

'But you will give them your opinion, eh?' Henry said, ignoring his uncle. 'And, knowing and loving you, all four men will choose what *you* choose. Tell me, how is that knowing the whole argument?'

'I shall not give my opinion,' Chris said hotly. 'But, if I should, 'twould be this: stay home and raise your families and work your land. The land is about all that will be left when Parliament and Royalist have finished killing each other. And I might say that I find your remarks nothing short of hypocrisy, Hal, when 'tis well known that you have instructed your own men which side to choose if they wish their leases renewed on Lady Day!'

'Chris, Chris,' William murmured. 'This is not the occasion for such words.'

'Why not? We are all friends together, of more than a decade. Why not speak candidly? If there were more talk and less action, perhaps England would be in agreement without bloodshed.'

'Parliament has presented its resolution for the dispute time and time again,' Henry said with cold clarity. 'And has been ignored by its anointed sovereign—time and time again.'

'Enough, my boy,' Walter said. 'Mary—pray collect your cloak, and we will bid Richard and Emma goodnight and wish Alice once again a happy birthday.' He rose with finality.

Alice got to her feet. She tucked her pet under her arm and went to the door to see her guests away. She was beginning to think that she did not know either of her childhood friends; certainly she had seen them both in rages before—the volatile Chris had often teased and provoked Henry into a show of stolid anger—but never before had she seen such passionate partisanship on both sides. It appeared to her now that they had both taken the leap into manhood without her noticing.

'Something else I never knew about you,' she murmured to Chris as she followed him out to the stable-yard.

'And what is that?' He was calm now, but his eyes were still a bright shining blue.

'That you are a Royalist.'

'Did I say that?' he demanded. 'I did not! I said only that I think all men should be free to make up their own minds about what is worth dying for.'

When his handsome mare was brought Alice fingered the grey mane. 'Making up one's mind is the problem, I suspect. I have known for a long time to be sure which road Henry intends to take, but I don't know about you. Nor, I think, do *you* know about you.'

'True words, little Alice. Civil war is a horrible thing. There is such a small division between one man and another of the same race. Yet, in this, friends, even brothers, hold opposing views. Can you imagine anything more terrible? To have to take arms against one's brother? One's friend?'

'You may have to do just that,' she said quietly, 'if you truly believe what you have said tonight.'

Chris glanced over at Henry, assisting his aunt into the saddle. The lady was not at any time an able horsewoman and after an evening of rich food and wine the sight of her attempting to mount a tired and irritable horse was quite comical. He had, however, no desire to laugh, was in fact a little disconcerted about his words earlier. Like Alice, he had not known that he felt so strongly one way or the other. Now he suspected that the thing must be thought of, decided upon. He mounted, then hesitated, gripping the reins. He said abruptly, 'If Henry should get his heart's desire and marry with you, he will have almost unlimited means to put behind what he believes in.'

'I know that,' she said composedly.

'Do you?'

'Of course. I have taken the trouble to find out that Henry will come into his fortune the day I accept him formally in marriage. I know quite well where a proportion of that money will go.' She gave him a mocking smile. 'Perhaps you think that is why he is so eager to extract my promise to wed him.'

'I don't think that. Any man would be proud to win you.'

'I have wrung a compliment out of you at last; this night has been a revelation in more ways than one.' She stood back as he turned his horse's head. She looked up at him. 'Friends may ask favours, isn't that so, Chris?'

He nodded, the moonlight full on his face.

'Then promise me you will not go to war without saying goodbye to me.'

He bent in the saddle to brush his lips against her face. 'I promise.' He moved away and Alice turned to bid farewell to the rest of her guests.

CHAPTER TWO

As the year turned full circle and Alice again began to contemplate her birthday celebrations, she wondered how the war had ever seemed less than very personal to the three families of Larkspur. For the last eleven months had seen great changes in the sleepy rural area.

Kent had been Royalist when the King raised his standard at Nottingham in 1642 and Parliamentarian a year later, following the military expedition dispatched there from Westminster. It was now partisan indeed to the government. Henry no longer spoke only in private of his convictions, and was lauded for them by most of the gentry who followed the lead of a growing number of neighbouring counties.

London—official London—had begun the conflict behind the throne, but by August '43, when the House of Commons impeached the Royalist Lord Mayor, the capital threw its weight solidly behind the government and remained so. Oxford was now the Royalist capital, for the King had ridden there at the head of his victorious army following the triumph of Edgehill and established his wartime court within its city walls.

Newsletters flooded out from both strongholds, keeping even the far-flung places informed. Alice read these blurred missives with a puckered brow. She had a naturally receptive mind for information and could see that Parliament had learned its lesson well from disasters at the start of hostilities. They had sent troops to Edgehill and Newbury poorly trained, poorly equipped and lacking in discipline. They had been no match for the King's armies, composed mainly of the sons of gentlemen, schooled from boyhood in the art of war-

29

fare, and had been duly routed. Now that tide was turning. More and more was heard of the meteoric rise to power of the Huntingdonshire squire, Oliver Cromwell. A minor force in the Long Parliament before the outbreak of war, now a combination of circumstances had produced in him extraordinary qualities of determination and leadership. His New Model Army, with its rigidly drilled batallions, its newly acquired weapons, its men bolstered by a code of behaviour instilled by Puritanical commanders, had come of age.

Of course the Crown had its high cards in the deadly game; few Roundheads could resist an assault led by the dashing Prince Rupert's Bluecoats, and the King had loyal commanders in Hopton and Montrose and half a dozen others, but increasingly their regiments were facing a united army of stolid farmers turned soldiers, who believed they had God on their side.

Alice had her own problems at Ashley. Her uncle had held to his belief that none of his men would be forced into service against their will, and some had decided to keep out of the fight under either flag. But many went and Alice, increasingly taking the responsibility for the day-to-day running of the estate out of her uncle's fumbling hands, was growing used to the young men roused by bugle and drum coming cap in hand to bid her goodbye.

To each she said the same words: 'Very well, Wat——' or John, or Thomas '—if you have truly thought on it, and still wish to go, then do so, and may God go with you. When 'tis over, come back to Ashley.' She remained inscrutable whichever side the man had chosen, but noted that most rode, or walked away wearing the red of the Roundhead army.

Struggling to keep the land husbanded with half the amount of labour, she was frustrated by the knowledge that Ashley—like every other estate now in England—had become a larder for the government army. Scarcely a week went by without a representative arriving to request a portion of what was produced.

She also had the added pressure that Henry Carrington put upon her. He had relentlessly pursued her since the New Year—riding over twice a week and using all his slow powers of persuasion to get her to accept the proposal offered the summer before. He was never harsh in his tactics, never bullying, and his unfailing kindness, with advice and encouragement in her running of the estate, made her realise afresh what a sterling man he was. There were times, she admitted to herself, when she finally gained her bed at night, when it would have been a relief to lay her head on his shoulder and say, Yes, Henry, I will marry you, and so give up the whole muddle that Ashley had become. What held her back? she wondered. What else was she waiting for? Henry had shown her again and again what a prize he was, just for the asking. But hold back she did, even though Walter Carrington lent his considerable support to his nephew's enterprise, exhorting Richard to direct his niece in her duty. Aunt Emma came puffing to her room at night to add her tearful pleas; even Chris Rokesby sent a teasing note to her one day: 'Not decided yet, little Alice? You and I must be competing for some sort of trophy awarded for dithering!'

Alice had crumpled up this missive and tossed it impatiently into the rubbish, but not before understanding that it was his way of telling her that he had made no plans to join the war.

On the afternoon that Alice sat down to write her invitations to her supper party—always sent out in the month before the date—her uncle put his head around the door of the parlour to ask if she would join him after the evening meal in the library. Alice smiled and said she would be pleased to, but sighed inwardly, knowing what the topic of conversation would be.

When the meal had been eaten and her aunt had

retired tactfully to her bed, Richard led the way into the library and asked her indulgence that he might light his pipe. He settled into his favourite chair and looked thoughtfully at her.

'Now, my dear,' he began, puffing the noxious fumes into the sweet breeze coming through the open window. Alice sat near him, the leather-bound book of Shakespeare's sonnets—Chris Rokesby's last birthday gift to her—open on her lap. She looked enquiring, but Richard surveyed her a few minutes more.

A year had made all the difference to Alice, he thought. Always a taking child—when she had come to him all those years ago she had been pretty—now she was a beauty. An unconventional beauty, he qualified, in his vague way. He had, in his youth, been a well-travelled man, and nowhere in the world had he seen a woman with quite that shade of bright brown hair—sometimes almost blonde, sometimes gleaming chestnut—combined with smoky blue eyes so luminous that they defied the candlelight shed by her own carefully made best wax candles, and a skin so perfect that it resembled full cream mixed delicately with the rose colour from one of Ashley Manor's prize rose blooms. As to her figure—a near-sighted man would be entranced by such curves.

He said resolutely, 'Dear Alice, you and I have always got along very well together. I know you to be a girl with a mind of her own—lamentably changeful in the past, but on no serious issue—and well able to arrange her own affairs. And that of Ashley—don't think I am unaware that you have most tactfully taken the burden of the estate from my shoulders in recent months. But. . .today I have again been subjected to one of Walter Carrington's tirades. My dear—Henry has been valiant enough in his efforts to win you. Now, I think, he must be rewarded or sent about his business.'

Alice sighed. Her fingers touched the smooth binding

of her book. It had fallen open at one of her favourite poems, dedicated to Will Shakespeare's famed Dark Lady. The old words—so romantic, so fervent in their sentiment—always touched her heart. She said, 'I know I must give my answer without delay, Uncle, but it is very hard. . .'

'Why so? Have you something against the young man?'

'Nothing,' she declared. 'He is everything a girl might wish for. But——' She paused, trying to find something acceptable to say, to explain the reluctance which she could not explain to herself, then said slowly, 'I find I have no wish to be married as yet.'

'No wish? This coming month you will be seventeen years old.'

'Are you afraid that you will be saddled with me for life?' She smiled.

'Nothing would delight me more—you know that. When your parents died I will admit that your aunt and I were a little disconcerted. We had no child of our own—what did we know about bringing up a little girl? But immediately you made a place for yourself in our hearts, and have been there ever since. But my sister-in-law, your mother Kate, was a born wife and mother. She would wish the same for you. It is my duty to encourage you towards it.'

'Am I like her?' Alice asked. She had seen a portrait of her mother—and her father—but somehow they had never seemed very real to her. Locked away in her heart she had other pictures too, put there in the early years of her life, but they too were indistinct.

'No,' Richard said, fondling his briar and remembering. 'You are not like her in looks or personality. To tell the truth, you are the image of your grandmother, your namesake—the first Alice Ashley. Sometimes I look at you and see my mother so clearly that it gives me the strangest feeling.'

'You were very fond of her?'

'Certainly, for she was that kind of woman—kind and joyous and. . .significant. But at the same time, when I think of her now, I remember her in later years when she had. . .lost something. I cannot explain it easily, Alice, but can only say that at the end of her life she was a sad woman. . .' Richard stared into the candlelight, his eyes full of memories. 'But——' he wagged the stem of his pipe at his niece '—you are not going to distract me from what I was saying. Now, miss, which is it to be? If yes, then let us make the announcement at your birthday supper. If no, then let us also have that above board and for all to know. I am sure that the Rokesbys are as interested in the matter as the rest of us.'

Alice turned the book in her hands. She had seen little of Chris or his family lately. She had been busy; she was sure they were in similar case. Oaks was the smallest of the three concerns but William Rokesby had been less than well lately, and the major work of his estate had fallen to Chris to undertake. It had been some time since the trio of young people had been together. The last time had been at the players' theatre in Maidstone, shortly before it was closed.

All the theatres and playhouses had been closed in the last year—and strolling mummers were no longer welcome on the village green. . . The performance that night had been one of Kit Marlowe's plays and Alice had been the guest of Henry and his aunt and uncle. Chris had been included in the party but had arrived late, during the interval, and had had little to say for himself. She remembered that Henry had taken him aside as they waited for their horses to be brought.

Approaching Chris to tell him goodnight, for she was to ride home with the Carringtons, Alice had seen that both young men were angry, and on the way home had asked Henry for an explanation.

He had dismissed the episode with a few words: 'Chris is a fool, and we all know that fools are punished first!'

She had thought those hard words and had replied lightly, 'You would like him to join your cause, Henry, but you never could talk him into anything he didn't want to do, you know. He is far too strong a character.'

Henry had become angry with her then, saying brusquely, 'And you never could see that a refusal to join the norm does not necessarily indicate strength of character!'

'You are fortunate to know what the norm is,' she had countered tartly; 'the rest of us are not so sure!'

He had placated her then, but they had spent the rest of the journey back in silence.

'There is no one else?' Richard asked her now.

'Of course not! You know I don't meet many young men, Uncle.'

'No,' Richard agreed thoughtfully. 'And I suppose that is really the problem. But let me assure you, my dear, that were there a hundred men to choose from, Henry would still be the best.'

'You are not alone in assuring me of that,' Alice said drily, thinking of Chris's words last summer.

There was silence between them for a while. Alice rose and thriftily pinched out half of the burning candles—it was necessary these days to practise small economies. Only today she had received a bill for the horses' feed she simply did not know how she could meet.

'So, what will you do?' Richard asked.

'I don't know.' Alice resumed her seat. 'Please advise me, as you see fit.' She had a longing to have someone else make her decisions for her—about how to keep Ashley land in order without the necessary help, how to pay bills when the farms now produced half what they used to, and what to do about Henry. If the last could be settled, she would never have to make a decision alone again——

Richard looked into her wistful face. He knew that he had not been of much help to her in the changed circumstances, for he was by nature a leaner. But he must do his best to help her to this advantageous marriage, and he was quite happy in his own mind that it was right. 'Why not accept his proposal, but state that you would like an indefinite time of engagement? That would give you time to think longer and be very sure of your intent.'

Alice considered. No one spoke of love, she thought suddenly. Not Henry or his Uncle Walter, nor either of her relations. But she did love Henry, did she not? Had *always* loved him—her friend and childhood companion. And what a relief it would be to her for one area of her life to be secure. Later that day she wrote him a short note, saying roughly what her uncle had suggested, and the next morning despatched it along with her invitations.

Acceptances arrived the following week. The Carringtons, overjoyed by the news Henry had given them, accepted with great pleasure. As did the Rokesbys, but Margaret Rokesby mentioned that they were sorry that Christopher would not be able to join them—he was going away for a short time and would not be back for that evening. Not be back? Alice examined Margaret's letter again. Across the bottom of the page Chris had scrawled in his reprehensible hand, 'I am sorry I cannot be there. But I will be back. I promise.'

Alice slid the note into the drawer of her desk with an exclamation of annoyance. It would be the first time for ten years that they had not all been together on that date. In her bedroom she stood admiring the spectacular sunset. Strange, she thought, how such light makes the familiar look mysterious. Beyond the drive each branch of the encircling trees, with its decoration of green leaves, was etched against the crimson sky; the corn growing straight and healthy in the patchwork of fields was a peculiar brownish purple— 'I will be back. I promise.' I promise. Now, why had he written that? Of course he would be back from whatever short trip he was making. I promise. . . He had used those words to her in another connection once. Turning slowly from the window, Alice wondered why his innocuous post-script should make her so uneasy. Perhaps she should ask him, and without delay.

The Rokesby manor, Oaks, was smaller in design than its two comparable residences, and infinitely older. Its foundations had been laid before the Tudors, before the Stuarts, and bore the unmistakable air of antiquity. As a child, Alice had examined the chipped marble statuary in the gardens—said to be relics from Roman times—with interest. Other clues to a dead civilisation existed in the old hall, which contained a faded coloured glass window of a Saxon king apparently enduring a painful death from arrows sprouting from his body and set into the old floorboards was an odd square of tiles, depicting a crude red bull which Richard Ashley insisted honoured the old religion of Mithras, god of the Roman legions.

Chris loved Oaks. The house, with its modest land and, Alice suspected, all of its tenants—many of whose families had been Oaks farmers for uncountable generations. She tethered her horse on the worn rail before the deep, shadowed porch and tapped on the door. The servant told her that the master and mistress were out visiting that day, but that Master Chris was in the stables. If she would come in he would send word——

'I will find him,' Alice said, and made her way through the gardens to the old stables. The gardens were not typical of current tastes. No orderly beds filled with stiff rows of flowers, no green yew tortured into the shapes of animals and birds, no ornamental fountain tinkling graciously amongst the wild roses. Instead there were drifts of lavender—blue and fragrant under the summer night sky—banks of lemon thyme offered its sharp scent, silver drifts of sage vied in colour with purple rosemary, jostled in their turn with savoury old herbs: basil, vervain, borage. Over all hung the sweeter scent of the new fruits of apple, plum and apricots from the orchards beyond the old crimson walls of the manor's boundary.

In the yard Chris Rokesby's grey mare was saddled and ready for departure. He was there, examining each hoof in turn, and straightened up as she came across the cobbles.

'Well, little Alice?'

'Well, Chris, what are you about?'

'As you see, I am about to undertake a journey.'

'A journey to where? And for what length of time that you cannot be back for the celebration of my special day as usual?'

Chris, satisfied his horse was in good fettle, turned her over to his groom. He rubbed his hands over his disreputable breeches. 'A necessary journey.'

Alice fixed her eyes on the boy walking the high-stepping mare about the yard. 'Where, Chris?'

He said quietly, 'I am for Oxford, Alice, and. . .the King.'

'I knew it!' Her heart turned painfully in her breast. 'And you promised to tell me if you were going,' she added bitterly.

'Well, I have,' he countered. 'For you are here, are you not?'

'I see. That cryptic line was supposed to inform me? Why not simply ride over as any other neighbour would and bid us all farewell?'

'I don't want anyone else to know,' he said casually.

'No one else? But surely your cousins?'

'Not even them. In fact, I have chosen this day
because they are away visiting. Perhaps you haven't
noticed, Alice, but just now those I am about to support
are distinctly out of favour in these parts. To go shouting
my intentions might result in my confinement.'

'But then. . .when it is discovered, may not things go
badly with your family?'

'I pray not. They need only say the truth—that I gave
them no prior notice of my intentions. Anyway, Will
and Margaret have no real affiliations, but 'tis no secret
that my roots are in the west, and there it is still
staunchly Royalist.' He gave Alice an unreadable look.
'Your roots are there too.'

'Mine?'

'Certainly. You are Cornish-born, my dear.'

'Of course, I know that.' Knew it, but never thought
of it, could hardly even remember the wind-blown
house on the ragged Cornish coast. Chris's branch of
the Rokesbys came from Bude, too, although he had
been born in Kent. She said,

'So it is secret, this thing you are doing?'

'Yes.'

'But you trust me with it?'

'You could always keep a secret,' he smiled. 'At least
you kept enough of mine when I was an unruly boy.
And you are keeping one of your own just now, aren't
you?'

She coloured. 'It is no secret. . . Henry told you?'

'Yes, indeed, last week. He was so elated he scarcely
could find the words.' Chris had found few words of his
own that day, before his friend's shining happiness. He
had known it would come, and surely should have been
happy for both of them, but somehow, somehow he had
kept thinking of Alice in the vinery at Ashley, Alice
speaking of romance and excitement——

'But you have not trusted him with your secret?'

He gave her another oblique glance. 'I fear Henry's sense of duty might impel him to delay me with more of his reasonable arguments.'

'They would be reasonable, wouldn't they? I can assess the recent reports as well as any other, and obviously it is possible that you might be about to choose a losing side. Why?' Latest newsletters had been gloomy from the Royalist point of view. They still had their troops and their courage, but squabbling in the higher echelon of the King's men had weakened their force; one report had dwelt at length on the poor deals foolish Loyalists had made regarding new equipment and supplies.

'Because I don't like to be told how to live my life,' he said shortly. The light was fading fast. His cousin had shown him her acceptance of Alice's invitation at midday, before she sent it away and left with William on her visit. If he was honest, Chris might admit to himself that he had waited all afternoon for Alice to come, but now he must be away.

'Odd words for a man about to join the army,' she said.

He signalled to his groom. When the mare was brought he caressed her briefly, before lifting his weighty saddlebags on to her sleek back. He waved the groom away. He had told no one of his men that he intended leaving for Oxford. He suspected, and rightly, that most of them would want to ride with him. Lately, some had tried to extract his promise that he would keep them advised of his plans. But he had not given that promise to any but Alice. . . 'Yes,' he agreed, tightening the girth to ease the extra weight upon the mare, who had seldom carried more than his own slim body. 'I must follow military orders until it is decided one way or another, but after—after, if all goes well, I shall be free again.'

'No one is free. There are laws in England now which must be obeyed.'

'I know that, but the constables do not yet come to remonstrate with a man in his home enjoying a pipe or a glass.'

She half smiled. How typical of Chris, she thought. Larger issues of state had left him unresolved, but the idea that another man might presume to question his personal habits—— 'You do not own a pipe, and are very moderate as to consumption of wine.'

'Stop pretending to misunderstand me. In the future, if they have their way, what is already begun will be the law soon enough. In Kent now the theatres and most of the taverns are closed. Public merrymaking is frowned upon, women may not wear their pretty gowns, or show their bright hair without fear of reprimand, nor men parade in their fine clothes for fear it will offend the all-seeing Lord. I like to serve God in my own way, Alice, and do not choose to believe that He is offended by the triviality of a gentleman in Flemish lace, tipsy on occasion, or a lady tying a red ribbon in her curls.'

She was silent before such vehemence. And yet, she thought, it was none of these trivialities which had tipped Chris Rokesby over the line of neutrality. Rather the idea that any Englishman could be ordered to change his life. Persuaded, advised, maybe—but forced? No. At least this was so for him. She herself did not like the Puritan insistence that this or that was sinful, but nor did she consider it worth risking one's life to argue it. Chris looked at her intently a moment, then swung into the saddle.

'So,' he said, 'you think I'm a fool. Well, perhaps we are all fools about one thing or another, and choices—howsoever they appear to others—are made for all sorts of reasons.'

'Tell me a little of your plans,' she said, her throat constricted. She had seen many men ride away in the last months, but none had torn at her heart in the way Chris Rokesby did, abandoning the home he loved to depart in shabby breeches and torn shirt to fight for the dubious principles he had just declared.

'Better not. I will only remind you that once you accused me of favouring a colour of coat which matched your eyes.'

The Prince Rupert's Bluecoats, then, she thought. And if he should gain access to such an élite band the more danger he would be in. She patted his mare's velvet head. 'Then I am glad you are well-mounted, but never knew you were a student of the German language.'

He smiled, obscurely pleased that she should have made the connection so easily. But didn't she always? He had spent the previous night lying in Molly Judd's passionate arms, but it had hurt him less to leave her than to leave Alice Ashley, with her innocent blue-grey eyes and candid tongue. This thought was so unwelcome to him that he would have touched his hat and moved away then, but she held his bridle, saying, 'You have not yet congratulated me upon my engagement.'

'It is customary to congratulate the gentleman concerned.'

'And did you?'

Chris grinned. 'I wished him luck, yes, and think he will need it.'

She swallowed. At this moment, when they were taking leave of each other and might never see each other again, she felt an inexplicable desire for a show of affection from him. But it had never been that way between them. Henry had always been the one with the helping hand over stiles and through rough nettles in their childish games, Chris the one with the derisive laugh that she could not keep up with him. They had always teased and provoked each other. It was foolish, then, to feel tears pricking behind her eyes—she had always counted it a point of honour never to cry before him. She looked up.

'Why, Alice,' he said softly, 'I believe you are really sorry to see me go.'

'Of course I am!' She was angry with herself and him. 'I may never see you again!'

He leaned forward in the dusk to examine her upturned face. 'I wrote that I would be back, and I will. I promised. But I am glad enough to receive the traditional soldier's farewell from a pretty and tearful maid. Will you kiss me, Alice?' he added laughingly. 'To complete the ritual?'

She raised a stony face, and he smiled and bent to kiss her cheek. Either he was less adroit than usual, astride the restless horse, or she turned her face at the critical moment but, however it was, their lips met and clung for what was only a few seconds, but which seemed a much longer and confusing time for the two, alone under a sky fast becoming speckled with dim stars.

Chris recovered first. His mare, knowing she was about to take the open road and impatient to be off, chewed on her bit and shook her head angrily. Her master shortened the rein. 'I must go now,' he said, his voice, too, less sure than usual. The moment, he thought, that is all it is—he was riding off into the unknown and his senses were heightened. Even knowing this, he also knew he would carry the touch of her lips in his heart forever. 'I must go now,' he repeated.

'I know you must,' she answered. 'God speed, Chris.'

He raised one hand in salute, hesitated a split-second, then spurred his mount and clattered out of the yard.

Alice allowed true darkness to come down before remounting her own horse and taking the road home. She did not hurry; her thoughts were too complicated and puzzling for her to want to ignore them. A year ago she had looked upon Chris Rokesby in a new light; now she must do so again.

Of course she had heard the whispers that the Rokesby boy was becoming a rake and too fond of women for his own good. But they had been indulgent whispers, in an age where a young man was expected to sow wild oats before marriage and keep a discreet mistress or two after. She had paid little attention to them. Now she thought about them more seriously. Chris had kissed other girls like that—and more, if the tales about Mistress Judd were to be believed. There was a whole other sensual dimension to his life that she, his oldest friend, knew nothing about. Irrationally, she was displeased by this thought. Also, she was suddenly forced to consider Henry and her projected marriage in this reflected light.

She had let herself agree to marry him without even contemplating this part of their relationship. If Henry would kiss her as Chris had just done—— Shocked, she realised that she was uncomfortable if Henry even touched her hand. . .

She drew up beside the slow-moving dark waters of the tributary of the Medway which fed the rich and fertile farmland in this area. The birds were calling to each other in the trees above, thick clouds of hovering insects hung almost immobile over the expanse of water.

What had she felt a half-hour ago? There were no suitable words, only the knowledge that Chris had a secret he could have shared with her—a heady and entrancing secret—if they had both desired it. But, of course, he did not wish to do so, for she was betrothed now to his best friend. And she did not wish it for the same reason. The evening wind brushed over the river and rose to cool her flushed face, but did not blow away these puzzling thoughts. It was in that moment, sitting on her well-trained horse and listening to the murmuring of the water and the rustling of leaves above, that Alice was glad she had set no definite day for her wedding.

Alice's birthday party duly took place, but did not have the crowning moment expected by several members of the party. Instead, the betrothal between Alice Ashley and Henry Carrington was announced, but no firm date for their union designated. Henry had smiled through the evening, apparently quite at ease with the arrangement, but the next morning had ridden over to take Alice to task about it.

'But why, sweetheart?' he asked. 'Why not a Christmas wedding, so appropriate and suitable? We are both decided—why delay?'

'I don't want to be hurried,' she replied composedly. 'It is the rest of our lives we are deciding on—can I not have a little time?' They were having this conversation in the library at Ashley. It was raining hard and Alice had reluctantly left her inspection of her crops, previously doing well in the brilliant weather, but now in danger of spoiling under the relentless downpour. 'Also, Henry, you know how things are here at Ashley. My uncle is the kindest and best of men, but. . . management is not his strong suit and, with so many hands gone, the estate requires all my attention these days.'

Henry smiled indulgently. He was proud of his future wife's skill in doing the work of ten men for her home, as long as she understood that when they were wed Richard Ashley must sink or swim without her constant supervision. He said, 'If you would only let me send some men to——'

'No!' she said decisively. 'Ashley has always been maintained by Ashley people,' she added awkwardly. It had been on the tip of her tongue to say that she was already working day and night to put food into the bellies of Roundhead soldiers. Help from Fox Hall would increase that bounty.

She would also have liked to say that if Henry had men to spare perhaps he might think of sending them to Oaks. Chris had been gone for three weeks. Within a week of his departure half his men at Oaks had left to follow him; the other half were preparing to go. When Alice had last visited, Margaret had been wringing her hands in despair. Her husband was ill, she had said fretfully to Alice, his farm hands scattered, and Chris had deserted them! Alice, hearing this last, could have cried remembering how the Rokesbys had adored their young cousin. Damned *war*, she had thought, riding home, how it laid waste affection and kindness—all the normal kindness of ordinary people.

Henry accepted Alice's offer of wine and sat down. Her refusal to set a firm date, he thought complacently, did not affect his plans. Under the terms of his father's will he inherited the bulk of his monetary estate upon his official betrothal. His father had been a forward-thinking man and had foreseen that his son would need ready cash to secure a suitable residence and make it ready for his bride. That and other sundry expenses. Henry would not be using any part of his inheritance for this purpose, of course—he and Alice would live quite comfortably in one wing of Fox Hall, which would in due course become his property upon his uncle's demise. Meanwhile, Henry had already set in train his heart's desire: the recruitment, the equipping and training of a large force of men.

This had not been difficult. All men enlisting with government regiments had been promised great rewards in the future when the war was won, but received little more than a sketchy suit of clothes and a weapon. Henry not only promised a reward of land when the conflict was decided but also lodged a small amount of money with each man, to leave with their families or spend as they chose. He also provided a complete suit of clothes—the dull red shirt and breeches, the buff leather coat which, in lieu of the old-fashioned armour, gave some protection from shoulder to hip, the helmet or montero of the cavalryman, together with the high boot of hide, well-seasoned with beeswax, and—best of all— a good horse for each man. Those in Carrington's regiment of cavalry felt themselves privileged indeed, and applications were steady.

Henry looked speculatively at Alice today. She had seated herself on the window-seat, apparently enthralled by the sight of the summer storm decimating her gardens. Should he tell her that in a few short weeks he would be ready to leave Fox and take up his duties as a commander in Lord Fairfax's band? No, he would defer that for another time. Also, he was reluctant to press her again about a wedding-date, feeling reasonably content with her consent to a proposal. He cast about for another topic of conversation.

'Chris Rokesby is gone, did you know?' he asked eventually.

'I had heard,' she said evasively.

'No one seems to know where,' Henry continued. 'I had a most distressing interview with his cousin William, who is ailing and does not need the added worry that Chris has thrown in his lot with the King.'

'Indeed?' Alice murmured. William Rokesby had been taken ill while out visiting the day Chris had left and had been brought home in a closed carriage. A condition of the heart, his doctor had declared, and Alice, on hearing this, had not been able to help being glad that the attack had occurred before he came home and discovered that Chris had decamped.

'Well,' Henry said thoughtfully. 'If he has done that he is more of a fool than I took him for. The news this week must convince anyone of who will be the ultimate victor in this affair.'

'What news is that?' she asked sharply.

Not noticing her tone, Henry described to her the events of the battle fought on Marston Moor. It had been the bloodiest so far fought and, although lasting only two short hours, had resulted in over four thousand Royalist casualties—the Earl of Newcastle's Whitecoats so decimated that the earl had exiled himself abroad.

'Where is. . . Marston Moor?' she asked fearfully.

'Oh—north—near York, I believe.' Henry looked into his glass. 'A great victory for Parliament.'

North. Perhaps Chris was one of the casualties, she thought fearfully. What is this? she admonished herself immediately. Your betrothed sits a few feet away, safe and sound and not in harm's way. Why your concern for another man? Because we have been friends for so long, came the swift answer. Henry and Chris and me. . . She said crisply, 'If you believe that Chris has joined the King's cause, I wonder that you are so obviously joyful about such news. Are you not worried about him?'

Henry laughed. 'Worry about Chris? One might more profitably worry about whether the sun will rise tomorrow morn.'

'He has been our friend for so long as we can remember.'

'And for all that time I never knew another better able to see for himself. I feel I have done my duty to him by offering him a place in my enterprise—he refused it, and now must suffer the consequences.' He gave her a sharp glance. 'And I feel I must point out to you, my dear, that I would wish for no past associations—for either of us—to conflict with my new position.'

'And what position is that?'

'I shall shortly be the commander of quite a substantial body of men, wholly committed to the Parliamentarian cause,' he said complacently. 'I shall, overnight so to speak, be rather an important person.'

She laughed. 'Dear Henry, don't be so pompous.'

He reddened. 'As my future wife, it is hardly becoming of you to speak in quite that way.'

She had the grace to blush too. Of course Henry expected her loyalty; naturally he was entitled to it. But loyalties could not be abandoned, shuffled around like cards; she wondered how Henry was able to dismiss ten years so easily. She was sure she could not. She said stiffly, 'I am sorry for being impolite. But, you know, our situation is rather like the larger one, don't you agree? Nothing has really changed between us three friends, yet we are now in effect enemies because men we do not know—have never met or judged—decree it so.'

He frowned. 'You are not part of this, Alice. To speak of. . .enemies. You are to be my wife in due course, and our future is to be together. Chris—in view of his recent action—has no part in it.'

She could hardly believe her ears. No part in it! A cool finger touched her heart. She was now betrothed, had committed herself to a man who could so easily dismiss a decade of friendship, and expected her to do the same—but surely what Henry had just said was an example of his prosaic view of life. She must not be judgemental, for it was not in his nature to be speculative; he dealt only in the actual and the immediate. She forced a smile and rose.

'All you say is true, Henry.'

He took her hands and kissed each in turn. 'So, I have a hundred things to do, as I'm sure you do. Let us dine together at Fox Hall in a few days, yes?'

'Of course.' She smiled again, but the meeting this day had made her uneasy in a way she could not yet define. Watching Henry ride away, she could not rid herself of the feeling that a year ago she had had two friends whose characters and feelings she had known as well as the palm of her hand. Now those two had assumed the guise of strangers.

CHAPTER THREE

IF WAR could be described as a chess game, the situation in the middle of 1645 was stalemate. Neither Royalist nor Parliamentarian had triumphed in terms of destroying each other's armies. Both were involved in internal squabbling within their high command.

In the Royalist ranks great changes had taken place in the previous twelve months. Wilmot, suspected of collusion with the powerful Parliamentarian leader, Essex, had been arrested and replaced by Lord Goring, who in turn had made way for Lord Hopton. Prince Rupert now had so many enemies at Court that every sensible proposition he made to his royal uncle was viewed with suspicion. His brother, the Prince Maurice, not as able a soldier as Rupert but equally loyal, was now so out of favour that he was openly defied and abused—— And so on and so forth—endless petty disputes, undermining the fabric of the crown's endeavour.

There was little more peace in the government faction. The bitter round of recriminations after the disaster in the west and at Newbury appeared to be self-perpetuating, each general blaming another for events. In the heart of Parliament's ranks, however, there was one absolute: Oliver Cromwell was now the man expected to lead the Roundheads to victory.

At Ashley, Alice had more personal but equally distressing problems. Winter had been struggled through somehow, the consequences of a depleted workforce evident in the amount of food available. The harvest had been poorly managed despite her efforts. Crops had spoiled from waiting too long to be gathered in; fruit had rotted in the orchards for want of hands to pick it; animal stock was almost daily poached by the commissary. The list of cares she had to bear went on and on, but somehow she managed. Her aunt and uncle, her household servants and her tenants did not starve, but she was weary.

At the beginning of the previous October Henry Carrington had completed his master plan and rode away from Larkspur at the head of his own regiment. The whole village had turned out to wave them away. They had passed Ashley Manor and Alice had stood with her aunt and uncle at the end of the drive to witness the parade.

I should feel *something*, Alice had thought, as she acknowledged Henry's correct salute as he passed her on his handsome chestnut horse. For Henry, and for all the familiar faces going with him. Why, there is Joe Pipe, and his wife about to deliver their first child so eagerly awaited! There is Matt Rawley—surely he is but seventeen this autumn month! And little Seton Smith, riding alongside his father Edward—goodness knows what Emily will do now, with both her men gone. . . But all she could feel was a sort of dismay that all these men and boys could not get on with their lives in peace.

What did all those who rode or walked past expect from their impulsive action? What they would not get would be the riches promised in land by the representatives of the cause they were rushing headlong to join, for if all the promises were fulfilled England would be bankrupt as to cash and its green land divided into squares no larger than a cottage woman's patchwork quilt. Even Henry had had to admit lately that, although he would honour the wages of those directly under his command, he could not hope to honour their claim to land, and those who were following his flag without specific invitation would get nothing at all.

'They look fine, don't they?' Emma Ashley had said,

her hands clasped to her breast, her ears ringing with the resonant beat of the drums, the musical note of the bugle.

'Very fine,' Alice had agreed but she had thought, How fine will they look when they limp home without an arm or a leg or, worse, are conveyed in a pine box? Some would not come back at all, for she knew that casualties could be so high now that many were consigned to faraway communal graves without benefit of markers. She had thought of Chris Rokesby's words about men staying home and working their land and raising their families, and had turned back into the house with sadness in her heart.

Alice was alone in the stable-yard when she received a message. She was grooming her own mount, pretty Jenny, one of only three horses to escape the commissary, and could not help glancing around at the empty stalls now and again and sighing. She scarcely noticed the ragged boy who came on foot and stood uncertainly just inside the gates. One of the Ashley grooms, young Jack Madesley, went to him and took from his hands the crumpled letter. The child melted away and Jack brought it to Alice.

'This'n for you, mistress,' he said, holding the grubby note between his finger and thumb. 'Thass not addressed to you right, but the lad knew your name and bade me give it you.'

Alice unfolded the single sheet of paper. There was no greeting, nor signature, but Chris Rokesby's distinctive hand leaped from the page:

My brave horse has foundered and I must walk now, unless you can help me. Also I am barefoot, and disputed land is as hard as any other. *A moi*, Blondel.

Three bare lines, yet they spoke volumes to Alice. Chris's mare, Julie, had been spectacular for her courage when put to any test—she must have been sore indeed to fall even in the hottest battle. The final line referred to a game she and Chris and Henry had played when they were children. It was a romantic echo from tales they had heard of long-dead Richard of England, the Lionheart of a thousand stirring stories. One had it that Richard was imprisoned by a European prince and confined in a high tower. His squire, Blondel, had walked the length and breadth of Europe, playing his lute beneath the window of every prison until he received answer from above. Chris had always been Richard, Henry the wicked prince, and Alice had been forced to play the loyal squire—more fitting to a girl, the boys had declared scathingly, although she had always pointed out that she was tone deaf and possessed no musical instrument—

She refolded the paper. A horse? Easy—she would willingly part with Jenny. Boots? She could manage that too. But where to despatch them? There was no clue in the torn letter as to its writer's whereabouts. But there must be a way. Everyone gossiped about an underground network all over England which supplied the Royalists. In these parts rumours abounded about the Evening Sun. Molly Judd and her father were said to be for the King. Molly Judd. . . Alice shrank from seeking help from her.

'Mistress?' Jack was still standing quietly by her side. 'Is there anything I can help you with?'

Alice hesitated. She must not involve any innocent member of her household in this.

'Mistress,' Jack said softly, 'let me help you.'

Alice fingered the note. It had passed through many hands to arrive at Ashley, it was soiled and battered, but Chris had taken pen in hand to write to her for help. She tucked it into the sleeve of her gown and looked at Jack carefully.

He was young, the same age as her maid Betty Mote.

He was also from the west, had in fact travelled in the same wagon from Bude as little Alice and Betty, his family being dead in the same plague as Alice's parents and it being thought useful to send a handy boy along with the girls. Last year Alice had noticed that he had a flair with horses and had promoted him to the family stables. She had also noticed that Jack had grown up in that year, becoming very tall and broad-shouldered. Whenever Jonas Spragg or his kind had come to Ashley they had had words with the boy, tried to persuade him of his duty to join their army. Henry, too, had added his word of censure. But Jack had resisted all efforts. She made up her mind.

'It is this way, Jack. A friend of mine—an old friend of mine—needs a horse and other provisions. I would like to assist him, but have no idea how to go about it.'

'Is it young Master Rokesby of Oaks?' Jack asked immediately.

'Yes, it is,' Alice said, astonished that he should have leaped to this conclusion.

'Then I understand,' he said quietly. 'What would you wish to do?'

'I would wish to send him what he asks for with all haste. If I only knew how to do it.'

'I know where you can find out,' Jack said calmly.

'And where is that?'

'The Evening Sun.'

'They are definitely of that. . .persuasion there?'

'They are. Between you and me, Miss Alice, they are the only house in these parts who are.'

'I see.' Alice felt in her pocket for the few knobs of salt she always carried when entering the stables in hot weather and offered one on her palm to Jenny. The animal inclined her graceful neck and nibbled it. Well, Alice thought, they would be. For wouldn't a tavern—and some said a bawdy house—be the first to suffer under Puritan rule? The Evening Sun had escaped closure thus far because it was the only ale-house situated on a road where travellers needed stabling facilities. Hard on these thoughts came another: had Molly Judd heard from Chris? Had he written to his mistress, if not to his friends and family?

Jenny, her titbit consumed, was still standing patiently. Alice reached to smooth her shining flank. How sad she would be to part with her lovely mount, whom she had raised from a long-legged filly and trained to instant command! The Ashley stable-boys had used to joke that little Jenny could be controlled by a silk thread.

She said resolutely, 'I believe I will take a ride now, Jack. Do you saddle Jenny and Primrose and come with me.'

It was only a short distance to Larkspur village. On the outskirts the Evening Sun showed its lights bravely in the gloom. The taproom was already full of customers—some travellers on their way to the coast and some local men, their working day done, come in search of a tankard shared with their mates and perhaps some other more dubious entertainment; Molly Judd had two comely sisters.

Alice paused in the yard at the back of the inn. She had never been near such a place in her life! Her aunt and uncle would be scandalised had they known what their niece was about this evening.

Jack said, 'I'll go in now and bring Sam Judd out to you.'

Alice sat her horse patiently, her eyes fixed on the back door. Within minutes it opened and a yellow slice of light cut across the yard. But it was not Sam Judd who trod carefully over the dusty ground towards her, but his eldest daughter, Molly. Alice watched her across the space which separated them. Molly was not a graceful or elegant woman, but she walked with a free and easy stride, her yellow hair loose about her shoulders. Her eyes, even in the half-light, were brilliant and bold. She looked up at the slender figure on the tall horse.

'My father is sick with the stomach grippe. You can say what you have to to me.'

Alice stared down at her.

'Do we discuss it out here?' Molly said roughly. 'Or will you come inside, Mistress Ashley?'

'I will come in.' Alice slid down.

She was led into a warmly lit parlour at the back of the taproom. It was well-furnished, with velvet settles and some silver on the tables. She sat down by the window. Molly offered her wine and, receiving a shake of the head, poured herself a full beaker and sat down beside her.

She is pretty, thought Alice reluctantly, her eyes roaming over the other woman's face. She waited for Molly to speak.

'Jack has told me what you want, mistress, and I can't help you in this.'

'You can't?' I have come for an important and specific reason, Alice thought, why then can I not prevent myself from being distracted by the thought that Chris and this girl have been intimate? Why do I keep thinking of them together, of what they meant to each other? She sat upright.

'We are watched. Night and day by those who suspect us. They can't prove anything, and I don't want them to be able to. If I send one of my lads away with a horse which is plainly not one of the hacks we keep at the tavern, and with bags full of whatever Chris has asked for, then I might just as well stand in the public square and shout, I am for the King!'

She calls him Chris in that familiar way, Alice thought with a twist of her heart, and is unable to keep the caress for his name out of her voice. She said impulsively, 'Have you heard from him? Have you received letters from him?'

Molly gave her ready smile. 'No, mistress, I have not. What would be the point? I cannot read, nor barely write my name.' So she declared the gulf between the man she loved and herself. 'But I hear things occasionally. Hear about young Rokesby, who has risen like a rocket in the Royalist ranks. Captain of Horse he is now. *Captain* Rokesby, and friend to the King's nephew, the Prince Rupert.' Her bright gaze challenged Alice to deny her the pride she felt in saying this.

Captain! thought Alice. An officer of the King in rag shoes, with no worthy mount! Her resolve hardened. 'Then how shall I go about this? Tell me, and I will contrive to send him that which he needs.'

Molly considered her. She was a good judge of character in both men and women—one could not run an inn without seeing the best and worst of humanity. She took her time over her assessment.

Soft and spoiled. These faults she attributed to Alice immediately. But also something else. Something strong and valiant, much as a silk thread could be more lasting and durable than the coarsest twine. And hadn't she taken the reins of Ashley from her dithering uncle and run it on half-help for two year or more? And hadn't Chris Rokesby always said that he would trust Alice Ashley with his life. . .? As to the rest? Well, Alice was not to every man's taste; she was too strong-boned and vividly coloured to please a fashion which liked its women dainty and pale. Even so, Molly decided without rancour, Alice Ashley would be significant, with those bones and those eyes, even when an old woman. 'There might be a way,' she said at last. 'If you were willing and clever.'

'Tell me.'

'What if you were to decide to go on a little visit? To a friend who lived some distance away? Naturally you would ride your handsome mare; naturally you would take a male servant. Naturally you would have all kinds of things in your saddlebags and trunk for your holiday.'

'You mean that *I* should take the stuff to Chris? But— I don't know where he is!'

'You might have that information by first light tomorrow.'

'I don't know if I could do it,' Alice said humbly. 'How do you know I would not be stopped. . . questioned?'

'Mistress Ashley of Ashley Manor? Whose family have sat on the fence for so long they must have sores on their rumps?'

Alice flushed brightly. She should be offended, of course, but the coarse words described the case, did they not? She said stiffly, 'Not decided would be a fairer description, Mistress Judd.'

Molly revealed her white teeth again in a derisive grin. 'Not decided, is it? Then you'd better do it soon, lady, else the war will be done before you do!'

Alice got up and took a turn around the room. The practicalities of the project were easy. She often visited Meg Allerton, who lived just beyond the borders of Kent. The two girls wrote frequently to each other and Meg's last letter, received only a week since, had begged her to visit—with no prior notice needed. . . She could show that letter to her uncle. . .

The noise from the taproom had swelled in the last quarter-hour; it was market day and very busy. Molly guessed that her sisters were in need of another pair of hands. She in her turn wondered about the relationship between this girl and Chris Rokesby. Nothing more than an old loyalty, she guessed, for there was a whisper about that young Master Carrington had succeeded in his suit for her. All to the good, that was, Molly thought, for no one would suspect that the betrothed of an ardent Roundhead would be carrying supplies to a Royalist. She said impatiently, 'So?'

Alice turned, her hands pressed together in a childish gesture. 'I'll do it,' she whispered. 'If I know where to go.'

'Good. What did Chris ask for?'

'Just a horse. . .and some boots.'

'Take food too,' Molly advised. 'Anything edible which will keep—dried stuff, you know. Our troops are half starved, and no one can fight a battle on thin air.' Molly got up and poured more wine. 'Drink this. You look as if you need it. You'll hear from me tomorrow first thing, and take Jack Madesley with you when you go. He's a big lad, and smart and resourceful too.' She reached and gripped Alice's arm. 'May God go with you.' She was gone in the next moment, leaving Alice to raise her glass to trembling lips.

The following day began misty, with great pillows of grey cloud heralding rain. At breakfast Richard said, 'I believe you would do well to postpone your visit to Meg, Alice. You will not wish to travel in poor weather.'

'Perhaps I will,' Alice said casually. Molly's promise of information as to her destination had not been fulfilled yet, although Jack was stationed in the yard to receive any messenger.

'I am very glad you're going to Meg's for a while, whenever you go,' Richard continued. 'With Henry gone, and. . .other friends away, you will be best occupied with a little enjoyment.' He paused to refill his ale mug, then went on, 'Have you heard aught of Chris Rokesby, by the way?'

'I have not heard where he is,' Alice replied, anxious to avoid a lie. It had not been hard to let her uncle think that she was going to Meg's—she had not actually had to say the words, for when she had shown Richard Meg's letter and announced her intention of going on a visit, Richard had leaped to the conclusion that it was to

Bicksby she was going. 'Has his cousin Margaret no news?'

'None. In truth, Margaret has been in a daze since Will died. When the physician was forced to tell her that it would be advisable for her to call Chris home if he wished to. . .bid farewell to his cousin she had no idea where to write. She is in a similar dilemma regarding William's death. It is a great sadness to her.'

Alice crumbled her breakfast bread without speaking. William Rokesby had passed peacefully away six months ago. At the gathering after the funeral Alice had comforted a tearful Margaret, who had been unable to believe that neither of Chris's best friends had been privy to news of him.

'Oh, Alice!' she had cried. 'Will loved the boy so! It was so miserable for him not to see him one last time. . . . Now you tell me, and Henry has insisted in his reply to the letter I sent him, that neither of you know where he is! If that is true, then how could Chris do this to all of us?'

Alice had soothed her as best she could, privately thinking that it was for the protection of his cousins that Chris had not kept in touch. . . Now, she supposed, if she found Chris, she would have the dismal task of telling him that his beloved cousin was gone.

The meal went on. As the dishes were cleared Alice saw Jack pass by the window with a purposeful air. She said, 'I do believe the sky is lightening a little, Uncle. My trip may not have to be put off after all.' She murmured an excuse and left the table.

Jack was in the porch. They exchanged whispers. The King's army was now camped at Market Harborough — or so Molly Judd's information declared, Jack said. The Prince Rupert was within that encampment, and if he was there so would be Chris Rokesby. Of course the information was several days old, but did Mistress Alice wish to make for there?

Alice had no idea what to think. She questioned Jack a little more.

"Tis this way,' Jack said judicially. 'The King and his nephew are there, and also Cromwell's troops. I think. . . Well, with the both of them in one place, seems to me. . .'

'We will go there, then,' Alice said, with more decisiveness than she felt.

'So I think—and, having decided that, we must leave without delay.'

'Jack.' Alice closed the door of the hall gently, so they could not be overheard. 'You don't have to do this, you know.'

'I know that. But tell me, Miss Alice, do you remember my old Grandfer—back in Bude?'

'I think I do,' she said, crinkling her smooth forehead. Many of her memories were vague, but Jack's grandfather had been the kind of character one did not forget. Josh Madesley—a constant trial to her father, a delight to the local children with his store of fascinating tales, indomitably loyal to the Ashleys, on whose land he had always lived, self-opinionated, and a devil—even in his sixties—with the dairy-maids.

'Well, *his* grandfather was at the back of an Ashley in crusading times. An Ashley from *your* branch, I mean— the Cornish Ashleys. Granfer Josh told me many a yarn of those times fighting with King Richard, and his father was with old King Hal at the Cloth of Gold tournaments in France.'

'I didn't know that.'

'No, well, another thing I guess you never knew is that Ashleys have always fought shoulder to shoulder with Rokesbys, and always on the side that wore the crown. Young Master Christopher's great-grandfather was killed fighting the French in Henry Tudor's army. His grandfather was knighted after some battle against the Spanish when Elizabeth Tudor went to war.'

'I didn't know that either!'

'No... Anyway, the thing is, our families—Rokesbys, Ashleys and Madesleys—have always been entwined in some scrap or other over the years and so I think I've the right to help you and Master Chris in this latest.'

They set off before the noon hour. Richard Ashley made no comment over Alice's insistence that Jack accompany her rather than one of the older grooms, nor about the excessive amount of luggage strapped to the extra horse they took with them. What Alice had stored away in that luggage had been the result of a conversation with Betty Mote and Betty's subsequent raid on the Ashley larders. Betty had been most intransigent when she'd found out that her mistress intended taking a trip without her.

'I go with you, Miss Alice,' she had said firmly. 'Now, just give me a minute——'

'No, Betty!' Alice had said.

'Then you tell me what's really going on.'

Mistress and maid had eyed each other.

'I can't,' Alice had said sulkily.

'You will, or not go!'

Alice had shoved a pair of leather shoes into her trunk and slammed the lid down. 'Very well, if you must know——' She had recounted events to Betty, whose round eyes became like saucers. 'So now you know!' Alice had said crossly. 'And perhaps you will allow me to get off now.'

'Yes, I will,' Betty had said slowly. 'And will wish you luck for the brave thing you are doing. But I'll say as well that I wish you had asked me to go with you, or at least trusted me with it all.'

Alice had lifted her trunk off the bed. 'It isn't a matter of trust, Betty, and you know it! You can't come with me, for how would Ashley fare with us both off on a

wild mission? You and I are the only two with a bit of
sense on the place.'

Betty had considered. 'Thass true. . . But, Miss
Alice, what you are doing—how will it set with Master
Henry?'

'I can't think about that now,' Alice had said,
exasperated. 'It's Chris I must think of. No horse, no
shoes on his feet—I can't bear to think of him like
that.'

'No more can I. But all the same. . .'

'Oh, don't lecture me! I'll find Chris and give him
what he needs, and be home before anyone knows
where I have gone. Including Master Henry.'

Once on the highway, Alice regained some of her
composure. The thing was done now; she had decided
on this course of action and must make the best of it. As
the day cleared and a brilliant sun burned away the
clouds she thought of Betty's words about Henry. It
would not, she knew, 'set' well at all with Kent's latest
gallant commander. Indeed, he would be absolutely
furious if he should hear of it.

He need never know, she decided. As far as anyone
knew Alice Ashley had gone on an innocent little
journey to spend some time with a friend. If anyone says
different, Alice thought brazenly, I shall deny it.
Choices, Chris had said, were made for various reasons.
What was her reason for this one? Habit, her inner
voice insisted. The habit of answering a call for help
from an old friend. Also, she could not believe that
Henry would really condemn her for her actions, not in
his heart. What he would be most worried about was
what Henry was always most worried about—how did
the thing look to others? He was obviously intent on
becoming an important figure in his county, and the
war would add lustre to that ambition. She would
support him wholeheartedly in this, but meanwhile she

had something to do and looked forward to it with apprehension.

The village of Naseby was situated in the centre of England. It was on a plateau two hundred feet above sea level, fed by streams flowing from both the Atlantic Ocean and the North Sea, and was a place of hills and vales. It was not, in the opinion of military strategists, an ideal place to stage a battle, but circumstances forced both sides to confront each other in this inconvenient location.

The New Model Army had been put to test in early June, when ordered to attack Oxford by Parliament. Deflected from this objective, on learning that Prince Rupert had attacked Leicester with such ferocity, and incensed by its eventual loss, Fairfax had swept into the Midlands to prevent further disaster. The two armies—Roundheads, commanded by Thomas Fairfax, strongly supported by Oliver Cromwell's cavalry, and Royalists, with King Charles at their head, equally firmly bolstered by Rupert's Bluecoat cavalry, had arrived in Market Harborough in June. It was on the eve of their confrontation just outside Naseby village that a friend of one of the Royalist commanders arrived to bring provisions and comfort. Alice and Jack had ridden hard for several days and paused on the outskirts of the camp.

Like all army camps it presented a scene of chaos and seething activity. White tents were erected; fires were burning on the open ground; men and horses, closely confined in spite of being in a vast area of field, jostled together. Alice, never having witnessed such a sight before, was frankly terrified by it. She might have hovered forever on the fringe of the camp had not Jack urged her on.

'However shall we find Master Chris in this confusion?' she asked.

'We'll find him,' Jack assured her. They had not come all this way, he thought grimly, and suffered the discomfort and trials of a journey across England in hot and dusty weather, to be baulked at the last. He drew ahead on his sturdy cobby mare and raised his voice.

'Captain Rokesby! Where is Captain Rokesby of Kent? Captain Rokesby!'

Blank faces greeted his calls. He and Alice rode on through the mêlée, Jack shouting out at intervals. At last there was an answering cry. 'Rokesby is in the end tent!' They rode to the end of the ghostly white shapes. Beyond, over the meadows, the sun was sinking in vermilion glory. Jack dismounted and lifted her down. He strode to the tent flap, thrust it aside and peered in.

'He's in there, Miss Alice. Now 'tis up to you.' He stood back.

Alice looked into the smoky interior. 'I can't go in there!' she gasped.

'I can't leave the horses and supplies,' Jack said practically. 'They'd not be here when we came back — and I can't leave you out here, neither.' He seized her arm and propelled her inside.

She looked around. Under the sweating canvas roof there seemed to be dozens of men, some in an embarrassing state of undress. On pallets on the bare ground those wounded the week before groaned and tossed. On the far side a small group stood around a makeshift table, talking. One of them was Chris.

Alice stiffened her spine. She cleared her throat and called out, 'Chris Rokesby! A word, if you please.' He turned, a blank expression on his face, then he was shouldering his way through the crowd to her side.

'Little Alice! What a surprise!'

'I can't imagine why you should be surprised,' she said with dignity. 'You sent me a message and I have answered. *A moi*, Blondel,' she added.

He smiled. 'That old battle cry. I don't know why I wrote that.'

She was thinking, How changed he is in just a year! Can a man approaching majority be said to be still growing? For he appeared immensely tall to her, dressed in immaculate grey with the regiment's coat of sky-blue, spotless lace at his throat, above which his face was pale and finely planed. About him the air of authority clung; the set of his head and shoulders declared the same. Only his eyes were the same: shining blue and candid in the flickering light shed by the lanterns swinging from the tent roof.

'You wrote that because you knew I would respond,' she said briskly. 'And so I have. Outside this tent is as fine a horse as can be obtained. On another are saddlebags, packed with a pair of Uncle Richard's best leather boots. Also anything else I could lay my hands on at short notice.'

He was staring at her. 'Sweet Alice,' he murmured. 'In my dreams you have featured and now here you are in the flesh. I can't believe it.'

'Sore and tired flesh,' she answered, wondering why she had never before noticed how attractive Chris Rokesby was. How blue his eyes, how glossy and rich his hair, curling over his high-standing collar. She looked at him tonight as if she had never before set eyes upon him. She pressed on with her polite speech. 'I am so tired I could sleep for a week.'

'I know well the feeling. . .you must rest and eat.' He looked around the noisy tent. 'Obviously not here. How many men did you bring with you?'

'One. Jack Madesley.'

'Little Jack!' Chris looked horrified. 'You came all that way with just a boy?'

'Big Jack,' she corrected him. 'He has been a-growing while you've been away, and is strong and smart as well. I trust him absolutely. . .with good reason.'

He was continuing his appraisal of her. 'He is not the only one to have done some growing—you are all grown up, little Alice.'

She coloured under his eyes and said quickly, 'I shall not be happy until what I have brought is in your care. Sometimes I have thought that we would never reach you with it still intact.' With that sentence she made light of the several narrow escapes she and Jack had had on the road, from men made desperate by a need brought on by the war which raged through England. The ordinary man, tending his farm and caring for his family, had found himself caught between two fires. On the one hand he could join the army of the government and perhaps be paid. On the other he could stay on his farm and give up his hard-earned profits to that same army. Either way his family might starve. Small wonder that he would see a pair of travellers on two good mounts, with another carrying weighty luggage which might contain edible or valuable goods, and chance his arm. Other than these usually respectable citizens were another more raffish breed. There were a great many deserters from both sides—men who had been promised riches to fight and been swiftly disillusioned. All in all it had been a hazardous trip.

Chris said, 'I can imagine—and if you truly have a likely horse out there I had better stake my claim before another does. Forgive me a moment.' He left her and returned to the table, touching one of the men on the arm. The man turned to attend to him. Alice saw that he was not the tallest of the group, nor the most significantly dressed, yet there was about him such an intense vitality that he made the others around him appear half alive. His eyes flickered over to her, then he smiled and nodded, and Chris came back to her.

'Who is that?' Alice asked as they left the tent.

'It is the Prince Rupert—my commanding officer, and as fine a man as I have ever met.'

'Prince Rupert,' she murmured. 'I had imagined him a little different.'

'Ten feet tall and exuding a bright light?' Chris smiled. 'Such is his reputation, I suppose, and he is correctly assessed. He is two years older only than myself, but could win this scrap for us if he were but allowed free rein.'

Prince Rupert of the Palantine, despite his age, was an experienced warrior. Before he was twenty years old he had earned honour fighting at the Siege of Breda, and two short years later had come hurrying to his English uncle's aid to support him as the civil war clouds gathered over England. His bravery and apparent invincibility since had made him a legend among his own troops and those of Parliament.

'I thought him rather like you,' Alice said slowly.

'No greater compliment,' Chris said lightly. 'Now——' They were out in the cool light. Jack was standing patiently on the spot he had found for himself in the shadow of the tent.

Chris ran his eye over him as he and Alice walked over the rough ground towards him. Yes, he thought, Alice had chosen well in her chevalier—he wished he had a hundred young men under his command with just that look in their eyes, that particular determined stance. He extended his hand. 'Jack Madesley—I would never have known you.'

Jack, who had been preparing to bow to the young master of Oaks, blushed and gripped the offered hand. 'Good evening to ye, Master Chris.'

Alice took Jenny's reins from Jack's other hand and gave them to Chris. She curtsied. 'For you, Chris, with my best wishes.'

'But—this is Jenny! Your own sweet filly. Surely you are not giving her to me?'

'I am. On receiving your message I reviewed what the

commissary had graciously allowed me to keep and decided that she was the best.'

Chris fingered the black mane. Jenny, who recognised him, whickered and lowered her head for his caress. Chris loved all living things, and horses—with their brave hearts and grace—first. His own mare had not foundered, as he had written to Alice, but had died horribly from wounds sustained trying to protect her master, who lay on the field of Marston Moor felled by a blow to the head. Chris had cried that day, not with the pain of his own considerable injury—from which he bore a four-inch scar beneath his black hair—but for the loss of such beauty and loyalty. Horses had a short life in the horror of war, and Chris thought he would remember their agonised screams above any other sound of battle until his dying day. He said, with difficulty, 'I remember the day she was born.'

'So do I,' Alice said, remembering. 'Her dam was in sore straits, Jenny being entirely the wrong way around for easy birth and, when my stablemen had despaired, you took off your coat, rolled up your sleeves and rearranged matters, and a few minutes later there was as pretty a foal as was ever seen lying on the straw. I *want* you to have her, Chris.'

'Then I thank you, sweetheart, and promise I will see for her with my life if necessary.'

'You will see for each other,' Alice said firmly. 'Now, we were discussing where I might rest and eat.'

'Yes. . .' Chris looked vaguely about him. There was, of course, accommodation for women in the camp. But those women were not the kind he could introduce a young girl to. 'I have it,' he said. All cavalier camps had their makeshift churches, where the fighting men could go for spiritual guidance before and after battle. Alice could rest there and he would find food for her. His servant, a slim, dark boy with a clever face, had followed him out. 'John—take charge of this horse, and of what is in the bags of her fellow. Guard them well, my boy.' John smiled and took Jenny's reins. 'Also,' Chris said, glancing at Jack, 'take this fellow with you and see him fed and bedded down for the night.'

Walking across the uneven ground towards the tent emblazoned with a black cross, Chris took Alice's arm. 'I didn't expect you to come in person, you know. Why didn't you send through the usual route?'

'The Evening Sun, you mean? I went there, of course, but. . . Molly Judd told me they are watched, suspected of sending aid through to the King's men.' Under cover of the darkness she flushed. She hoped he would not ask for Molly—she didn't want to hear the same note in his voice as she had heard in Molly's.

'I see. I hardly know how we are to continue fighting if all such avenues become blocked. The opposing army grows in strength each day.' He sounded almost despairing.

'Would that be such a terrible thing?' she asked reasonably. 'If this squabble ended all the young men could go home and——'

'Don't ever say that to me!' he said harshly. 'I have seen my friends die—and horribly—before my eyes, in what you dismiss as a squabble. If we should lose, their deaths will have been in vain, and we in the King's army still alive will lose everything.'

They were passing one of the many fires lit around the camp; in the dancing light his eyes were dark and brilliant.

'But Chris,' she faltered, 'you will still have Oaks.' She stopped, her heart thudding. Now she must convey the news that she had dreaded telling, and shrank from it—the more so because she felt it so terrible to add to his burdens. 'Your cousin—your cousin, William. . .'

'I know, Alice,' he said tiredly. 'Months ago I had a message.'

'I'm sorry,' she said painfully. 'I loved him too. But

your cousin Margaret told me. . .told me that in his will he left Oaks and. . everything to you.'

Chris could have laughed at her innocence. He had inherited nothing, he knew bitterly. A Royalist soldier? If he escaped with his life and returned home to Kent it would be to find his estates sequestered under the new laws. Under government law now no man who supported the throne could own land, or if they could it would be as the result of paying an exorbitant fine, and there was no ready cash at Oaks. He kicked at the dried mud under his feet with his scuffed leather shoes. He had taken them from a dead Roundhead after Marston Moor. They were two sizes too small and he hoped to God that the boots Alice had for him would fit better.

There was a way for him to retain his property, a way taken without shame by many of his comrades who had quietly asked a sympathetic supporter of the other side to allow the deeds of their property to be transferred to them and so escape confiscation or fine. Two months ago, seeing the ways thing were, Chris had written to Henry Carrington and asked him for this favour. He had had no reply.

'Chris?'

He looked down at her anxious upturned face. A year ago he had examined this same face in the gentle light of the stable-yard at Oaks. Tonight he saw the same beauty he had seen then, with an added mature loveliness. Beneath that attractive skin he could still identify the leggy child that Alice had been, the valiant spirit so determined to keep up with two older and stronger boys. She had ridden for five days to get to him with what he had in an idle moment asked for, had suffered on the way, he had no doubt—no one could travel in these times without danger—but retained that bright beauty. 'She looks a likely lass,' Rupert had said when Chris had excused himself from the counsel of war fifteen minutes ago. Likely, yes, thought Chris, and also loyal and brave and probably the best friend he would ever have.

Earlier, caught off-guard by her sudden appearance, he had told her that he dreamed of her. It had not been a courtly compliment, but the truth. Since leaving home and joining his regiment he had frequently conjured her face before sleeping. Before a battle he had done the same and had conceived the superstitious fancy that if he thought of Alice Ashley before commencing the bloody business ahead he would come through it safely. And so far he had. Now, here she was in the exquisite and creamy flesh he had dreamed of. Surely before this confrontation—declared by many in the camp to be the deciding one between the two forces—it was the best of omens.

'My dear,' Alice said gently. 'If I am tired, I believe you are more so.'

'Tired? Yes, I am tired. At any given time I could lie down on the bare earth and sleep for a day, a week, forever. . . But——' he gave a short laugh '—I have no right to that accommodation. I have been serving for a mere twelvemonth, others here for four long years.'

'You are very young,' she said helplessly. He looked so tired, and it was a tiredness of spirit rather than a physical need for rest, and it tore at her heart to see the carelessly debonair Chris so discouraged.

'Young? I am the oldest in my platoon! Our drummer-boy is but twelve years old, my brothers in arms yet to see their nineteenth birthdays——' He broke off as he saw her distressed expression. He must not. . .must not. . . But how good it was to see her! To talk to her! He had not realised until this moment how often in the past he had brought his problems to her and how often she had comforted him. It was a strange thought: Alice—so changeful, so light-hearted. He said, 'I don't know why I am saying all this to you.'

''Tis because you know you can,' she returned gently.

'And because you know I will understand. Now, where am I to sleep? Tomorrow will obviously be one of those days before which a good rest will be needed.'

On impulse he bent his black head and rested it on her shoulder. Against the rough material of her riding habit he murmured, 'Tomorrow? Tomorrow, at first light, you and Jack will be safely away from this place. On the road back to Ashley.'

CHAPTER FOUR

WHEN 'tomorrow' had come and gone, and Alice was
able to think clearly again, she decided that one day an
account in the round would be written of the Battle of
Naseby. Some historian and scholar would sit down in a
quiet room, pen in hand, and write of the strengths and
weaknesses of the two opposing armies, of the position
of their troops and how they were deployed, when and
where and how various men had left their footprints in
history's sands. He would write that the Prince Rupert
had not wanted to fight this battle at all, that—as the
most talented tactician in the Royalist lines—he had
known it could not be won. He would write of mistakes
made, of courage and cowardice in the face of the
enemy; he would also put down the dry facts and
statistics of a major landmark in the great civil war in
England. But he would have no first-hand knowledge;
he would not have been there. Alice was, and for her
the events of the day were restricted to her own actions
and reactions to the actions of others.

At dawn on the fourteenth of June, 1645, Jack
Madesley came to the padre's tent and advised her that
Master Chris had instructed him to make sure she took
the road home without delay. Refreshed by her sleep in
the quiet tent and her companionship with the gentle
old man of God, Alice told her servant that she would
stay and see what she could do. For the wounded, she
said. For wounded there would be, and in large
numbers.

Jack, torn between wishing to carry out the orders of
a man he admired and not being able to withstand a
determined mistress, did his best. He told her of the

horrors to come, of the unspeakable sights she might see, of how he felt personally responsible for her as his master's niece. He also told her that he thought Master Chris would probably hang him if he did not make her comply.

To everything she had a reasonable answer; to the last she gave her glinting smile and told him that she would make it right with young Rokesby. She then asked him what he would do that day, given a free choice. Jack had his answer ready.

'If I had the choice, then I would take arms and join the fray, Miss Alice.'

'Then do so. And may God attend you.'

When the boy had gone Alice reviewed her resources. She had a cool head and a practical nature. Any small injury at Ashley had, for as long as she could recall, been brought to her for making well. She could stanch bleeding, bind a wound, offer comfort as well as any other. She splashed her face with cold water from a bowl on the table, also bearing a font of blessed water. She tied back her hair and left the tent to do battle of her own.

But, even armed with a vivid imagination, she could not ever have imagined such horror as she was called to witness that day. The camp surgeons in the hospital tent accepted her presence without comment. She was not the only woman who found her way there that day. Some were respectable matrons and mothers, who had followed Thomas or Richard or John to the site of the great battle, and who turned to to assist in any way they could. Some were the reverse of respectable—hardened prostitutes, camp-followers—which any army of men attracted as a dog did fleas. But there was no distinction during the conflict at Naseby between those women reared gently or otherwise.

Any young man—and so many of them were scarcely more than boys from the Royalist fallen—thought of home when brought into the medical tent, and thinking of home brought to mind their mothers and sisters. Alice, out of her depth among soldiers with terrible injuries, found the role of comforter most in demand. Throughout the long morning she held hands damp with pain and fear, smoothed back hair from faces distorted in agony, and talked. Talked until her throat was hoarse—of better times to come, of holding on and being brave, of May-tree blossom, pink and dancing under a spring sky, of anything that came into her head to take her charges' minds off what they had seen and experienced that day. And all those words were spoken above the sounds of strife, the cries of men mortally wounded, of screaming horses, of the crack and thunder of guns and the strike of cold steel against cold steel.

'May God forgive them all,' muttered the white-haired padre, who had come hastily to Alice's side to ease the path of a young man for whom the harassed surgeon had pronounced the death sentence.

'One wonders where God is on such a day,' Alice said grimly.

'My child!' Even in this dire moment the old man was prepared to remonstrate against such a remark. 'We all have free will, after all.'

Do we? Alice questioned silently, bending to offer water to a boy who could surely be no more than sixteen and already about to leave this tiresome world. Was her decision to come to this place free will? No, rather it seemed inevitable that she would eventually come to choose a side. Well, she had chosen now, and she wondered where that left Henry Carrington, her betrothed, her future husband. Was Henry out there somewhere? As imperilled as any of the men who had been brought into this place? A frightening thought, for she loved him, did she not? Had agreed that in the future she would love and cherish him above all others? Why, then, did he seem less real to her than this broken boy on the makeshift pallet before her? Less substantial than any of the young men who had most bitterly confronted death that day? Don't think of that, she adjured herself, for these are extraordinary circumstances and 'tis not fair to ask yourself any questions.

At around noon Chris was brought in, bleeding from wounds above the heart and in his right thigh. Alerted by some sixth sense, Alice made her way to his side in time to see the surgeon rip open the dusty shirt.

'This,' the doctor said, 'will heal well enough. But the leg—it must come off if the man is to live. It is already almost too late and the wound is putrefying.'

John, Chris's body servant, was at his elbow, his boy's face marked with tears. 'Sir—I brought him in as soon as I was able. We were separated in the fight, but I searched for and found him. . .'

The surgeon brushed him aside. 'That is as may be, boy, but this limb must be removed immediately.'

John turned disconsolately away.

Alice said, 'Amputation? No!' She dipped a cloth into the bucket of water by the pallet and pressed the cold linen to Chris's forehead. He was unconscious, his mouth drawn back in pain, his long eyelashes fluttering. 'Not that!'

'It will surely turn bad if left,' the surgeon insisted. 'And its poison spread throughout the body. I have seen a hundred such cases.' He turned to his assistant, holding his box of instruments, their sleek, sharp blades bloodied by many hasty operations that day.

'I will not allow it,' Alice declared.

The doctor paused. 'Only a close relative may make such a decision. Are you such?'

'I am,' Alice said breathlessly.

'You are. . .wife? Sister?'

Alice hesitated, her heart beating wildly. Which capacity would bear most weight? 'I am his wife,' she said finally. 'And forbid you to perform such an operation upon my husband.'

'Very well,' the surgeon said. 'But I cannot answer for the outcome of such foolishness.'

'I will answer for it,' Alice said faintly. 'What must I do for him now?'

'Clean both wounds with alcohol,' the surgeon said, his attention already turning to the next emergency. 'Keep him quiet and change the dressings frequently. I believe, myself, that cleanliness is paramount in these things. . .' He moved away.

Alice, left alone with Chris, drew a sharp breath. Now what had she done? She had no right to decide life or death for him! Yet into her mind slid memory of a conversation she had had with Chris two years ago. One of the Ashley men had put a pitchfork through his foot during harvest. The wound had turned septic and the barber surgeon had been summoned in haste to perform his grisly duty.

Matt Worsely had recovered in time, but the next time Chris had seen him limping about the estate, he had said to Alice, 'My God, better he had died than suffer such mutilation!'

'He is alive,' she had protested. 'And will be well taken care of here.'

'Even so,' Chris had declared passionately, 'I would rather be dead than half a man.'

Alice bent over the lifeless body. She could see that the surgeon had spoken good sense. The chest wound was no more than a long scratch, but the leg—the gash was six inches in length and the lips of the angry-looking injury already beginning to fester. . .

'Mistress Alice——' Jack materialised at her side, covered in mud and barely recognisable through the layer of dust on his face.

'Jack! I'm glad you're safe.'

'So am I,' Jack said laconically. 'What's to do here, then?'

'Master Chris is badly hurt—'tis his leg. I have forbidden that it be taken off, but now I—— It needs to be stitched and I have sent the surgeon away.' She began to cry weakly.

Jack gripped her arm. 'Bear up, Miss Alice. If it needs a bit of thread, you can do that, can't you? You've done it often enough before.'

'Oh, Jack, only on little cuts—and once on my lap-dog when it was in a fight—those were mere scratches compared to this!'

'The job's the same,' Jack said calmly. 'What do you need?'

'A needle, coarse thread, but I——' But Jack was gone, to return almost immediately with the necessary implements. He also had a bottle of brandy tucked under one arm.

'In case he should wake while you're practising doctoring on him,' he grinned.

Alice marshalled her wits. She threaded the needle in the flickering light of the lanterns suspended overhead, lit to try to dispel some of the dust and smoke-induced gloom. She carefully cleaned the gory wound and began to make neat stitches.

Jack glanced sideways at her. She looked like a child, he thought, bent anxiously over her embroidery for fear a stern mother might whip her if her efforts were not good enough. The tip of her tongue appeared between her parted lips as she concentrated; her hair had long ago escaped its demure linen cap and lay on her shoulders in gold and brown curls.

'There.' She snipped off the thread and straightened up. 'I think that will do. Now the bandage, but first—— Oh, I should have asked the doctor for some soothing balm.'

Jack tipped a little of the brandy on to a cotton swab.

'This will do. Good for any ill, within or without. We'll get the other presently.'

As she wound the length of linen around his thigh Chris stirred and opened his eyes. He smiled when he saw Alice.

'Alice. . .what are you about?'

'Probably murder,' she said tartly, relief that he had emerged from his coma and was able to speak sharpening her tongue. 'How do you feel?'

Chris grimaced. 'My chest is sore and my leg is numb.' His bright gaze shifted to Jack. 'Well, Jack, you were in the thick of the fight, were you not? But unscathed, I see, unlike my foolish self.'

'Unhurt, thanks to you,' Jack muttered. At one point in the battle he and Chris had been alongside each other; they had exchanged a few swift words before being overwhelmed by the enemy. Jack, willing but unskilled, had been hard-pressed to defend himself, and within moments had been unhorsed and fighting for his life on the ground, two Ironsides intent on despatching him to his maker. There had been a shout from above and then Chris Rokesby was beside him, his sword flashing about the business of death. Chris had then hauled him to his feet, remounted and plunged back into the mêlée.

'How went the day?' Chris demanded now.

Jack swallowed. 'It is lost to us, sir.'

'Lost?' Chris murmured. 'Then the cause is lost.'

'I fear so,' Jack said awkwardly. 'I have heard that there are five thousand officers of the King taken prisoner.'

'And myself not among them,' Chris said bitterly.

'You have done your part,' Alice broke in. 'And now must rest.'

'Have you heard aught of the Prince Rupert?' Chris ignored her, his eyes on Jack.

'He is away safe. His Majesty too. Or so rumour has it.'

'Away to fight another day,' Chris chanted in the sing-

song voice of delirium. Two hectic spots of colour lay on
his cheeks. He closed his eyes.

A few hours later Alice and Jack moved Chris into the
warm night. It was a move strongly resisted by those
around them, but Alice insisted. The tents containing
the wounded were crowded, noisy and horrible with the
cries of the mutilated soldiers.

'He must have quiet!' Alice said fiercely. 'The doctor
said that to me. Help me take him out, Jack. The night
is warm and there will be more ease for him beside a
camp fire than in this hell.'

She had her way and, choosing a spot on the outskirts
of the encampment, she wrapped Chris in blankets and
sat down to watch over him for the rest of the night.
Towards dawn she raised heavy eyes as a small party of
men came quietly over the ground towards them. One
of them was the Prince Rupert. She got unsteadily to
her feet as he bent and jerked the covering from her
charge.

'Chris? Chris Rokesby?'

She stepped forward. 'This is Rokesby, sir. What do
you want with him?'

The man's bold eyes swept over her. Were it not for
his reputation he could have been the gentle romantic
prince of a hundred fairytales, handsome and youthful.
He said, 'I wanted to be sure he had survived the day,
mistress. You are?'

'Alice Ashley of Kent,' she said, managing a crooked
curtsy.

Rupert put out a hand and helped her up. 'Chris
always did have a pretty taste in ladies. What is amiss
with him?'

'He is sore wounded in chest and leg,' she said. As
she spoke Chris moved in his cocoon of blankets and
struggled to rise. Rupert was swiftly on his knees by his
side.

'Rokesby, lie quiet now.'

'Rupert? You here? I had heard you had escaped.'

'I had. Have. I am not here and you haven't seen me. My spirit is simply checking up on old friends.'

Chris laughed shakily. 'You are tricky, my prince, even in this desperate hour.'

'Desperate indeed. . .' Rupert put his arms around his friend and laid him back on the warm wool. 'What do you now, Chris?'

Alice had come to stand above him. 'I am taking him home, sir.'

Rupert glanced up. 'Very wise.'

'Not so,' Chris said. His leg was on fire now, the blessed numbness of the savage thrust worn off, and his chest ached abominably, but his brain was miraculously clear. 'I am with you, sir. We will disappear from this dismal place and appear in another to fight again.'

'No, no, Rokesby. We lost today. Not only the battle, but also the war. My uncle Charles is already fled to Oxford to consider the future. Had he asked me, I could have told him what it holds. It is over. *Over*. All bar the shouting, as you English say.'

'I cannot believe that,' Chris protested.

'Nevertheless, 'tis true, my dear friend. But what concerns me in this moment is where do you go? Home? As your pretty lady says?'

'Home?' repeated Chris bitterly. 'Where is that? My home is now an enemy stronghold. I would rather die here among my comrades.'

Alice made an instant decision. Where the thought came from she had no idea, but it sprang into her mind. 'Not home to Oaks, Chris, but to my—our—home. To Gull's Nest on the Cornish coast.'

'Cornwall?' Rupert said quickly. 'The west is still ours, Chris. Go you there and we might well meet again for the final reckoning.'

The effort of talking, of feeling an emotion too strong

for any man in his weakened state, had taken its toll.
Chris sank again into unconsciousness.

Rupert stood up, looking down silently. Then he said,
'It is true? You are for the west, mistress?'

'Yes,' said Alice firmly.

'Then take this.' Rupert reached into his short coat
and withdrew a purse, clinking with coins. 'And may
God care for you, and one of the bravest men I have
ever known, on the journey.' He swept off his feathered
cap as he bowed low. 'Good luck, sweet Alice, take care
of my friend.'

'I will,' promised Alice, her throat constricted. 'He is
rather like you,' she had said to Chris about the prince.
Now she felt that more strongly than ever. To look at
them they could be brothers, she thought, but they also
shared other qualities: courage, kindness and charm of
manner. Added to these was something less easy to
define—a charismatic aura which brought men—and
women—to their side in fair weather or foul, prepared
to stake their lives on their leadership. She watched the
prince melt into the darkness with his guards, then sat
wearily down again to continue her vigil.

At mid-morning the next day rumour swept the decimated Royalist camp that the victorious army were
preparing to clean out the remnants of the enemy camp,
take any able-bodied men prisoner, and drive off the
rest. Any war was about territory, and this land was now
indisputably Parliament's. Jack, who had been here and
there since early light listening to gossip and also seeing
what he could 'liberate' in the way of useful provisions,
came to Alice and said quietly, 'If we are to move, Miss
Alice, it must be soon.'

Alice rubbed the sleep she had finally achieved out of
her eyes. Before dropping into oblivion she had asked
herself over and over again what had possessed her to
say that she would take Chris to Gull's Nest. She had

only the vaguest knowledge of where exactly it was, and
no idea at all how to get there. And even if the journey
could be made, with a severely wounded man, and his
enemies on every road, what would they find when they
arrived? Occasionally her Uncle Richard had mentioned her inherited estate in Bude, usually in sentimen-
tal terms as his childhood home—but she had little
knowledge of its whereabouts or condition. Hesitantly,
she explained the situation to Jack. To her surprise he
threw back his head and laughed.

'So you're a Cornishwoman after all, Miss Alice! I
have often wondered if you were under that——' He
stopped and turned brick-red. 'Please excuse me, I must
be mazed by the battle and all.'

'Don't apologise,' Alice said hastily. 'After all you
have done in the last days. . . Only help me explain to
Master Chris when he wakes that I have made a promise
I cannot possibly keep.'

'Why can't you keep it?' Jack asked quietly.

'Because I have not the faintest notion where in
England I have sworn to take him to.'

'I have. I was only a little lad when I came with you
and Betty to Ashley, but I can find my way back all
right.'

Alice looked at him. His blush had receded, and his
eyes were bright and hopeful. She said, 'Even so, how
can we move him without causing more injury? And
surely if we do we will be accosted by—by those who
defeated us yesterday?'

'He won't take no more injury from sitting a horse,'
Jack said steadily. 'He's tough enough to stand that. As
to being stopped by those b—by those Roundheads,
they have other business on their minds right now.'

Most of Fairfax's troops had moved on; those who
remained to complete the operation of herding up the
Royalists at Naseby were a relatively small force, and

necessarily must confine their activities to sorting out
any potential future threat.

Somehow they got Chris astride the horse Jack
provided—had stolen, to be strictly honest, and he had
chosen well. The poor animal would be no temptation
to any man, nor would be the two mounts that Jack and
Alice had made their own. Alice said sadly as they rode
slowly away from Naseby, 'I hate to leave this place
without knowing what happened to Jenny. You know
nothing of her?'

'No, Miss Alice,' Jack lied. He had seen Jenny's
body, just a carcase among the other poor innocents of
the slaughter. She had been pierced through the chest
by a musket-ball, probably at the moment her rider had
been thrown from the saddle and sustained his own
injuries. Jack did not relish the thought of telling either
that rider or his mistress of her end. . . 'Some other
cavalier has taken her to make his escape,' he said
comfortingly. 'We'll not begrudge him, will we?'

'No, indeed,' Alice sighed. 'But it hurts me all the
same.'

Too easily hurt, sweet pretty lady, Jack thought. But
how proud he was of her for not showing it! And for
what she had done yesterday, and for daring to chance
herself again today in getting her friend to safety. Were
they just friends, she and Master Chris? wondered Jack,
normally the least speculative of young men. In the
past, growing up together at Ashley, Alice and Chris
Rokesby had always seemed to rub each other up the
wrong way, teasing and arguing, but she had proved her
mettle in coming here to this place.

Jack adjusted himself more comfortably in his saddle,
upon a horse overburdened by both his weight and that
of makeshift bundles of food and supplies, and looked
onwards and forwards to the West Country.

* * *

The little party arrived at Gull's Nest two weeks later. It had been a horrible journey, Alice thought, looking up at the outline of her birthplace—black and stark against a radiant sunset. The weather had chosen to turn in those weeks—to heavy rain, which made the roads impassable rivers of mud, thereby preventing their progress for several days at a time. Chris had been, in turns, rational and bitter, or delirious and too ill to move—in both moods he had been uncooperative. It had taken all her ingenuity to subdue him and all her kindness to bear with him.

Now they were here. Chris, whey-faced and drooping in the saddle, and Jack, desperately weary and thin from the lack of nourishing food in the last ten days. Herself? She had not minded the discomfort, the poor accommodation—for, despite her ready hand with the gold Prince Rupert had provided, inn-keepers were reluctant to take in a man so plainly in the grip of fever—or the grinding hardship of eight hours at a time in the saddle in churning mud and drenched by rain.

What she had minded was that the man she was making this desperate journey for was a stranger. A cruel-tongued, disappointed, awkward stranger. Was it her fault that his cause had failed? she had asked herself many times. Was she to blame for the humiliation of defeat? Calm reason answered no to both these questions, but Chris Rokesby appeared to lay all the blame for his ills at her feet. In the past fortnight he had alternately railed and upbraided her, or turned a stony face to her sympathy.

'Shall we ride on up?' Jack asked, urging his tired horse alongside hers.

'I suppose so. I think I will go a little ahead, and you bring. . .him, after.' She dug her heels into her mare's flank and hastened up the weed-filled drive.

She had awoken to a rosy dawn; the capricious English weather had decided that she would take her first sight of Gull's Nest for twelve years at the end of a perfect summer's day. Her riding habit, soaked yesterday under torrential rain, had dried on her body throughout the hot afternoon, but she was still chilled and aching from too many hours in damp clothing and longed for hot water and a comfortable bed to rest in.

Outside the deep stone porch she dismounted stiffly and raised her hand to grasp the iron pixie which served as doorknocker. As she did so the door opened and a woman, candle in hand, stood staring at her.

'Why——' Alice stared back in astonishment, for the woman could be Betty Mote! Betty, grown old and thin—but the bright dark eyes, the cheerful smile were identical. She said hesitantly, 'I am——'

'I know who you are, Miss Alice,' the woman declared. 'I'd know you anywhere.' The woman bobbed. 'Are you alone? Surely not!'

'No. . . There is my manservant and another gentleman. Up the drive apiece. You are?'

The woman looked disappointed, or as disappointed as anyone with so cheerful a face could look. 'I'm Lizzie Mote, miss, your Betty's mam. Don't you know me? Well, 'twas a long time ago you left, but I would know you, as I said, anywhere. How's my Betty, then?'

'Betty?' Alice was mystified. 'She is well and. . . But, forgive me, I had no idea she had a relative here. She never——'

'Mentions me? No, I suppose she wouldn't.' She flashed her undaunted smile again. 'See, me and her pa weren't wed. I was let down, as they say, but Old Mistress Ashley—your pa's mother that was—you won't remember her, for she died afore you went off to your uncle——'

The story appeared to be getting more and more complicated. Alice leaned against the stout doorpost, her head swimming with hunger and fatigue. Lizzie clapped a hand to her mouth.

'Now! Here I am with my nonsense and you half
faintin'. Land sakes!' She was looking over Alice's
shoulder along the drive. "Tis a day for ghosts and no
mistake! But it can't be.' Chris, tired of waiting, was
approaching, slumped low in the saddle, but shaking off
Jack's steadying hand. 'Old Reckless Rokesby,' Lizzie
murmured. 'But no, he is dead and in his grave more'n
half a century.'

'That is Christopher Rokesby,' Alice said weakly.

Lizzie sped past her through the porch. As Chris
made a clumsy attempt to dismount she offered her wiry
arm to support him. He remained upright with difficulty, leaning against her, unable to put any weight on
his injured leg. Jack sprang from his horse and came
around his other side. Between them they brought Chris
into Gull's Nest.

In the hall, Chris was deposited gently on to one of
the faded settles and Lizzie disappeared through one of
the doors. She returned with a glass containing a
glowing dark red liquid and put it into his hand. He
looked up at her, bemused, gulping at the liquor.

'I don't know who you are, madam,' he said, remov-
ing his battered hat. 'But I am eternally grateful to you,
for both your strong arm and your good wine.'

'Raspberry cordial, Master Chris, and as good as any
French wine,' Lizzie said, responding as any female of
any age did to her unexpected visitor.

Alice had remained standing in the doorway. Grateful to *her*, she thought resentfully. And I have cajoled
and most gently bullied you over hundreds of miles of
hard road! Held you in my arms when you cried with the
pain of your wounds, sat up of nights in horrible dirty
rooms — Jack came to her.

'I will attend to the horses, Miss Alice,' he said
quietly. 'You must take a little food now, then find a
bed and sleep.' He said peremptorily to Lizzie, 'This

lady is very hungry and tired. Please give her some
attention at once.'

'That I will,' Lizzie returned cheerfully. 'And fully
intended to, as soon as this poor lad was off his feet.
And don't you be givin' me stern orders, Jack Madesley,
for I was changing your napkins not so long ago.'

Jack blushed. 'You know me then, Liz Mote?'

'Of course I do,' Lizzie said, for the second time that
day. 'In spite of all those extra inches. It's quite a
reunion we're havin' here.'

Chris had fallen asleep sitting up, his empty glass held
loosely in his fingers. Alice shifted her weight to her
other foot, wishing she could do the same. Lizzie
grasped her arm and led her across to the stairs. 'You
first, Miss Alice. Then Jack and me'll see to the poor
gentleman.' They began to climb the stairs.

She won't be calling him that when he sharpens his
tongue on her, thought Alice, scarcely aware of reaching the upper floor. Lizzie opened a door at the end of
the passage.

'This was you mam's room, God rest her. She would
be glad indeed to know you were to lay your head on
her pillow.' She went to the vast curtained bed and drew
back the coverlet. 'Might be a touch damp—I'd no idea
to expect you, you know.'

'It doesn't matter. . .' Alice sank thankfully on to the
plump mattress. The linen was clean, but worn and
patched; the cover, once bright with embroidery, was
now fawn and grey. In fact the whole house is practically
to rack and ruin, she thought. What a shame. Almost
forgotten memories of the beauty and grace which had
existed here in the past drifted before her closed eyes.
Yes, she remembered this room—remembered the dia-
mond brightness of the windows pierced by morning
sun, the yellow pools of light lying on rich Turkey rugs,
remembered the high gloss on the elegant French
furniture and the soft outline of a figure sitting up on

this very bed among dazzlingly white lace. Remembered. . . She slept.

When she awoke it was pitch-dark beyond the undraped windows. Lizzie had set a single candle burning on the table before the dark glass and the flame wavered uncertainly in the wind which blew through several cracks in the glass. Alice sat up, her aching muscles protesting. How long had she slept? Long enough to be refreshed, and now she was ravenously hungry. Someone had put a plate of little cakes and a beaker of milk beside her bed. She bit into one of the cakes. It was as hard as wood and lacking in either sugar or any spice, but it took the edge off her appetite and the milk was good—cool and creamy.

There were several stubs of candles in pewter holders on the table as well, she lit them from the one burning and the room became less shadowy. Her trunk had been unpacked and its contents folded and laid on the chest below a mirror. On the wash-stand she found a cracked jug of tepid water. She washed away some of the grime of travelling, changed her dusty clothes and picked up one of the ivory-backed brushes on the dressing-table. It was yellowed with age and the initials AA, fashioned out of silver, were tarnished and dark. Alice Ashley had been her grandmother's name as well as her own, she thought, drawing the bristles through her tangled hair. How strange to be here in this place using this brush.

A faint tapping on the door disturbed her. She called, 'Come in,' and turned to find Jack in the doorway. He smiled shyly.

'I hope you're feeling better, Miss Alice.'

'I am.'

He stepped in and looked around. 'A dismal place now, Gull's Nest, isn't it? In the old days it was counted the most beautiful house in these parts.'

Alice found a dusty length of ribbon in one of the

drawers and threaded it through her hair. 'It is dismal,' she sighed. 'I wonder why Uncle Richard didn't sell it years ago.'

'It wasn't his to sell. . . And perhaps he thought you might want to come back here some day.'

'I wonder why I have now. . . It would have been better to go home, Jack. Chris should have been taken back to his cousin Margaret. How is he?'

'Well enough,' Jack answered shortly. 'Well enough, anyway, to refuse to allow Lizzie to touch his dressings.'

Alice frowned. 'We will see about that. Which room is he in?'

'The room at the far end.' He stepped back hastily as Alice marched past him. 'But I would leave him be. He's in no mood for——'

But Alice was out of the room and flying down the passage. Without knocking, she opened the door at the end of the gallery.

'What the hell!' Chris was lying flat on his back in the bed. He lifted his head and saw her advancing on him. 'Go away, little Alice, I am not fit company for anyone.'

'I have come to look at your wounds,' she said.

'I don't want them looked at! I don't want them touched—they hurt like—like anything, and I could not answer for my temper if you insist.'

'I have been exposed to your temper for thirteen long days,' she said crisply. 'I am sure I have no more to learn of how evil it can be.'

A smile tugged at his mouth. He had only patchy recollection of the last two weeks, but some moments were clear enough in his mind. 'I have given you a hard time, have I not?'

'You've been abominable!' she said, not smiling in return. 'I can only find it in my heart to forgive you as you were so seldom in your right senses. Now, must I call Jack to hold you down while I examine you?'

'No, don't do that, for Jack is as disillusioned with me

as I am with myself. I am suitably ashamed, Alice. You need not rub it in.'

'All I intend rubbing in is a little balm,' she said in softer tones. 'If I can remember where in our luggage I packed it.'

He gestured to the table. 'Lizzie brought it up, I believe. . . I'm afraid I was very rude to her when she attempted to apply it.'

Alice sat down on the edge of the bed and looked at him. 'You were always very disobliging towards anyone trying to help you. When you were twelve you bit the surgeon who was summoned in haste to patch you up when you fell from the tall oak at the end of your manor's drive.'

He laughed wryly. 'Yes, I remember that—and your scathing remarks for my doing so. I suppose I have always tried to hide my hurt, always considered it a weakness on my part to be hurt at all.'

'Then try to turn over a new leaf,' she said briskly, 'for 'tis arrogance, you know, to believe you are invincible.' She lifted aside his shirt and viewed his shapely breast. Here the flesh had healed well; in two weeks the wound had closed and looked healthy enough.

Colour rising in her face, she eased open the blood-stiffened gap in his breeches to look at his leg. She untied the bandage she had with difficulty applied two days ago in the malodorous tavern they had been forced to stop in. Here was a different story.

Conscious of his eyes fixed on her face, she tried not to reveal what the sight made her feel. The livid wound was terrible to see—swollen and angry-looking, dark streaks veining out from the gash, her neat black stitches almost hidden in the puffy flesh. Involuntarily, she bent closer.

'Don't worry,' he said drily, 'it has not yet reached that state. I have smelled gangrene often enough in the past year and can say it is not yet apparent.'

She lifted her eyes to his face and said painfully, 'The camp surgeon wished to remove the leg. I wouldn't let him.' She thought guiltily of the lie she had told then.

'So it was your intervention that saved me from that. I did wonder. . .' He took one of her hands and held it against his cheek a moment. He kissed her fingers without speaking.

In the silence she could hear her heartbeat quicken. Puzzled, she stared at him.

There was a movement behind her and Jack said, 'Miss Alice, I remember there was an old man in the village who was reckoned a miracle-worker as far as healing went. Job was his name—if he is still alive——'

'Find him and bring him here, Jack,' Alice said, white-faced.

Old Job came limping up to Gull's Nest a half-hour later, brought by Lizzie's kitchen boy, Thomas, the only servant apart from herself employed in the manor. He was simple-minded, but capable of straightforward duties, and required no payment for his services except for room and board.

Lizzie had been mortified by the glances she had seen Miss Alice giving the poor condition of the house, for she had done her best with very little for more than ten years. Robert Ashley had made his money early in his lifetime, then speculated with it, losing much of its substance. He had sold off the outlying land shortly before his death and left the house to his only surviving child, Alice, with little cash for its upkeep. His brother Richard, Alice's guardian, had thought of selling the property many times and putting the resultant monies in trust for Alice, but never had. Perhaps, as Jack had said, he had thought she might one day want to come back to the place she was born.

Out of his own pocket Richard had sent the house-keeper, Lizzie, enough to keep her as caretaker—which duty she had carried out with scrupulous application—but there had been no extra for any but strictly necessary repairs. Lizzie felt it very keenly when she looked around the battered shell that her old home had become.

Alice took Job up the stairs with the gravest misgivings that he would be able to do anything at all for Chris. He was such an unprepossessing old man, dirty and apparently half-blind, but she was by this stage prepared to try anything. For Chris had slipped back into delirium again in the last hour, his fever noticeably worse. Alice, standing at the side of the bed and watching Job peer dubiously at the ghastly wound, could feel the heat of his body from where she stood.

Job grunted and gestured to Jack, who waited impassively, holding the old man's bag. The bag was made of stiffened hide and was of good quality, though shabby, and Alice wondered how he had come by it. After silent minutes of examination Job took out a flask of dark cloudy liquid and something else. Alice looked with horror upon the glittering knife. Without glancing at her Job said, 'Out you go now, mistress. This boy here can do what is necessary.' He gestured at Jack. When she hesitated he said testily, 'I want no fainting women here.' His voice and the phrasing of his words was educated; Alice felt a flicker of hope. But——

'You do not intend to—to. . .'

He gave her a scornful look. 'I like my patients in one piece, lady.'

Alice turned and left the room, closing the door behind her but remaining in the passage listening. But whatever carpenter had wrought and hung the oak doors of Gull's Nest had made them close-fitting and at least three inches thick. There was no sound from within.

Lizzie found her there when she came with a tray

holding a bottle of brandy, glasses and a bowl of bread crusts soaked in milk.

'The old man asked for these,' she said, putting the tray on the chest which stood against the wall. 'I had to send to the tavern for the bottle. I'm sure I don't know what the landlord thought, but he gave it to Thomas without asking for payment.'

'I have money,' Alice said. 'He'll be paid tomorrow.' She was still rigid with straining to hear what might be happening beyond the door.

Lizzie opened the bottle and poured a little into a glass. 'You have this. Even a Rokesby can't down a whole bottle by himself,' she grinned.

Alice took the offered glass and almost absent-mindedly tipped the brandy down her throat. It burned like fire and she gasped.

'That'll put heart into you, though what your mother would have said, I daren't think. What about some food now?'

'Later, when—when I know he's all right. Tell me, Lizzie, how do people around here feel about the war? I mean, if they knew Master Chris was here, and had fought for the King?'

'They don't know that, do they?' Lizzie said practically. 'And won't unless we tell them.'

'But if they did?' Alice insisted. On the journey here there had been many tales whispered—they were hanging Royalist soldiers on any pretext now. 'Is the west still for the King?'

'Around here, yes. O'course we have our share of rebels too.'

Alice half smiled. In Kent it was the King's men who were the rebels—somehow it made such a nonsense of the whole thing. Civil war, as Chris had said, was a desperate matter. 'Should we hide him?'

Lizzie looked outraged. 'Hide a loyalist in an Ashley

house? Now, that would make your grandma mad, and your ma and pa too!'

After what seemed an age, but was in reality only a half-hour, the door behind her opened, and Alice looked fearfully at Job who plodded out. His eye lighted on the brandy and Lizzie poured a stiff measure. He tossed it back at a gulp and held his shaky hand out for more. Lizzie pursed her lips and repeated the measure. Job set the glass back on the tray and smacked his lips appreciatively. He said, directing his words to Alice, 'The leg will be better, in time. About the fever, I am not so sure. It may be part of it; it may not. Don't you touch my good work—just make him take his physic and stay still.' A smile crossed his weatherbeaten face. 'If you can. I'll be back tomorrow to see him again.'

'But he will be all right?'

'Any man who can ride for a sennight with that leg won't come to grief lying soft abed,' was all he would commit himself to. He stumped off down the gallery, leaving the two women staring after him. Alice turned into the bedroom.

Chris was propped up in the bed, his leg raised on a bolster. The material of his breeches had been cut completely off and only a light bandage covered the wound, at the edges of which Alice could see traces of blood. His eyes were closed, but she fancied he felt a little less hot. He opened his eyes as she withdrew her cool hand from his forehead.

'I recall your remark about murder, Alice,' he murmured. 'Who was that unspeakable old curmudgeon?'

Jack was covering a bowl of water, stained with red, beside the bed. He said, 'I've never seen anything like it, Miss Alice. The old fellow said that the bad flesh must be cut away instantly and he carved Master Chris like a table fowl——'

'Spare Miss Alice—and myself—the details, Jack,' Chris said lightly. 'And get rid of that bowl containing half my life's blood.' As Jack smiled sheepishly and picked up the bowl, he added, 'And thank you, my friend, for your patience. I seem to remember calling you several offensive names when you held me down earlier—forgive me for those.'

When Jack had gone out Alice hovered at the foot of the bed, aware of the closed door and the man on the bed, bare to the waist, his leg exposed from thigh to toe. Reading her thoughts, he said mockingly, 'Too late for modesty now, Alice. I imagine you have seen more of me already than is suitable for a maiden. Or so Henry would think, I'm sure. How is he, by the way?'

She looked at him blankly. Henry had not crossed her mind for days now.

He raised his eyebrows. 'Surely you applied to him before racing to my rescue?'

'He wasn't there to apply to,' she said with dignity. 'He and his men have been gone from Fox Hall for nine months. Had he been there I would of course have told him, and he would have understood.'

He laughed. 'If you think that you know little about one of Cromwell's Ironsides, and even less about Hal. He would—far from understanding—have been more inclined to lock you in your room and mount an armed guard on the door.'

'I am not married to him yet,' she said sharply. 'And even if I were he could not order my actions, or tell me what to think.'

'Then I see squalls ahead for both of you. . . Why didn't you marry him before he went? I'll wager he asked you to.'

'He did, but—but I didn't want to be hurried. Then he was so busy recruiting and—— I don't think I have to explain myself to you, Chris Rokesby!'

'No, indeed, and you are probably very wise. Marrying a soldier off to war is a risky business. He might come back maimed as I or not come back at all.'

'You are not maimed,' she said indignantly. 'Job said to me that you would be well.'

'Perhaps I shall, but not for some time.' His mouth twisted and the bitter note invaded his voice again. 'I am a lot of use to the King in this state, am I not?'

'If you are going to feel sorry for yourself, then I have little sympathy. Perhaps you would rather be one of the young men I had the misfortune to witness dying before my very eyes a short time ago!'

Anger flared into his eyes. 'Damn you, Alice, the experience has apparently not curbed your thoughtless tongue! Don't you think I remember them? Every minute I am in my senses I see them. . .my friends——' He broke off as Alice burst abruptly into tears. 'Ah, my dear, don't cry. I should be shot for damning you, after your bravery has saved my miserable hide.' He reached out a long arm and patted her hand awkwardly. She snatched it away.

'You have not even thanked me!'

He blinked, thinking that no one could change their mood as swiftly as Alice. He had a sudden memory of one night on the road when, as he cried out in agony, she had taken him in her arms and rocked him against her breast until he slept. He could smell the perfume of her now. . . He said slowly, 'We must not fight with each other. I have had enough of fighting for the moment. Instead we must decide what is to be done.'

Alice sniffed and shrugged, annoyed with herself for the weak tears. She prided herself on how seldom she resorted to them—a childhood spent in the company of two boys had made it a point of honour not to employ this feminine weakness. 'What is there to be done but wait for you to be well? Then we will speak of what happens next.'

'But should I stay here? The name of Ashley is famous in Cornwall for its support of the crown—or so my cousins always said. As soon as word is abroad that there is a young man at Gull's Nest, the Ironsides will be on the doorstep to round me up.'

'They did not bother us on the journey here.'

'One glance into my face probably assured them that the only place I was bound for was the graveyard. It will be different once I begin to recover. I would have given my life at any time for the cause I fought for, but I am not giving it in the service of some fat Dutchman in the West Indies, or a white swine working poor blacks in the sugar islands.'

'What do you mean?'

'There is a brisk trade in Royalist prisoners these days,' he said cynically, 'as slaves.'

'Englishmen selling their fellow Englishmen for slavery! How dishonourable!' Alice was bright with anger.

He shifted uneasily. He thought, I must be less sick than I imagined to notice how entrancing she is when aroused. What if she were aroused for another reason. . .? Such a thought was betrayal, he rebuked himself, of her inocent friendship, and of his loyalty to Hal. He said, 'Well, honour is usually a casualty of any war.'

There was silence betwen them, disturbed only by the sound of the sea wind seeking entry into the room. The windows rattled and a stray current of air lifted the hair from Alice's forehead. Her thoughts mirrored his and she had the sensation of standing on a familiar shore as a tidal wave swelled in the ocean. When she was with Chris now her feelings were confused, the past obscured by the fancy that she no longer knew him.

'I have heard,' she said at last, 'that many Royalists have transferred their property to a Parliamentarian friend—to keep it safe against taxes and confiscation. If you did that, you could go home when the war is over.'

'I have heard of such transactions,' he said casually.

'Then why not do that?'

'Whom would you suggest I ask? Henry? I am afraid

that would strain his conscience too far.' He had no intention of telling her that he had already asked it of his friend. Also, if Hal had been absent from Fox for nine months, it was possible that he had not received his message. . .

Alice rubbed at a healing burn on her wrist. On the journey here they had been refused shelter by the only available tavern in a village in Devon and had been forced to pass the night in the open. The day had been wet and the night cold so Jack had lit a fire to warm them. Alice had gathered wood and, in putting one of the unwieldy branches on the blaze, had been caught by the flames. Chris caught her hand.

'Don't do that.'

'It itches. . . No, not Henry. I was thinking of myself.'

'That would amount to the same, wouldn't it?'

She avoided looking at him. ''Twould be a solution in the short-term.'

'I hope you have not nurtured me day and night in the hope of acquiring my property.'

'If you could be serious for a moment. It would solve a problem, and you can trust me.'

He shifted uncomfortably again under her candid eyes. What on earth had been in that potion that Job had forced down him? It had had not only the effect of pain-killer, but aphrodisiac as well. . . 'You have done enough for me already,' he muttered. 'Besides, Oaks must be my cousin Margaret's now.'

'But she has not inherited it, has she? If you are sensible she need never know of our arrangement. It would be our secret.'

'Secret like Jubal?'

'Oh, don't remind me of that!' she exclaimed, laughing.

Jubal had been one of Chris's hounds. When still a puppy it had shown evidence of being vicious and, after several incidents, Will Rokesby had reluctantly ordered it to be put down. Chris had smuggled it over to Ashley, where Alice had kept it under her bed for a day, until Jubal had all but bitten the nose off a maid unlucky enough to be investigating the strange sounds in Miss Alice's room. There had been an almighty row, with Richard Ashley much embarrassed and Alice declaring a lapse of memory as to how the puppy came to be in her bedchamber. The inquisition had gone on for some hours, but she had not given Chris away, and when the dust had settled somehow no one had remembered Jubal's execution order and he had grown up to be as good and faithful a dog as any Chris had owned. It came to her now that Henry had not been privy to this secret; neither Chris nor Alice had spoken of excluding him, but——

'I know exactly how to go about the transfer—I read it in a book only a while ago. I will see to the writing of the document. Now, Lizzie will give you a little bread and milk, then you must sleep.' She rearranged his pillows and covered him closely. 'Are you quite comfortable?'

'Quite,' he assured her. 'Comfortable and very grateful to you.'

'At last, some gratitude.'

CHAPTER FIVE

THE next day was wet again. Alice had never seen such weather in July. She no longer puzzled over the lack of flowers in the gardens, for what could live under such conditions? The wind from the raging sea literally ripped the few surviving plants out by their roots, stripped the bright green summer leaves from the trees and sent them dancing over the ground. In the fresh light of morning she was surprised how close the ocean was, could hear the waves crashing thunderously on to the shoreline almost under the house.

A wild place, she thought, hugging her robe around her as she surveyed the scene from her window, but I don't dislike it. Unaccountably, it answered some previously unknown emotion inside her—she who liked order about her—some reckless desire to be out in the rough and teasing wind, pitting her strength against such elements. But perhaps it had been there all the time, waiting for Chris's plea for help to enable it to surface. Otherwise she would not have had the temerity to answer. Lizzie tapped and came in with a mug of chocolate and gave it to her where she stood. It was faintly musty-tasting and Alice guessed it had been long in the kitchen, for such beverages were expensive.

'It is a stormy day,' she said, sipping the hot liquid.

'Oh, this is calm to what it will be in a few months. This is no gentle place at any time.' She began to potter around the room, picking up Alice's discarded clothing and laying it neatly on chest and chair. Alice knew she wanted news of her daughter.

'You asked me last night how Betty was. I told you

102

she was well, and she is. I can also tell you that I have no better maid, and no more trusted friend.'

Lizzie's face was radiant. 'I do thank you for that, Miss Alice! It has been a heartache to me all these years to have no word of her.'

'You were telling me yesterday how that came about.'

'I was, but shouldn't have been.'

'But as you did,' Alice prompted.

''Tis the usual story, I suppose. Betty's dad was a casual labourer here and took off at the first sign of trouble, and old Mistress Ashley wouldn't have me dismissed as your ma wanted.' She smiled apologetically. 'Your ma was rather. . .strict in such matters. Anyway, Mistress Ashley let me stay, and when Betty was born she let me care for her in the proper way. Then she died, but in her will she mentioned me and said I was to have a home here with my child as long as I wanted. I was happy here, specially after you were born, for your mam was sure of my being a good nurse by then and I had the care of you as well as my little girl.' Here the tale came to a halt as Lizzie looked wistful, thinking back on happier times.

'Then, all of a sudden, both your pa and ma took with the summer plague. Oh, it was a dreadful time! Both dead and me demented, thinking you must take the sickness. But you didn't, and then came the question of who would be your guardian, and where you would live and all. . . The upshot of it all was that your Uncle Richard in Kent agreed to have you. After that was the sad time for me. See, you and Betty were raised together. She was older, o'course, but always your slave. So, when it came to the point I said to the lawyers, "Send Miss Alice off to her uncle if you must, but she does not stir off this place without my Betty." And I told Betty straight, "Don't you be looking back, or writing, or. . .anything." That's how it all came about. . .' She tailed off.

Alice was entranced by the story, told so simply yet so sincerely. She said, 'I wish I had known of this—of such loyalty—to give up your own child, Lizzie!'

Lizzie blinked back a few tears. 'Ah, well, as Jack's old grandfer used to say: Ashleys and Rokesbys—they both inspire loyalty.'

'They were close, the two families?'

'Here in Cornwall? My, yes! That was in your grand-mother's time, of course.'

'What was she like, my grandmother?'

'Oh, like you! To look at. The same hair and eyes and——' Lizzie struggled to convey what she remembered of the first Alice Ashley. 'She was alive. Sounds funny, I know, for all above ground are that, I suppose. But she made you think of bright sun and warm wind and in wintertime of how the snow fairly crackles with a life of its own.'

Alice smiled. 'You have a way with words.'

'I'm not usually handy with them, but. . . You had to know her really, miss. I wish you had.'

'So do I. Was she happy? With my grandfather?'

'He died when she was quite young. Before that——' Lizzie hesitated. 'Before that there was a lot of talk about her and Lord Rokesby.'

'Master Christopher's great-uncle?'

'Mmm, yes. There were two Rokesby brothers here in the old Queen's reign—Charles and Toby. Toby was always the more settled one. He married young and had a son, Master Chris's father. He married away from Cornwall, then he died, and his wife, and Master Toby, and we heard here that the son was to be raised in Kent. I guess that's how he came to be your neighbour, Miss Alice.'

'Why was there talk? About my grandmother and Charles Rokesby?'

'Well, your grandfather and he were neighbours——'

'But there isn't a house for miles!'

'There used to be. Along the cliff aways. Great big house. It burned down and some said he did it—Charles. Came home drunk one night from Gull's Nest and torched the place.'

'Why should he do that?'

'I'm coming to that. See, as I say, Edward and Charles were friends from the cradle, and when your grandma came to live at Gull's Nest—she was a distant cousin or something, and had lost her parents—they all become friends, grew up together and, when she and your grandpa married, stayed friends. Then this evening there was some trouble over cards—I'm not sure exactly how it was—and Edward called Charles out. Can you imagine that? And them like brothers! Anyway, Lord Rokesby rode home after they had set the date for dawn the next day, and the next anyone knew Rokesby Manor was ashes and the master of it perished in the flames. Some of the house servants gossiped about the argument not being about cards at all, but about Mistress Alice.' Lizzie's eyes were large remembering these events. 'Still, the old master was in his own grave not long after that and your grandmother lived to be quite an old woman. The business with Reckless Rokesby was more than forty years ago. A long time ago.'

Yes, thought Alice. A long time ago. But how she wished she knew the whole romantic story. For it was romantic, she knew; she had sensed that the moment she had entered this house. There was drama here, and heartbreak, and all the other emotions human beings were prey to. My grandmother and Chris's great-uncle, she thought. She too brought herself up.

'Have you been in to Master Chris this morning?'

'I have, and he is sleeping like a baby. Do you dress now and come down to breakfast, miss. You didn't eat enough last night to keep a bird alive. Jack has been out gathering new-laid eggs and there is bacon in the smoke-hole.'

'I'll be down presently.' Alice washed and dressed, her mind turning on what Lizzie had said. How I wish I knew the whole story! she thought again. For so much of it would parallel my own life, surely. Two boys, one girl. Herself and Chris and Henry.

Reaching Chris's door on her way down the gallery, she opened it quietly and looked in on him. He was dead asleep, one arm thrown back over the pillows, one hand cradling his cheek. He looked perfectly at rest and she closed the door and continued on down the broad staircase. Various problems occupied her. First she must write to Meg Allerton, and advise her to keep up the pretence if any from Ashley should send a message to Alice. Then she must finish writing the document she had begun last night regarding Oaks. Thirdly, she must see what could be done to make Gull's Nest more comfortable to live in for a while, for in daylight its dilapidations were even more apparent.

The day passed busily for Alice. She had always enjoyed housekeeping; she was a born organiser and, knowing herself how things should be done, had always been well-served at Ashley Manor. But Ashley was a country gentleman's home, smooth-running and well-staffed. Here, there were only two pairs of hands—Liz Mote's and the boy, Thomas's.

She set to work in the hall. It was not greatly changed, she suspected, since the house had been built in early Tudor times, save that a false ceiling and large hearth had been added as had become fashionable when men and women became tired of living in one space with a central smoky fire. Above had been added the long gallery and extra bedchambers. To the left and right of the hall the summer and winter parlours. The large expanse of window along the west side of the hall, with its tiny panes—some coloured in amber, violet, red and green and bounded in lead—was still intact, as were the wide honey-coloured boards of its floor, laid here and there with worn rugs, their vivid colours now mostly a uniform tan. Alice opened the door on to the porch, ignoring the flurry of raindrops which entered, and set to work with a stiff broom. She then polished every stick of furniture, relaid the fire and, satisfied, began on the two parlours.

After she had attended to her bedroom, and listened a moment outside Chris's open door, a thought came to her. In none of the chambers were there any pictures. When she had brought her own portrait from here years ago her uncle Richard had admired it, and in later years had remarked that her father's collection of paintings was quite famous. Where were they now? Alice wondered. She called to Lizzie.

'Why, they are all in the portrait gallery, Miss Alice— the long gallery as it's called. I have the key somewhere.' She felt in the pocket of her apron for her bunch of keys and extracted one. Alice slipped it into her pocket. Her uncle had told her that it was a tradition in the Ashley family for each member to be painted once in their lifetime—some of the pictures dated back to medieval years. Artists would travel from one country to another, seeking work at any of the great houses. Occasionally some penetrated as far as Cornwall.

With the sun about to set she tidied herself and opened Chris's door softly. He was awake, his eyes fixed on the glow through the window. He said sulkily, 'Well, at last you've come to see if I am alive or dead.'

Alice lit the candles, their frail flames no match as yet for the shining splendour outside. 'I have been in several times—each time you were fast asleep.'

'Then those must have been the few times I closed my eyes this day. I have been alone for hours.'

She set one candle by the bed. 'Lizzie tells me that you ate a very good lunch.'

'You did not even take trouble to see if I could achieve that.'

'I went to the stables,' she said placatingly. 'Jack has been trying to create some order there. They keep only one ancient horse here—it was necessary to provide accommodation for those we brought here. Is your leg hurting you?'

'Yes.'

She picked up the flask Job had left; it was still three-quarters full. 'Then why have you not taken your physic?'

'I don't want it,' he said petulantly. 'It takes away the pain, but makes me feel half-witted.'

'Dear me, what a difficult task for such innocent-looking stuff.'

'Stop laughing at me. You know I hate to be alone, and I hate being stuck away here with nothing to do.'

'You have something to do—getting well again.' She found a spoon, unstoppered the flask, and carefully poured out the drops. She held it out; he turned his face away.

'I won't take it.'

'If you don't, I shall go away, and forbid anyone else to come near you.'

He opened his mouth, accepted the spoon and swallowed the medicine, shuddering.

'Do you want a sweetmeat to take away the taste?' she asked.

A few strands of dark cloud floated over the dying sun—now the room was crimson, now yellow with candlelight and dark with shadows. Either effect enhanced her, he thought. 'Stop provoking me and talk to me. What have you been about this day?'

'Exploring. Cleaning. I like this house, Chris. I feel that I have come home.'

'You have. Why exploring? Don't you remember it?'

'No, I don't.' She puckered her smooth forehead. 'Do you know what I was thinking while I was working? That I was probably so upset when I left, because of my parents, of course, and leaving my home, that I did not *want* to remember. Could that be so?'

'Perhaps. You are luckier than I am, for my family home doesn't exist any more. Not Oaks, but the Rokesby home here in Bude.'

There were no chairs in this room so after a moment she sat carefully on the bed. 'Lizzie told me about that.'

He was conscious of her weight beside him, not only because it jarred his leg. 'What did she say?'

'That your great-uncle himself had burned the house to the ground.'

He smiled. 'That is an old family story certainly—spoken of with great disapproval by my cousins.'

She looked sideways at him. 'And the rest—did they speak of that?'

'You mean the old tale of him and your grand-mother?' he asked, amused. 'Did Lizzie rake up that yarn too?'

'Is it a yarn? I thought it most romantic.'

'Ah, romantic. . . I never saw it so. It was said that my great-uncle and your grandfather were the best of friends, as blood-brothers, until your grandmother came between them. She had known them both most of her life. She married Edward Ashley then, ten years later—with two young children—decided that she had made a mistake, thereby ruining the lives of two good men.'

'But how cruel you are! One cannot help falling in love!'

'One should decide upon whom one loves before the die is cast.' There was an odd note in his voice—perhaps of warning, perhaps of—— What? Again Alice had the sensation of an undercurrent of some powerful force swirling about her. 'What else had Lizzie to say of the old days?' he enquired.

'She told me about herself, and very sad it was. She was in love with a man who betrayed her and when she—er—when it was clear that he should stand by her, he ran away.'

'Hmm. And Betty is the result? Yes, I guessed—the likeness is extraordinary. Still, Lizzie was more fortunate then than she would be today.'

'How so?'

'Really, Alice, and you betrothed to a Puritan! Don't you know it is now a punishable offence to—er—need a man to stand by you?'

'How shameful! As if a girl in that position had not enough to try her.'

'Your views are very liberal—also dangerous in the current climate. Keep them to yourself—especially when Henry is around.'

'You are always bringing Henry into our conversations!'

He watched her until she turned to look at him, then held her eyes. 'Should I not? Naturally, I thought him a welcome addition to them.'

The sudden change in his tone—from idle teasing to deliberate—affected her. She got up and went to the window. The sun had disappeared in a blaze of fire. The afterglow lit up her clear-cut profile, exaggerated the length of her eyelashes, and her hair was like a shining cape upon her shoulders. She attempted to rearrange her thoughts, questioning why mention of her betrothed, her love, was so unwelcome at this moment. And could find no reasonable answer.

Chris was in similar confusion and he, too, sought some answers. Propinquity, he decided, was damnable! It bred unreal feelings and emotions which, in this case, he resented and feared. Partly because he had just begun his active masculine life before the war, but had been deprived of satisfaction since, and knew that there must be no sweet dalliance with Alice Ashley just because she was to hand—for she belonged to Henry Carrington, and was therefore out of bounds. Partly because his new feeling towards her was not just desire, but something entirely more complex and confusing.

His childhood friend was still there—she was the one who had come hot-foot in response to his request for help. That person had come with no thought, he was sure, of what she was getting herself into, but with the usual thoughtless instinct to support a friend. But with her had come another Alice—the Alice who had out-faced the surgeon and forbade him to mutilate him. The Alice who had—according to Jack Madesley—survived the hazardous journey to Naseby and, once there, comforted and rallied dying cavaliers throughout a hot July day; the Alice who had most tenderly held him on the bitter road to Cornwall. But knowing all this of her must not—must *not* encourage any more intimate relationship between them.

When Chris had first begun to drink in the Evening Sun, Molly Judd had treated him with scorn. Soon, however, she had made time to sit with the handsome heir to Oaks and they had begun a passionate affair, the beginning of which he had initiated but which had soon found her more than willing. But how long since he had given Molly a thought, except in kindly admiration for her part in the underground support of his cause? Since Molly there had been several girls. Not the poor, raddled creatures who followed the camp—he would have none of them—but nice girls he had met in Royalist houses in various parts of the country. There had been nothing serious, just an eloquent exchange of whispered affection, and a few kisses begged and given to a young man who might die at any time. They too had been forgotten swiftly enough.

But Alice was different. They had years of shared memories, years of comradeship. Pictures of their child-hood came to him now: Alice as he had first seen her, brought to visit his cousins by her new family—six years old, pink and cream and gold, but apparently unable to speak, only to look with great eyes at more strangers. Alice at eight, running wild at harvest-time, intent on work or mischief, or both. At twelve, with a newly acquired manner and dressed in lace and silk. At thirteen, fourteen. . . And more personal memories: Alice putting her cold hand in his when they had run away together one day and, having found themselves in Beech Wood, so familiar in daylight, so terrifying after dark, saying comfortingly, 'Nothing can *really* happen to us while we are together, Chrissie.' Alice asking his help because her pet dog was ill, and laughing, always *laughing*, with her particularly joyous laugh, when he described to her some misdeed for which he was to be punished. . .

When they had ceased to fight with pinches and punches, they had continued abrasively to try to get the better of each other with verbal heckling. But they had been unified instantly by any threat from outside, and she had always been his lieutenant in the endless games of chivalry they played. It occurred to him suddenly that Henry had been the outsider then; it was Henry who had been forced to enlist one of the boys from the estates to champion him.

'What are you frowning about now?' Alice asked, coming back to the bed. 'It will be a long convalescence if you are intent on sulking about your enforced idleness.'

'I wasn't sulking, just thinking of the old days.'

'Oh, the old days.' Alice dismissed the happy past. Why must he think of them? Everything was different now, changed by circumstances as well as personal events. She wanted to begin again with him, although she did not actually say these definite words to herself. She said impatiently, 'Shall I get you a book? It would help to pass the time.'

'You know I don't read. Besides, I want to get up for supper.'

'Nonsense!' She paled. 'You are not well enough. Old Job will be here later and I would not care to have to explain to him why I allowed you to leave your bed.'

'I am not answerable to him! I really do feel better,' he added.

'It is only the miracle drink making you feel so. I have not half carried you here on that tedious journey only to have all my work undone. But——' A thought struck her. 'If you must take a little break from bed, we could visit the portrait gallery.'

'What is that?'

'My father and his, and his too, kept pictures of the Ashley family in a room along the passage. I have the key but have not yet looked in. It is only a step along the passage.'

'Then let us go.' He sat up.

'Not so quickly! First I will find you something to lean on.'

'I'll lean on you.' He swung his legs off the bed, trying not to wince as his thigh objected with throbbing pain.

'Thank you, but, thin as you are, you are still a dreadful weight.' She had found what she sought in one of the long cupboards—a stout, smooth walking-stick with a knob of chased silver.

'The very thing,' he said wryly. 'Now I can truly look the part of a cripple.' Nevertheless, he took it from her and rose, testing his weight on his injured leg. It was painful, but however much it hurt he must get out of this room for a time, or run mad.

The key of the gallery would not turn for Alice. She struggled for a time, then said, 'You try—it must be years since anyone went in here.'

'Years, indeed.' He succeeded in turning the rusted lock and the candle she held shed its light on a dusty floor. She went in and held it higher, then almost dropped it; its pale light had shown her dozens of ghostly faces staring down from the walls. She stepped sharply back, candle-wax dripping on to her fingers.

'Careful!' Chris exclaimed. 'You almost had me over. Give me the light.' She handed it over and he glanced around. In the centre of the long narrow chamber there was a table set with old silver candle-sticks, tarnished and black, but each still holding a thick white taper. He hobbled over and began to light one from the other. With each fresh blooming the room grew brighter.

'What a beautiful room!' Alice exclaimed. This room had been the original Elizabethan long gallery and was intricately carved and exquisitely panelled in a pale wood she had never seen before. Even with the thick dust overlaying the furniture she could see that each surface of gilded wood was inlaid with flowers and birds and fruit of different colours. And the pictures! There must be fifty or more, all of uniform size, all hung in matching gilt frames the exact same distance apart.

'Where shall we start?' Chris asked.

Alice was peering at the one nearest the door. 'Here, I think—from the dress I believe it to be medieval.' She rubbed at the little plaque. 'Yes, "John de Mornay Ashley".' The portrait showed a man of medium height, dressed in leather tunic and dark hose, a hooded bird of prey on the leather bracelet on his wrist.

'A fine-looking man,' Chris commented, 'and noble too, if he is entitled to the ownership of that falcon.'

'Here is his lady opposite!' Alice ran across the room.

'She looks as if a strong wind might blow her away.' Chris examined the dainty, wand-like figure, dressed in clinging white, a golden cord about her minute waist, a horned and gauzy headdress perched on her fair head. 'All the women are in white—she must have set the tradition.'

They progressed on down the room. Down the ages, thought Alice. At the end she stopped. 'My father,' she said, looking up, a catch in her voice.

'Then this is your mother,' Chris said from the far side of the room. 'And next before her your grandmother, the first Alice Ashley.'

Alice went slowly across. She looked at her mother's portrait first—the sweet, smiling face looked back. She turned to the picture that Chris was studying so intently.

'It could be you,' he said. 'Saving her dress, you are twins.' Here was no easy subject, he thought, but how exactly the artist had captured the mixture of grace and energy in the slender body, the expression of mischief and intelligence in the straight blue-grey eyes. Even the hands were identical—slim and white but capable-looking. It had been the fashion then for ladies to wear their hair uncovered—the shining brown mass hung past her waist, a few strands blown over one shoulder. She was so real. Chris felt that at any moment the parted lips would speak.

Alice, he thought, his confused mind slipping a cog, at twenty and serenely happy. So might the girl beside him look with the right man. But, he knew, a bare five years later this same model had been in an unhappy marriage and causing endless pain in consequence.

'It gives me a strange feeling,' Alice said at last. Chris moved painfully; standing had not been comfortable for some minutes now. She said, 'You had better sit down a moment before we go back to your room.'

She was taking refuge in ordinary conversation because the feeling she had had on entering Gull's Nest was now intensified, and what the house had said to her in that moment could have been explained to her by the dim ghost on the wall before her, if she could only speak. She helped Chris over to a settle by the wall and he lowered himself gingerly into it. Alice, wandering about the room, noticed another portrait, face against the wall.

'Here is another. I wonder why it was never hung.' She turned it around to face her—and stared. If Lizzie had seen this picture, and she must have done, no wonder she had cried, 'Old Reckless Rokesby!'

'Probably because there is not a square inch of space left,' he said. 'Why—what is wrong?'

She turned the canvas about until it faced him. 'Twins, you were saying? Well, here is yours. It must be your great-uncle.'

'Sweet Jesu!' The reference escaped him before he could prevent it.

The likeness was as extraordinary as that between Alice and her ancestor. Both shared the same expression of sweetness mixed with daring. This pictured face had little in common as far as indication of personality went with the happy-go-lucky Chris. And yet, thought Chris, studying it carefully, in a few years perhaps the despair of the last two weeks would grow and consume him, and produce in his own face just the lines of disappointment and disillusionment as were apparent in this portrait. Charles Rokesby had lost his love, a love he had had no right to, of course, but as valid a reason for despair as any other. He himself had lost his reason for living. Dramatic, yes, and Chris could not imagine ever speaking such words out loud, but they were true just the same.

He had gone to war almost gaily. On a whim because he had an aversion to anyone telling him how to live his life. Within a month he had been as wholehearted about the matter in hand as the whole of his strongly individual personality could be. For the first time he found himself in the company of other men who felt as he did. His companions were very English—tolerant of their fellows, fond of their horses, pretty women, a glass and occasionally a pipe, and with a desire to live in peace. They had—as their ancestors had—unconsciously drawn a line for themselves and, pushed up to and beyond that line, they resisted violently and were prepared to back that resistance with their lives.

So many had died. So many of the gallant and amusing and attractive cavaliers, and each time he had lost a friend he had said to himself, Press on, fight on, and at the final reckoning they will be avenged in victory. That hope of victory was dead now. If he had not known it at the defeat of Naseby, he had known it when he heard it from Prince Rupert's lips, for Rupert would never lie to him—they were too fast in their friendship.

Many months ago, when he had offered his services to the dashing young nobleman, he had been accepted with courtesy, but also cynicism. Chris has seen in the other man's eyes the thought that here was another of the gentry of England who thought it politic to take arms to protect his class, his rights, and would maybe be good for a year or two of duty. Chris had seen all that upon their first meeting and had known that he was accepted into the ranks of the celebrated Bluecoats for his superb horsemanship and his ability to ally that skill with a talent for the hit-and-run swordsmanship that the regiment was famous for.

Short weeks later Rupert had revised his opinion of this particular young man, for Rokesby was tough and able and clever, and also a born soldier. He could look over a potential battlefield and and see its advantages and the reverse instantly. He could walk among his men and know immediately who would perform well under fire, and who would not. He also had those essential charismatic qualities for any man in authority—a light touch with the nervous, a rallying joviality for the unwilling, a disciplined and strong example for the wild. Added to these attributes was an extra ingredient: Chris Rokesby was always good company. In sweet or bitter conditions he could turn any situation to gaiety, and Rupert loved him for it. If Chris considered the Prince his friend, so it was for Rupert. It was the reason he had risked his liberty searching the wounded at Naseby for

his comrade, why he had assessed Alice Ashley so
carefully in the light of the camp fire and decided she
would be suitable proxy to see his friend to safety,
why—in the future—he would hope that Chris would be
beside him the final and doomed confrontations of a lost
cause.

'What are you thinking of?' Alice asked, letting the
portrait of Charles Rokesby slide to the floor.

'Oh. . . Nothing in particular. . .'

If it were nothing, thought Alice, lifting the portrait
and replacing it against the wall, why did he look so sad?
It was an expression which did not belong on her
friend's face, and she hated to see it there.

'Why is that picture here, do you think?' Chris asked.
'He was no Ashley.'

'I've no idea. But it is a fine portrait—painted, I
would think, in later life than any of the others. Your
great-uncle must have been in middle-age when he sat.
All the rest were caught quite young.'

'What do you think of it?'

Alice sat beside him. Little swirls of dust from the
velvet seat of the settle flew up and laid again on the
faded print of her gown. 'He looks sad,' she said
consideringly. 'And cynical, as if he had refused to
compromise and so suffered. And also as if he had
allowed events to twist and shape his life into a pattern
alien to his nature.' She thought over the words she had
just spoken and smiled a little. 'But that is love, Chris,
undeniably frustrating and tragic for so many.' How she
knew this she could not have said, but it was so and she
felt it strongly.

He smiled too. 'Perhaps there was something else on
his mind other than his Alice.'

'I don't think so,' she returned quickly. 'He looks to
be in his mid-thirties when captured by the paint—just
the age when he must have known that he loved her, but

known too that it was all too late. It is a salutary lesson for us all.'

'In what way?' He was acutely aware again of her beside him. She had accused him of being too thin, but she too had lost weight. Even so, he was more than conscious of the soft pressure of her body against his.

'Not to tarry where one's heart is concerned, I suppose,' she said thoughtfully.

There was a moment's silence, then Chris said, 'Alice, are you still set on your marriage with Henry?'

She was brought back to the present with a jolt. 'I have promised it. Why?'

'If you are not sure. If you are not certain sure, then——'

'Then?' she asked, her heart pausing in its steady beat. It was a strange moment—in this room with centuries of her ancestors gazing down on them out of their frames with unseeing eyes, their lingering hopes and dreams suddenly oppressing her, and Chris speaking to her as he never had before. As if her answer was terribly important. . . As she thought this her mind shied away nervously. She said, 'You are his friend, Henry's friend.'

'I know that. Can never forget it. But I am also yours and ask you again—are you certain sure of this marriage?'

There was the sound of flying feet in the passage and Lizzie flung open the door, one hand pressed to her side, her breath coming in short pants. Alice said in alarm, 'What is wrong?'

'Ironsides,' Lizzie gasped. 'I seen. . .their. . .dust from the. . .top meadow. They passed me at. . .full gallop—and I took the short-cut here.'

'Get your breath,' Alice said.

'No. . .time! Master Chris must hide; it's him they're coming for.'

'But you don't know that! I think——'

'Don't think! Just help me get him into the hole. Then we'll clear his bedroom.' Lizzie skimmed across the gallery and tried to pull Chris to his feet. He folded his arms.

'I will not hide. I will see them.'

'No!' Lizzie said, still pulling. He brushed her off as though she were a fly.

'Leave me be, woman!'

Lizzie appealed to Alice. 'I know what I said, but I was wrong, miss. The rebels are all over the west now, and in Launceston they've got a whole regiment, with some stationed here in Bude. There's a man—a Captain Parget—determined to root out anyone even suspect of having a feeling for the King. The foreman from Sykes Farm was just this minute telling me in the meadow. . . Captain Parget has swept up half a dozen just this day— wounded and able alike. He even dragged off little Bobby Eliott, who is but fifteen and only was a drummer-boy before his father was killed and his mam asked for him to come home—— Oh, we're wasting time!'

'I think you had better keep out of sight,' Alice said hesitantly to Chris. 'Lizzie, where is this—hole, you said?'

'Off the hall. Your great-grandfather had it made to hide the priests; he was of the old religion. Come, help me with Master Chris, and I'll show you.'

'I don't want to go there,' Chris said violently. 'I'm not going into any hole to hide from any damned Roundheads. Better men than I have stood their ground and died. Better men are even now aboard stinking ships bound for the Sugar Islands. I will not hide as though ashamed of what they fought and lost for.'

A few moments earlier Alice had been thinking how much older Chris seemed, how different from the boy she used to know. Now that boy reappeared, his defiant tone the same as during any of their youthful escapades. She said coolly, 'Very well, it is your decision. I must prepare to be taken myself, of course. For I am what is pleasantly known as a Malignant, and as such 'twill be the Launceston gaol for me.'

She looked at Lizzie, who said fervently, 'That is *true*, Master Chris.'

Chris looked from one to the other. The seconds flew by, during which the sound of a commotion in the stable-yard could faintly be heard through the closed shutters. Chris hoisted himself to his feet.

'If I must, I must,' he muttered. Alice took his arm, but drew back from the furious glance he gave her. She gestured behind his back to Lizzie, who put her shoulder under his, and the two made surprisingly swift progress out into the passage and down the stairs. Through an open window in the hall Alice heard the raised voices of authority, then the slow voice of Jack Madesley.

Jack will delay them as long as possible, she thought, trying to be calm.

Lizzie hurried to a stretch of panelling on the right of the hearth and felt with trembling fingers for one of the carved Tudor roses which studded the walls. She twisted it, there was a grating noise, then a portion of the wood swung open. 'One step down, Master Chris,' she said, helping him negotiate the steep step and tumble into the dusty space beyond. Then she pulled back the panelling. Alice looked in vain for any evidence of the door which led to the priest-hole but could see none.

Lizzie seized her arm and hustled her to a chair. She ran to the desk and opened a drawer, caught up a piece of embroidery and thrust it into Alice's hands.

'Sit there,' she said urgently, 'and work as though nought were amiss. I'll see for his room.' She was gone, flying up the stairs, her skirts held high.

Alice looked blankly at the piece of work she held. Whoever had begun it had been a talented needle-woman. It was a hunting scene, almost complete save for the poor little doe, her heels a hair's breadth from the snapping jaws of the pack of hounds. The noise from the yard was louder now; heavy footsteps approached the porch. She withdrew the needle, with its speckling of rust, just as the door was flung open and two men entered. Behind them could still be heard Jack's protesting voice.

Alice rose, with every evidence of being startled. The taller of the men crossed the floor until he was only a foot away. He was slim, with a fair, open face, curiously at odds with a pair of watchful dark eyes. He looked her up and down, then removed his hat.

'Captain Parget of the Twenty-first Foot, Fairfax's Own, mistress,' he introduced himself.

Part of Alice's mind registered the title he gave her. The terms mistress and master were not so commonly used these days—the Parliamentarians disliked both, and missus and mister were now the favoured forms of address. She managed a smile and a polite curtsy.

'What may I do for you, Captain?'

'I'm sorry, Miss Alice,' Jack said from the door. 'These men forced their way in——'

Without taking his eyes from Alice's face, the captain said, 'No force was used, but your man was reluctant to allow me to carry out my duty.'

Alice resumed her seat. The silk picture had fallen from her lap when she jumped up; Captain Parget bent and retrieved it. She accepted it with another smile. 'Do sit down, Captain, and tell me what that duty is.'

'Thank you, but I'll stand. I have reason to believe you are harbouring a member of the rebel forces. It is my duty to take him prisoner, and advise you that you have committed a serious offence against the ruling government.'

Alice produced an expression of amazement. 'A member of the rebel forces? There has been some mistake, Captain, there is no member of the rebel force here.' Not quite a lie, she thought guiltily, at least only from one viewpoint. 'Forgive me, I have not introduced myself. I am Mistress Ashley, and Gull's Nest is my family home.'

'It is my understanding that this house has had no owner for many years.'

Alice inserted her needle and finished off the doe's little tail—very badly; it was a sin to spoil such delicate work. 'That is so,' she agreed. 'I have lived in another county since my parents' death. But Gull's Nest is mine and I am visting my property with a view to disposing of it.'

'You choose to visit now, with your country at war and travelling so hazardous?'

Alice continued her work, adding a quite unnecessary and awkward-looking portion to the tail. She said mildly, 'I am to be married soon, Captain, and naturally wished to review my assets before—— However, that is of no interest to you, I am sure.' Out of the corner of her eye she saw Lizzie coming down the stairs, innocently casual. 'Please order a search of the premises if you feel you cannot accept my word that no rebel is housed here.'

'I fear I must do that. Sergeant——' He gave the order.

Alice sighed gently and laid aside her embroidery. 'May I offer you some refreshment?' she asked politely as the sergeant called in his men.

'Thank you, no.' The captain's eyes roved around the hall.

'I will take a little of the raspberry cordial,' Alice said. Lizzie bobbed and disappeared into the kitchens, elbowing aside two of the soldiers who were beginning their search there. She brought the drink and Alice sipped it. Lizzie Mote's cordial was made to an old recipe—the soft fruit, freshly picked, steeped in cheap alcohol for many days. A sharp aroma of brandy drifted on the air. 'Can I not persuade you to try this, Captain? It is very good on such a warm day.'

'I have eschewed all strong spirits, mistress. Not only for the sake of my belief, but also because one needs a clear head in these times.'

'Very wise,' Alice said. 'Especially as you obviously have such disagreeable duties to perform.' From above came the sound of doors thrust roughly open, and furniture being carelessly moved about.

Unprovoked, Captain Parget continued his careful assessment of the hall. 'I have heard,' he said, 'that many of these old houses hereabouts have secret places—priest-holes and the like.'

Alice's heart began to thump. 'Indeed? I heard no mention of such here at Gull's Nest when I lived here as a child,' she said truthfully.

The captain wandered to the hearth and, bending, looked up into the chimney. He rapped his knuckles on the panelling to the left. Alice watched him, Lizzie's potent brew turning to ice in her stomach.

'The man we seek is in fact a family friend of yours from Kent,' the captain went on. 'Christopher Rokesby—now Captain Rokesby of the Prince Rupert's Cavalry.'

'Chris Rokesby? Yes, I have known him for many years.'

'And were responsible for his safe escape from Naseby—or so I am informed.'

'Who can this informant be?' Alice forced a light tone. The captain had ceased his scrutiny of the walls and now paced over to the writing-desk under the window. He is very young, thought Alice, no older than Chris, but as intelligent and dangerous. Her heart began to race as he absentmindedly shuffled the papers on the scarred top. Among them was the deed of tenure for Oaks, as yet unsigned by Chris. Before he could answer her question she rose and asked another.

'I wonder if you may have come across my fiancé, Captain? Henry Carrington, in command of his own Kentish battalion within Lord Fairfax's regiment?'

Captain Parget let fall the papers and turned sharply. 'Hal Carrington of Kent?'

'Indeed. You know of him?'

'I know of him. He is held in the highest regard by. . . many. Well, mistress, I had no idea. . .' His manner was magically transformed from the suspicious to the deferential. His troop was now reassembled in the hall.

The sergeant said respectfully, 'We have found nothing, sir. And no trace of any man being in the house.'

'Wait for me outside,' the captain dismissed him. When the men had tramped out he said to Alice, 'There are four horses in the stable. My information is that only one belongs at Gull's Nest.'

'Two were ridden here by myself and my manservant—the other used to carry necessary provisions,' Alice said quickly.

'Yes, I see. Well, it seems I was misinformed on all accounts, Mistress Ashley. I beg your pardon for disturbing you.'

'Not at all. I will see you out.'

At the door, the captain replaced his hat and bowed over her hand. 'I shall be stationed in Launceston for some weeks, mistress. May I ask leave to call upon you another time in a more acceptable capacity? I feel it my duty to offer my services to a brother officer's future wife.'

'Your duties appear to be rather arduous already,' Alice remarked.

A hint of colour showed in the fair skin of his face. 'I should have said it would be a pleasure rather than a duty.'

'Then, by all means, do dine here one evening,' Alice said courteously. She paused in the stone porch until the captain had swung into the saddle and led out his band, then turned inside and slammed the door. Lizzie hurried out of the kitchens.

'Well done, Miss Alice,' she said cheerfully. 'You are a cool one.'

'Not so cool.' Alice touched her hand, burning hot and damp, to the other women's cheek. 'Had we better release our captive?'

Chris came out of his hiding place smudged with dirt and choking from lack of air. He sank into a chair by the hearth and Lizzie pushed a stool under his injured leg. 'Sit you there, Master Chris, and I'll fetch the cordial — it will brace you.'

'Brandy will do the job better,' he muttered. When it was in his hands he swallowed off two glasses and looked up at Alice. 'I imagine you are pleased with your performance?'

'Shouldn't I be?' Yes, she felt she had managed very well, but apparently was to have no applause for it.

Chris slopped out another glass. 'Oh, Captain dear, have you come across my betrothed?' He mimicked her prim tones exactly. 'Oh, Captain dear, do dine with me any time you wish.'

'I didn't call him dear,' she protested. 'Nor did I invite him to supper — he invited himself.'

'And where shall I be while you romance the good captain? Crouched like a rat again in that stone box——'

'Romance!' she interrupted him heatedly. 'How dare you suggest that I would behave in any such way? Really, Chris, you are ridiculous! What would you have had me say and do?'

'I would have had you show him the door, and I would have had myself help him through it at the point of my sword!' He poured yet another glass. Alice removed the bottle and placed it on the table.

'Even the combined forces of Ashley and Rokesby

cannot deal with eight armed men,' she said with more restraint than she felt.

'Don't underestimate yourself,' he replied bitterly. 'I'm beginning to think that I never knew you at all, Alice. In the past week you have shown a part of yourself you kept most successfully hidden for twelve years.'

'I did what had to be done,' she said patiently. 'As to his coming here again, I very much doubt that he will.'

He laughed. 'Then let me tell you that even from my disadvantaged place I could recognise a desire on his part to excel in his—duty—towards his fellow officer's betrothed.'

Losing her temper at last, she said furiously, 'And what are Captain Parget's intentions towards me to do with you? No one has the right to speak to me as you have just done, saving Henry, and I know he would never presume!'

Henry's name dropped into the conversation had a sobering effect on Chris. Confusing too. Hidden in the stifling space behind the hearth, he had heard all that was said in the hall, and irrationally it had angered him. First Alice's feigned amazement of the charge—whoever would have suspected her of being such an accomplished liar? Not he, for Alice had always been terminally honest, scorning any direct lie as beneath her. Later, he—more sophisticated in such matters than she—had identified the change in the unseen man's attitude to her. He thought it had had little to do with her introducing Henry Carrington's name, and had much resented it.

But why? He had no claim of that sort on Alice, should only feel a profound gratitude to her for her courage in the last fortnight, and an affection for their association in the past. But, when a a certain note had crept into the voice of the man behind the panelling,

Chris had been ready to leap out of his secret place and
contest it. With no possible right to do so. . .

Added to these disquieting thoughts was the real
physical pain he was in. The pain in his leg had been
exacerbated by his trip to the portrait gallery and the
hasty flight to the foxhole. Now, despite the brandy, it
had an invading life of its own; his whole body was now
owned by it. He let slip the glass from his fingers and it
shattered in glittering shards on the floor. Alice leaned
over him, dismayed.

'My dear, this is very bad for you! You said yourself
we must not argue. Let me help you back to bed.' She
put a gentle arm around him and her hair brushed his
face, fragrant and warm.

'Let me be,' he murmured, shocked by the instant
desire he felt to put his own arms around her.

'What is this?' They both looked to the door. Job
stood there, his shabby case in hand, a forbidding
expression on his face. He advanced into the hall and
planted himself before them. 'I told you to stay abed,
young sir,' he said to Chris. 'I told you to keep him
quiet,' he said to Alice.

'We have had a small crisis,' she placated him.

'I heard about it,' Job acknowledged. 'Folks talking
as shouldn't! He examined his patient. 'You hid him
away, did you? And might have to again. Is there a bed
you can make up for him down here? Makes no sense at
all to have him trekking up and down stairs.'

'In the winter parlour,' Alice said. 'We can make his
bed in there.'

'Do it, then,' Job said briefly. He opened his bag and
took out a bottle of viscous black liquid. Delving
further, he found a wooden spoon with a deep bowl.

CHAPTER SIX

AN HOUR later Alice sat down to a solitary meal of bread and hard cheese. Chris was safely tucked up in the parlour, a strong dose of opium within him, his wound freshly dressed. Before he had drifted off to sleep he had taken Alice's hand and kissed it.

'Please forgive me, I was quite mad with pain and the shame of running before the enemy. No excuse, I know, for berating you who have been so brave and resourceful.'

'Sweet words,' she had returned grimly. 'But if you and I are to survive any of this we must put aside our usual dealings with each other and work together.'

'Our usual dealings. . .?' he had repeated, half tipsy on both brandy and physic. 'Were they so bad? I never in my life have trusted a woman as I trust you, darling. 'Twas therefore the greatest shock to hear you both untruthful and——'

Darling? This was something new—he had never used an endearment to her before. 'And——?'

'And indulging in the kind of flirting unworthy of you.'

'How self-righteous you are! I wasn't flirting, and if it sounded like that it was because I wanted to disarm him. Underneath, I wanted to spit in his eye!'

He had smiled. The evil-smelling mixture might have again taken away his sense of control, but it had also vanquished the pain. 'Why didn't you, then?'

She was tucking the covers around him. 'He wasn't the sort of man you do that to.'

'What kind was he, then?'

129

'Very young, very handsome, and somehow all of a piece. He is certainly no fool.'

'Handsome? You noticed that, in spite of the situation?'

'Of course I did. I am not blind. Besides, I do notice things like that now.'

'Why especially now?'

She had looked at him without speaking. The words had slipped out, without having been prepared in her mind first, but were true none the less. For instance, she had never before noticed how very blue Chris's eyes were, how palely fine the skin of his face and throat, how glossy his hair, even streaked with sweat. She had laughed to cover her uncertainty and said lightly, 'Well, I am growing up, I suppose, and 'tis late enough in happening. Many girls my age are married already, beginning families—— But that is enough talk. You are half-asleep, and need to be left alone to recover your strength.'

He had struggled against the encroaching sleep. He wanted to have this conversation now, it was very important to have it *now*. . . His eyelids had drooped and he slept.

Alice had blown out the candle and gone in to her supper, half relieved, half regretful that the subject raised was left unfinished. Had Chris always been so easy to talk to? Surely not, for they had never got very far in any conversation without disagreeing. They were still quarrelling, of course, but now it was different somehow. She ate her sparse meal without tasting it, puzzling over this difference and resolving to pursue it again tomorrow.

That conversation was postponed, however, for at some time during the night Chris took a turn for the worse and by mid-morning the following day he was in a poor way indeed. Perhaps it was the inevitable infection

entering with his severe injury, kept at bay so far by the
resistance of a healthy body; perhaps not. He was by
turns burning hot and shuddering with cold, and Old
Job came stumping up to the house and shook his head
dubiously. He uncovered the wound and discovered it
to be no more inflamed, but the man appeared more
sick than on arrival.

'I did my part,' he grumbled to Lizzie who, on rising
early and investigating the muffled groans from the
parlour, had sent Thomas running through the mist for
the old man. 'I said keep him *still*, and in one place, and
let my physic heal him. But no, I come here after
working on him for an hour and find he's been gallivant-
ing around the house, and then stuck in a cold stone
place——'

'How did you know where he was?' Lizzie demanded
suspiciously. Alice had told her that Captain Parget had
come to Gull's Nest armed not only with weapons but
also with knowledge, and Lizzie wanted to know who
had blabbed about Ashley affairs.

'I've got ears, haven't I? And there's enough talk
about to hang a man. But no one knows about the place
you hid him—at least not exactly where.' This was
probably so, thought Lizzie. The old master had only
told her when he knew he was dying, and the child, Miss
Alice, had not known. 'It's not the first time I've been
called to Gull's to tend a wanted man,' Job continued,
'and, cleric or layman, I've usually managed to save
them. But this time I am not so sure I can do much.'

'You must!' Lizzie exclaimed. 'Why, young miss will
be heartbroken if anything happens to him.'

'Hmm.' In spite of his rough way with Alice, Job had
formed a favourable opinion of her. Pretty in an unusual
way, and probably silly like all women were, she had yet
impressed him and made him think of words almost
forgotten from his rather grand education—an education not taken advantage of when he had decided that

the drink was too important to him. Loyal and courageous and high-stepping were the words which came to
his mind when thinking of Alice Ashley.

Along with all the other rumours about the village
now was one which declared that the young Ashley lady
was engaged to marry with a Roundhead. Lizzie's
statement seemed to deny this, but perhaps the young
lady had not yet made up her mind. Howsoever the
situation was, Job determined there and then that he
would do his level — and sober — best for Chris Rokesby.
He said thoughtfully, 'I'm not so sure, you see, that 'tis
his poorly leg causing the trouble. He's come from a
soldiers' camp, or I miss my guess, and those places are
breeding-grounds for a whole lot of ills.'

'You're saying it might be something else? Something
catching?' Lizzie asked fearfully.

'I am, and I'll say this too: I'll do the tending — you
too, if you've a mind — for you and I are too long in the
tooth to be caught. But you'd be wise to forbid the little
lass the sickroom.'

Alice was horrified when Lizzie told her the news.
'But I must do my share of the nursing,' she said firmly.

'You'll not! Fevers are funny things; Master Chris
could well get better, no trouble, then I'd have the job
of explaining to him why you're flat on your back, or
worse.'

They wrangled over it in whispers outside the parlour
door, but Lizzie had her way in the end. 'But,' said
Alice determinedly, 'if he should ask for me, I want
your promise that you'll tell me. Promise, now.'

'I promise,' Lizzie said, thinking she would use her
discretion over *that*.

In fact, during the next few days Chris did not call for
Alice. He spoke, in the grip of delirium, a lot about
someone called Hal. At other times he shouted for
Rupert — or some such name — and, in weaker moments,
cried bitterly for someone called Blondel. But Alice

Ashley's name did not pass his parched lips and Lizzie was glad enough about that, for neither she nor Job had much hope of saving their charge, and whatever ailed him was virulent.

During this time Alice wandered disconsolately around the house. She deliberately kept out of earshot of the winter parlour, so painful to her were the muffled cries of pain from within. Instead, she found solace in preparing the meals for the two nurses, keeping the house fresh and sweet, picking and bottling the first of the summer fruit and walking the flower-scented lanes and the flat sands of the seashore.

An unexpected find during the second week of the crisis kept her mind partly occupied during the long evenings in her room. Thinking she would turn out her bedroom, she opened the chests and cupboards and rooted about among the old clothes. At the bottom of one chest, under a pile of lavender-strewn linen, she found a silk-covered diary. Opening it, she discovered it to be 'Alice Ashley's Journal, begun this day of our Lord Fifteen Eighty-One.' It was many pages in length and written in a barely decipherable hand, in ink much faded by the years. But it told its story, and that story made fascinating reading.

Calculating roughly, Alice decided that her grandmother must have been fifteen when she first wrote in her 'gift from my godmother on my saint's day'. The last scrawled entry had been made 'this day, this most dreadful day, January Fourteenth, Sixteen Hundred.' Leaves had been added to the original thick diary. Years—sometimes as many as three—separated the entries, but it was a complete, if disorganised account of a headstrong and passionate woman's personal life.

Poring over it in the light of one candle, her mind on events down the broad stairs, Alice was transfixed by what she read. Alice Courtney Ashley had been born during the old Queen's reign—Elizabeth I—to loving parents who had indulged her for the first years of her life. Alice smiled when she read the early entries—nothing apparently changed, she thought, for all those years ago the first Alice had worried over the condition of her skin, the fact that her thick hair would refuse to curl in wet weather, the trouble she had maintaining a dutiful attitude in the schoolroom. Then the writer had suddenly lost both her parents and been consigned to the kind charity of Gull's Nest under the protection of distant cousins. Two friends had dominated her childhood and young womanhood—her cousin Edward, and the son of their nearest neighbours, Charles Rokesby. The comparison of this alone, Alice thought delightedly, was uncanny, for her own life had been so shaped by two young males.

In her seventeenth year Alice Courtney Ashley had accepted as her betrothed her fourth cousin Edward—'my dear and handsome Ned, who has courted me with unswerving devotion for two years now', and was duly married the following spring. Charles Rokesby, 'teasing me as usual, both before and after the wonderful ceremony,' had stood as best man to the groom, and the occasion was, by the evidence of Alice's pen, 'a joyful and—owing to Charles's behaviour—a somewhat riotous affair.'

There followed a long interval, then the journal picked up the story shortly after the birth of her eldest child—a sickly girl named Katharine—and followed it through the babe's first year, until little Kate was laid 'with my copious tears' in the graveyard, dead at eleven months from the croup. Another gap, then Alice took up her diary again to record the birth of her first son, Robert, and again in the following year to announce most joyfully the birth of her second, Richard. These boys being her father and her uncle, Alice thought to herself. There followed the mundane but compulsively readable details of Alice's young motherhood, her delight in her growing boys, and references to affairs, both personal and from the world, during the next eight years.

Then came a change in the tone of the journal. Alice was obviously growing unhappy in her marriage. Her husband was kind enough; she wanted for no material thing, but he was distancing himself as he grew into middle-age. His business life took him away from home to the sea ports, where he owned fleets of merchant ships. He was away for long periods and during this time his friend and neighbour, Charles Rokesby, was a frequent visitor to Gull's Nest and a welcome companion to his lonely wife. Alice's words summed up the situation at that time. 'He is so amusing and clever, provoking me to think a little above my normal preoccupation with household cares. He brings out the best in everyone he is with—in the most annoying and disguised way sometimes, when his comments are directed towards me.' Alice paused here and glanced at the dark window. Why did this thought seem so familiar to her? she wondered. She bent her head again to the book.

Now there was another change. Alice wrote less frequently, but what she put down was increasingly riveting, until, 'He is so often here, Charles, and I see now that I am falling in love with him. This is not a new emotion, rather a remembered love, grown and matured with the years. Each day it grows in strength for me, and I know 'tis also so for him, but there is nothing to be done. Nothing. Charles cannot be accused of betraying his loyalty to Edward in either word or deed, but he is miserable, and so am I. . .'

There followed several pages of self-accusation from an essentially loyal and honest woman in the grip of a compelling passion, and little heartbreaking notes which brought tears to Alice's eyes: 'Tonight as we sat at supper I noticed that he drank far more than is usual for him, for he has always been only a moderate drinker. I know it is because he is suffering, but can say nothing to comfort him. At midnight when I saw him from the house he could scarcely mount his horse and I longed to lay my hand upon him and say, "My dear, 'tis the same for me. If you are in pain, so I am." But that—naturally—I could not say, for to do so would not only be disloyal but would also add to his burden. . .'

Alice had reached this sad page in the journal on the twenty-first day of Chris's battle for life. That morning Lizzie had shown her one of the newsletters which the government spread around the country and it, too, made bitter reading. There had been the most terrible disaster for the cavaliers at Langport and Parliament made much of it in their writing. Lizzie had also told her that rumours on the local grapevine said that, following the rout, the Prince Rupert had strongly advised his king to sue for peace. Charles had refused and taken himself off to Raglan Castle in Wales, hoping to swell his diminishing force with Welsh and Irish troops. He had ordered his nephew to Bristol garrison and told him to hold it at all costs. Rupert, his advice ignored, as it had been on so many other crucial occasions in the past, was reputedly there now, trying to gather his scattered men and hold the remaining Royalist territory with his—and their—life-blood.

Alice held her breath on hearing this last. Her geography was sketchy. Where in relation to Bude was Bristol? Near enough for Chris, if he knew his friend and commander was mustering his cavalry, to leave Gull's Nest and join him? This last thought would seem to be laughable, for Chris was no better, and Lizzie and Job still gloomy. Either Alice had more faith in their efforts than they did, or she simply refused to believe Chris could be so lightly dismissed from life. Whatever, she gathered up the pages of the newsletter and put them on her dressing-table in her bedroom, and forbade

Lizzie to gossip about the rest with Job while in the sickroom.

July became August. Chris rallied briefly, then was laid low again. His grumbling doctor was truly at a loss to explain how any fever could inhabit a body for so long without killing its host. Alice, still forbidden to go near, continued to cook and clean and make friends with her immediate neighbours on the three surroundings farms. Shy at first, they were soon making time to visit her, apparently not disturbed to find the mistress of the once grand Ashley house with her sleeves rolled up, baking bread or turning a fowl on the kitchen spit. They offered little gifts when they came, some honey or a freshly made lardy cake, and some of the older men and women who remembered remarked her likeness to the old mistress, and spoke fondly of her.

Alice had now finished reading the old journal, and had cried as she did so. The last few pages concerned a dreadful scene which took place at Gull's Nest one raw January day when Edward Ashley was on one of his rare visits to his home. The Christmas season had been drawing to a close and had been one of gaiety at Gull's Nest, with their friends from near and far enjoying Ashley hospitality for weeks, and one of the gentlemen appointed the Lord of Misrule and relishing his duties. At the grand ball which marked the cessation of jollity he had instigated the novelty of the couples exchanging husbands and wives for the evening. Each man's name was placed in a tub and each woman closed her eyes and withdrew a slip and Alice Ashley, 'by the most malignant fate,' drew out Charles Rokesby's name. They had been forced to spend all the hours together, dancing and dining and playing the games as partners.

'Torture most exquisite,' was how Alice described it, and at the end of the night as the dawn crept in through the closely drawn drapes, the Lord of Misrule bade his 'married couples' to salute each other with a kiss. 'We would have ignored this instruction,' Alice wrote, 'but, by chance, the Lord was at our elbows and insisted. Dear God, 'twas torture to spend the evening in Charles's arms and sit drinking and eating with him so close, but this—— He was, as was usual with him nowadays, rather tipsy, and I, well, I was for once in similar state. We came together as lovers and, if all mortals are entitled to a little of the gods' rapture, I received my share at that moment. Even so, we might have covered our lapse had not some malicious lady pointed us out to Edward, and when I was released from Charles's embrace—from heaven, I could almost say—it was to find my husband's eyes upon me. Dear Ned——' Here the lines of writing were smeared and almost unreadable, but Alice held the book to the candle flame and read on. 'I saw him look at me, and then at Charles, and the mixture of scorn and torment and rage in his eyes made me want to cry out. He said nothing, but took Charles's arm and led him outside on to the lawns. We had had a heavy snowfall recently, so unusual in Cornwall, and through the window I saw their figures, black against the white. I saw Ned raise his arm as if to strike Charles; I saw Charles stand ready for the blow which never came. Instead Ned brushed him lightly across the cheek with his hand and after a moment's more talk Ned turned back into the house, shivering. He passed me without a word and said to the first gentlemen to hand, "I have issued challenge to Rokesby. We meet in two hours' time." Then he walked away without a word, and in the silence I heard the muffled sound of hoofbeats on the frozen ground and Charles rode by on his black horse at breakneck speed.

'The company sought their beds, but I remained in the hall, and as the hours passed and a timid sun rose in the crystal sky I saw smoke on the headland. Shortly after one of our men came to tell Edward that Rokesby Manor was razed to the snowy ground and that Charles had been found in the ashes. Ned came to me then, and advised me that Charles—his friend—had had to admit that he loved me, that he *worshipped* me, and that he had had no choice but to call him out. "Now he is dead," Ned said. "And if I must live with that, so must you. I shall never address another word to you again, Alice, as long as we live." He then turned and left me on this dreadful day, this most dreadful day——'

Alice had laid down the journal, her heart twisted in pity for all three of the characters who had featured in the pages. What had she said to Chris? That love was undeniably tragic and frustrating. . . It had been so for her grandfather and his wife, and the man who came between them.

The next morning she was poking about among the overgrown beds in the garden for any sign of the roses her grandmother had written of so often in her journal—about picking and arranging them around her home—when she heard hoofbeats at the back of the house and Captain Parget came into view. Alice looked wildly towards the house, hoping that Lizzie was alert. Jack had taken her mare for re-shoeing and was not in the yard. She took off one of her white gloves and waved it to deflect the rider from approaching the front porch and he saw her and came, still mounted, across the daisy-strewn lawn. With relief she saw that he was alone. He dismounted and uncovered his head.

'Mistress Ashley, I hope I find you well.'

Since the gardens were revolving alarmingly, she lied when she curtsied and said that she was.

'I thought I must fulfil my promise to you and satisfy myself that you are in need of nothing. Also remind you of yours to invite me to sup with you.'

'I would be delighted,' Alice said, smiling. Really, lying is becoming second nature to me now, she thought regretfully. 'May we say one day next week?'

'I fear I shall be gone by then—in truth I have no other night but tonight. I shall be busy with my duties before we leave.'

'Then it must be tonight.' No proper food was the least of her worries, she thought as he thanked her gravely and remounted.

'We will be just two?' he queried, replacing his hat.

No, indeed, she thought, there will also be a raving Royalist outlaw in the adjoining room. 'My maid will be there as chaperon,' she said haughtily.

'Of course, I did not mean——' Captain Parget suddenly looked his years. 'Well, until tonight, then.'

Alice watched him canter away. How she would manage tonight she had no idea. She dropped the stick she held and went back into the house.

Lizzie had insisted to both Job and Alice over the last month that each night she prayed for a miracle with regard to the young man she had nursed and grown so fond of. That day her prayers apparently reached their destination and were kindly received, for Chris began to show signs that he would recover. At first Lizzie had not believed it possible when he sat up at noon and demanded something to eat. Tentatively she felt his forehead.

'Don't paw me, woman!' he said irritably. 'Is it your intention that I shall starve to death? No solid food has passed my lips for near a month.'

Lizzie blinked. Could he, then, remember the passing days while he had lain so desperately ill? 'You have been out of your mind all during that time; how do you know how long?'

'The view from the window suggests it,' he said, with no softening of his tone. 'I came here in late June, now it must be August, for the apple trees will soon be to fruition.'

'How clever you are!'

'Shall you stand there marvelling at my intellect, or fetch me something to eat?' he demanded aggressively.

'I must first tell Miss Alice; she will be so happy.'

'Will she?' He could in truth remember little of the pain-filled weeks but knew, without quite knowing how, that Alice had not been near him during the whole of that time. 'If you must do that then I need to wash and change my shirt at least. I am not fit company for anyone. And shaving gear, if you please. I must look like a wild man.'

Lizzie fetched what he needed gladly, although she thought that the young man's appearance would not be as disturbing to her mistress as his attitude, which had obviously not been improved by his brush with death. Still, his rise from the almost-dead was most opportune. All morning she and Alice had been puzzling over how to entertain the enemy and keep him from being aware of Chris Rokesby's presence. Now it seemed that the problem could be solved—a man in his right senses could keep quiet upstairs in one of the bedrooms. The lesser worry over what to serve on the table had been unexpectedly righted too. Two plump ducks had been shyly presented by Joe Sykes and were even now plucked and trussed and awaiting the spit.

More important than these considerations, thought Lizzie, hurrying out to the dairy where Alice was making a batch of soft cheeses to serve at her supper party, was the fact that the invalid was on the mend.

Alice was overjoyed. She dropped the wooden battens she had been shaping her dainties with, brushed her hands over her apron, and flew back to the house. She opened the parlour door and discovered Chris sitting on a chair by the window, tying the laces of a clean shirt. He had shaved hastily and in doing so had nicked himself in several places, which had not improved his temper. His eyes swept over her—very blue, very unfriendly. He said, 'Well, you are here at last.'

The radiance faded from her face. 'What do you mean, at last? Oh, Chris, how glad I am to see you better! I have been frantic with worry.'

'Frantic? I am sure it does not show.' She was more lovely than ever, he thought. She had gained back her curves, and on her throat and bare forearms had a light dusting of sunburn. He had said to Lizzie that he was hungry; now he thought, I have been hungry for only one thing. One person.

Alice swallowed. She saw that the almost fatal illness had left its mark on him, on the handsome face and shapely body. He was now bone-thin, with fine lines etched about eyes and mouth. Even so, her heart fluttered. The sun, high in the sky, flooded into the room and turned his hair to a gleaming helmet. As she stood there a few lines of her grandmother's journal came to her: ''Twas no special occasion, Charles and I were but enjoying a glass of wine together in the winter parlour one evening when I looked at him and knew. Knew that he was my love, that my heart had finally recognised him as the one.'

That is how it is for me, thought Alice, stunned. In the very same room with that man's descendant. The realisation took all her breath; she stood there dumb and let it take over her body, her mind, her soul.

'What's the matter?' Chris asked. 'I know I look like hell—I should have engaged the services of a barber, my hands shake now like a toper's. But——have you nothing to say to me?'

'Yes,' she said slowly. 'I have something to say.'

'Pray do so. I have not heard your voice for some time, nor felt your hand on me while I was so sick.'

'I was forbidden the sickroom,' she said hotly. 'No one knew what ailed you and 'twas felt better I should not be exposed.' The words sounded unbelievably sterile in the light of her new knowledge. If I had known

what I know now, she thought, nothing on earth could
have kept me from his side.

'Well, pray do come in now and visit awhile,' he said
with studied courtesy. 'Tell me what you have been
doing all these weeks.'

It was difficult for her to believe that he could not
know how she felt at that moment; she felt that she must
be shining with her revelation, but he obviously did not,
for his voice was both cold and antagonistic. She went
hesitantly into the room, but before she could speak
Lizzie came in behind her.

'Miss Alice. I have put the ducks on to roast, and laid
up the table. What will you wish me to do about. . .
Master Chris?'

Chris stood up. He was shaky, weak from lying supine
for so long, but managed to hide it. He got as far as the
stool before the spinet and sat down abruptly. 'Roast
duck? I am very partial to it. Is there some celebration
in the offing?'

'No,' said Alice. 'No. . . At least, Captain Parget is
coming to supper tonight.'

Chris drew his fingers over the strings of the instrument. 'I used to have quite a talent for this. Do you
remember?'

'Yes, I remember.' Chris had always played on her
aunt's ancient spinet at Alice's birthday parties. Beauti-
fully. Some his own compositions. An odd accomplish-
ment for a man, or so Walter Carrington had always
said.

Chris frowned at the discordant notes resounding in
the air. 'It is sadly out of tune. . . So Captain Parget is
coming to supper. No need, then, for me to enquire how
you have spent your time lately.'

'It is the first time he has been here since that day,'
she said defensively. She turned to Lizzie. 'I will arrange
everything with Master Chris. Please attend to the

supper.' Lizzie retreated, a little offended by Alice's
tone, and Alice tried again. 'Chris, I must talk to you.'

He gave her a black look. 'If you are about to suggest
that I retire to the hole in the wall, please don't. If you
are engaged tonight, naturally I will take myself off
upstairs to one of the bedchambers to allow you free
rein.'

'Please don't put it like that. We must be careful, you
know.' She wanted to tell him what she knew of the
progress of the war, but was afraid to. If he was capable
of leaping out of bed the very first day he was able to it
was likely that he would feel equal in a few days to
rejoining—or attempting to—his old regiment. Along
with this line of reasoning ran the bright thread of her
love for him. The war, the danger, receded before the
importance of her discovery.

'How is it careful to have an Ironside to supper?'

'I could not refuse to have him. . . Parliament is
strong here now in the west, and Captain Parget eager, I
am sure, to continue his persecution of what he calls
rebels. I have no wish to arouse his suspicions——'

'Have you really not seen him again until today?'

'I have not. His sudden appearance this morning
nearly made me do what I have never before—fall in a
dead faint.' There, just the right kind of light tone to
placate him—when her one desire was to tell him, I love
you, I love you!

He half smiled. 'I can imagine. Why did he suddenly
appear, do you think?'

'His regiment is leaving the area soon.'

'Do you know where it is going?' he asked quickly.

'Why, no.'

'Ask him tonight.'

She turned away. This evening would be hard enough
without attempting to play the spy. She said, 'Do you
want me to help you upstairs? Lizzie could bring your
meal there and then we must set this room to rights.'

'No, I'll eat in the kitchen and then take myself up. What was it you wanted to say to me earlier?'

'Oh. . .nothing. At least, it will keep. Now I must look over the table and change.'

The only dress she had brought with her was one of fine cream-coloured wool which she wore in warm weather at home when simplicity and practicality were appropriate. In spite of its modest material and colour, it was cut in the style of two years ago and was more rounded in the neck than was fashionable now. It also had a frivolous edging of lace about the bodice and the cuffs of the elbow-length sleeves. Not a style that the Puritans favoured at all. She had noticed on her infrequent visits to Bude that ladies now wore a collar which was really more of a cape and covered them from under the chin to the neckline of their gowns and was firmly tied with cotton ribbon. They also wore hideous enveloping linen bonnets, hiding their hair completely. Well, thought Alice that night, I have neither collar nor bonnet, and Captain Parget must take me as I am.

She pulled back her hair, fastening it at the crown of the head and allowing the weight to fall in its accustomed ringlets. She had no gems to decorate her ears or neck, but that would no doubt meet with his full approval—even ladies of some social status only wore very unostentatious jewellery these days. Perhaps just a brooch in which was enclosed a loved one's piece of hair, or a simple string of pearls. They hardly needed any show of finery in any case, for in the past two years the grand balls had not been held, the theatres and places of entertainment had been closed, and social events now centred about church gatherings. Still vain enough to regret the light coat of tan she had acquired through careless exposure to the brilliant sunshine lately, Alice turned from her glass and went down the stairs.

At sunset Thomas, who was to help Lizzie wait on table and was washed and brushed for the occasion, came to the parlour to tell Alice that two riders were approaching the house. Two? Alice hoped that one was a servant and the good captain had not chosen to bring a fellow officer. Entertaining one stranger was as much as she felt equal to—also, the ducks would not go round. . . She rose and went into the hall and stood waiting, wishing she could fortify herself with some of Chris's brandy. There was a peremptory knock on the door and Thomas hastened to open it.

Captain Parget entered first, bending his head under the low beams across the opening. Behind him another man did the same, and when he straightened up Alice flushed, then paled. 'Henry!'

'My dear.' Henry came across the room and took both her hands and raised them to his lips.

Captain Parget said, 'I was for letting you know that a joyful surprise was in store, mistress, but Colonel Carrington forbade it.' He spoke in a jovial tone, but was a little disconcerted. The colonel had arrived unexpectedly that evening at the barracks, and John Parget had told him of his supper engagement and urged him to come with him, saying that he would advise Mistress Ashley without delay. Barely acknowledging the other man, Henry had said that he had every intention of visiting Gull's Nest—that it was, in fact, the reason he was in Bude—but that no notice was necessary for Mistress Ashley. Now the two were reunited, and Captain Parget viewed the reunion with dismay.

He had met Alice only twice but, not inexperienced with women, had formed the opinion that she was a passionate and affectionate girl—with the right man, of course. Yet here she was greeting her betrothed for the first time in a twelvemonth and as stiff and remote as an icicle. It looked as though there might be a difficult evening ahead, and John Parget wished he were not a part of it, if only for the sake of his career.

When Alice had mentioned her fiancé as being Henry Carrington of Kent, he had known the name. Who in Parliament's ranks did not? For Carrington had risen very fast and very far—not in the fighting ranks, although he had held his own in various battles, but in the more select diplomatic area. Now he was of the élite, sponsored by no less a man than Cromwell.

'It is a surprise,' Alice said faintly. 'Joyful, of course, but also. . .surprising.' Closing the door and inviting the men to be seated, she surveyed her friend and future husband. He was plainly dressed in snuff-brown, with no lace or ribbons or any finery at all about his costume. His hair was clipped very short and lay close to his head, an exercise which had subdued its bright colour, for cropped hair was always darker. His face was pale, his hands soft and white, and an air of time spent in dim and smoky rooms in an atmosphere of conspiracy clung about him. She could not help comparing him to Chris, whose hands were so rough, whose body was scarred with half-healed cuts, who brought the wild freedom of living in the company of masculine danger into every room he entered now. She released her hands from his and said to Thomas, 'Please bring refreshment for the gentlemen, Thomas.'

'Yes, mistress.' Thomas bounded away to get the jug of cooled spring water which Alice had thought appropriate.

When he returned, Henry said, 'I believe we might do better than that. John——' Captain Parget produced two bottles of wine and put them on the table with a sheepish air. If the newly promoted colonel thought it acceptable to take a little wine, then certainly it was not for him to dispute it.

Accepting a glass thankfully, Alice sat herself and looked expectantly at Henry.

'I am sure,' he said, 'that Captain Parget will not mind if you bring me briefly up to date, Alice. When last on leave I visited your aunt and uncle. They told me you were visiting Meg Allerton. I then proceeded to call on the Allertons, only to be told by Meg that you had suddenly decided to come to Bude.'

'Yes. . . A sudden whim, Henry. To see Gull's Nest and make up my mind whether or not to sell the property.' More lies, she thought bleakly.

'Without consulting me?' Henry asked her, frowning.

Had he always had that interrogatory way of talking to her? Surely it was something new and rather disagreeable? Also new was the air of authority now stamped on him. It was there in the deference that his captain showed, in the way young Thomas leaped to obey his request for water to dilute his wine, to lay another log upon the fire.

'However,' Henry continued, 'I am sure you simply had not thought the matter out carefully. I have to say that I think it was most i'l-considered of you to take the road in these uneasy times.' He allowed the reprimand to sink in, then went on, 'Alice, Captain Parget has informed me of his previous visit here, and of the reason for it.'

'Has he?' Please don't ask me if Chris is here, she begged silently. For I shall have to lie to you again. A horrible thought struck her. Chris knew Henry's voice so well; what if he should come hastening down the stair to greet him? 'Twould be disaster, for if Chris had changed in the war years, so had Henry, and Alice intuitively knew that the two men were now poles apart. While Chris, with his usual tolerance, could disallow the fact that his friend was now the enemy, Henry never would.

I never really knew either of them, she thought, and yet was prepared to accept one in marriage. Even without her secret and startling new feeling for Chris she could never marry the man before her—why, he was as alien to her as. . .as. . . Well, she could not think of a suitable example.

'Naturally,' Henry went on ponderously, 'I told him such disloyalty was impossible for you. Towards the government, and towards me.'

Alice was saved from having to reply to this remark as Lizzie bore in the ducks, garnished as best she could from the vegetable garden. She placed the platter on the table and the three took their seats.

The meal progressed pleasantly enough. John Parget showed an unexpected sense of social grace and tried to amuse the other two diners with various anecdotes. Henry smiled frostily at his efforts; Alice was genuinely entertained. It came to her that at the various parties and suppers she had attended with Henry, Chris had also been there to provide just the leavening of light nonsense that Captain Parget supplied tonight. Henry, she realised, had little sense of humour and no small talk at all. Why had she never noticed that before?

Lizzie brought in a mounded dish of early raspberries and a jug of thick yellow cream. Alice dispensed the red fruit and offered the well-ground sugar, thinking, That alone would be a gloomy prospect for the future had I intended to honour my promise to him. But, of course, I do not. . . She shrank from the task of telling Henry, though, and then knew something else about him. He was now a man to be wary of. But how terrible to be afraid of the man you had planned to marry! How terrible not to be able to picture him being kind in the many vulnerable situations a wife would find herself in.

Winter-stored apples and Alice's home-made cheese, served with wrinkled walnuts gathered from the old trees standing sentinel to the house, completed the meal, then John Parget rose.

'I do thank you for the excellent meal, Mistress Alice,

and now will take my leave. You and the colonel will wish a little time together.'

'Please do not hurry away,' Alice said. She had no wish at all to be alone with the colonel.

'I fear I must. I have various duties to attend to.'

Alice had to let him go. It had obviously been arranged beforehand that he would tactfully withdraw and leave the affianced couple to their own devices. She took him to the door and accepted his praise of the evening. Closing the door, she returned to the table and helped herself to another glass of wine.

'That will be your fourth glass,' Henry commented.

'Will it? I'm afraid I was not brought up to count such things.'

Her tone was combative and he noted it. All evening he had been noting and disapproving of her. Firstly, her gown was most unsuitable; the bodice showed off her sweet curves too obviously. Secondly, her hands and the lower half of her arms were touched with a golden colour very unbecoming to a lady. Most of all, her ready response to the kind of supper table conversation that young Parget had indulged in had been most distasteful. However, he had no desire to argue with her. He pushed back his chair and held out his hand. 'Come, let us sit and talk together.'

Reluctantly Alice allowed herself to be led to a chair by the hearth. The weather was too warm for a fire, but Lizzie had thought a blaze would dress up the room a little. Alice stared into the flames.

Henry seated himself opposite. 'I was,' he said, 'most distressed by Captain Parget's report that you had—on his intelligence information—helped Chris Rokesby to escape from Naseby and were harbouring him here.'

'Were you?' Her tone did not encourage further discussion, but he pursued it.

'Although I denied the possibility of your being capable of such treason—to your country and to me—I find I must ask you now if there is any truth in the matter.'

'So ask me.' Alice finished her wine and rose to pour another. She had eaten heartily of the good food that night but knew that the alcohol was making her less cautious than might be sensible.

'Have you seen Chris since he left Oaks?' Henry asked bluntly.

'Yes, she has.' Chris was on the stairs. He had been on the gallery above for some time, in two minds as to whether he should go down. Now, with Alice under fire, he had decided he must. He stepped carefully down the remaining steps and came to the hearth. 'So,' he said, his eyes on Henry, who was staring at him as if confronted by a ghost, 'if you have any more remarks on the subjects of *treason* and *betrayal*, please address them to me.'

Henry picked up his empty glass and looked into it. He could not really have believed Chris was here, he thought, otherwise he would not be so stunned by the sight of him. He struggled with two distinct thoughts. Here was Chris—his friend and comrade—desperately changed and ill-looking, and here was Rokesby, whose name and reputation were by-words now among Cromwell's fighting men. He got up slowly out of his chair, trying to reconcile these two separate images. There was a deadly silence. Chris broke it.

'What Alice did,' he said deliberately, 'she did for our remembered friendship, Hal. Yours and mine.'

'It must be so, I suppose.' Henry found his voice, but not his composure. 'But Chris, you are a wanted man. What do you expect me to say or do?'

'Little,' Chris said, holding his friend's eyes. 'But it is a thing between you and me. Alice is not involved.'

'Certainly I am,' Alice said crisply. Her heart had been in her mouth when Chris came down the stairs. She had seen the instant conflict in Henry's eyes. 'I came to your aid on my own behalf. I am as much your friend as Henry's.'

Both men turned to look at her. Henry in annoyance that she should so declare herself, Chris in admiration that she should.

'This is *my* house,' she went on, 'and I decide who may be *harboured* therein.' She walked carefully to the table and, taking Captain Parget's empty glass, filled it with wine. She took it to Chris. 'Shall we sit down?' There was another silence.

'You have the floor, Alice,' Chris said ironically.

'Very well. Henry—I insist Chris must remain here until fully recovered and able to leave of his own accord. What do you say to this?'

Attacked in this way, and by the woman he loved, Henry was nonplussed. His mind, not agile at the best of times, fumbled for the right reply. As a serving officer in the government army he knew what it should be, but as a lifelong associate of these two volatile personalities he doubted his ability to enforce it immediately.

Chris watched him, amused. Poor Henry, he had only just began to comprehend what an unusual and complex woman he had decided to take to wife. 'Hal,' he said, 'if you can close your dutiful eyes for a few short days, I will be away from here.'

'Where to?' Alice demanded. 'When you are scarcely able to walk!'

'I am stronger by the hour. And cannot state my destination in the present company, except to rebuke you for leaving various papers about the house.'

So he had read the newsletters, thought Alice resentfully. And knew that Rupert was in Bristol.

'The war is lost, Chris. What is the point in getting yourself killed when nothing will be gained?'

'It is not lost until the last man surrenders—also our support should not be discounted. Ask Henry if this is not so.'

Henry, well-informed as to the King's attempts to raise troops from England's nearest neighbours, remained silent. What Chris would do he would do, whatever the opposition, but Alice must not be part of it. Henry thought it already beyond belief that she should be having this conversation in front of himself. He considered his options.

Rokesby was hotly desired by the Ironsides, not for transportation, as so many of his fellows had been, but to be executed as an example to other young men who—if the Prince Rupert gave up the fight, if the young Prince Charles's flight to safety were made known, and the King remained beyond the border—might feel they still had a strong rallying point. Henry did not altogether support this theory; he was convinced that Parliament held the highest cards, not least in their belief that God was on their side. No one man, or men, could make a difference.

'If Alice,' he said directly to Chris, 'agrees to leave this place and return to her home, then I will hold my hand for five days. On the sixth I will come for you, with hand-picked men to take you.'

It was, thought Chris, a generous offer, and one he had not expected.

Infamous! thought Alice, to hold my affection for Chris to ransom in this way. Spit in his eye, was the phrase she had used in regard to John Parget; she wished she could now perform that vulgar action on Henry. Both men, having known her for so long, now expected an explosion. Instead she said coolly, 'I will go, Henry, if it buys Chris some time. But I will not forgive you for making the condition, or forget it.' She rose unsteadily, walked to the foot of the stairs, and began to climb them.

Both men expelled their breath, and Chris laughed. 'I told you not to underestimate her.'

'She did help you to escape from Naseby, didn't she?'

'If it compromises her to say yes, then no, she did not. If you can look upon her action neutrally, then yes, she did. And damned glad I was of her courage.' Chris went to the table and held up the bottle. Henry shook his head.

'How badly are you wounded?' he asked.

'A couple of scratches.' Chris dismissed the last weeks of agony. 'But, by God, Henry, your army is well-drilled! Is it abstinence from the good things in life that makes your men such tigers? If so, I might take the pledge myself.' He swallowed the contents of his glass.

Henry smiled thinly. 'Perhaps. That and the surety that we are right.'

'How pleasant that feeling must be. But then you always did feel that, didn't you? Even when you were barely breeched you could convince yourself that your way was best.' There was an indulgent affection in his voice. 'For myself, I am always inclined to think I am wrong—wrong, but prepared to take the consequences.'

'You may well have to do just that unless you are away from here on the day I have specified. I must go.' He got up and looked around for his hat. Chris produced it from the settle by the door. He examined it critically.

'This is what you are looking for? Not something I could have imagined you wearing two years ago. That is one of the things I believe I most dislike about the opposition—their dreary taste in costume.'

He presented it with a bow and Henry put it on, remarking sourly, 'You were hardly an example of elegance yourself in those days.'

'Perhaps I have changed. Indeed, I know I have—in many ways. So, it is goodbye, then, Hal. Now, what is it you want to ask me before you go?'

Henry avoided the straight blue eyes. 'I do not have to ask it, I am sure.'

'No, you don't. I said to you, and meant it, that if my

feelings towards Alice became something other than friendship, you would be the first to know. You could have heard every word which was passed between us in the last week without dismay.'

Henry delayed putting on his soft leather gloves to extend his right hand. Chris gripped it, saying, 'And if you are at all worried about the spirited display she just showed, believe me, had our roles been reversed—yours and mine—it would have been your battered body she dragged west. Were you there—at Naseby—by the way?'

'No. . . I was in London on. . .business. There are more ways of winning a war than taking sword in hand.'

'Really? I wish I had known that before I chanced my frail talent for warfare.'

'I have not heard that the talent is frail, indeed——' Henry hesitated; it did not become an officer of his persuasion to advise a loyalist officer, but. . . 'I have heard the reverse. You are a marked man, not only by the good Captain Parget, but by others. You would do well to bear that in mind before making your next move.'

Chris considered this a moment, for he thought the advice sincerely meant. He also suspected that Henry knew exactly what he was speaking of. He had immediately detected that Henry was no longer of the rank and file in the new order, but had probably turned administrator and politician. Well, thought Chris with an inward smile, he would definitely be in his element in such company, although how tedious their gatherings must be.

It did not occur to Chris to be fearful of his old friend. Intuitive in so many ways, he failed to see beyond the Henry of their past association but something made him say slowly, 'We have come a long way, Hal, since the days at Oaks and Fox and Ashley. Happy days. . . When all this is over, will there be anything left of those days, I wonder? For us?'

Henry turned at the door. He knew what Chris was asking of him, but could not answer. There was no going back once a choice was made, or so Henry Carrington believed. They had each made their choice and must live with it. But how their being together again—he and Chris and Alice—brought the memories back! Upon this thought sprang another: they had usually been ranged against him in those times too. He said stiffly, 'I cannot wish you luck, Chris, for that smacks of superstition and even collusion, but I shall ask God to look kindly on you.'

'Thank you.' Chris followed him out into the moonlit night.

When he was mounted, Henry said, 'I shall send one of my men here tomorrow to escort Alice home. I hope she will be ready to go.'

'I will make sure she is,' Chris promised.

CHAPTER SEVEN

HAVING said that she would leave Gull's Nest, Alice, waking the next morning with a thick head and a tremor to her hands, knew that she would have to make good her promise. She did not want to. Not only because she was afraid to leave Chris to his own devices, knowing he would instantly make ready to fling himself back into the fight, but also because she had grown fond of her heritage and its neighbours.

Lizzie had said little when advised of the plan; she had had an ear pressed to the kitchen door during the discussions of the previous night so it was not news to her, but she was relieved when Alice said that she had no intention of selling and might well be back when conditions were easier. In sympathy with her young mistress's set face and obvious unhappiness, Lizzie comforted her by swearing that she would ensure that Master Chris was as well as he could be before leaving and obeying Henry Carrington's ultimatum. They had talked in the early morning in Alice's bedroom while Alice was brushing her hair, and impulsively Lizzie had taken the brush and drawn it energetically through the glinting strands.

'Don't you worry now, Miss Alice, I'll see for him and make certain he takes as much food as I can muster and all the good warm clothing I can borrow or steal. 'Twill be bitter winter soon enough.'

Bitter, yes, thought Alice, and for me especially. I may not be going into battle and danger, but I will feel as if I am—back at Ashley with only my imagination for company. She waited until Lizzie had tied her hair with a ribbon, then rose. 'I must dress now.'

157

'And I'll get your food right quick. Master Chris is in the hall already, eating his.' Lizzie hovered a moment, picking up Alice's nightgown. 'Miss?'

'Yes, Lizzie?' Alice was stepping into her white dress. Later she would change into her riding habit for the journey, but had resolved to leave it until the last possible moment before departing.

Lizzie blushed bright pink before she got the words out. 'I know it's not my place. . .but. . .you love him, don't you? Master Chris, I mean?'

Alice fixed her eyes on the sun climbing up into the blue sky. She said nothing.

'I seen it in your face, miss,' Lizzie went on with a rush. 'And it seems to me——'

'Whatever I feel,' Alice interrupted her. 'There is nothing to be done. I am still officially betrothed to Henry Carrington, and he is Master Chris's best friend.'

'Nothing to be done!' Lizzie's flush receded, but her voice was outraged. 'I'm nothing to you, my lady, and cannot even claim an old servant's rights—although I held you in my arms when you were not an hour old—but seems to me. . .seems to me that one life spoiled be better than three.'

'What do you mean?'

'Dear miss,' Lizzie said patiently, 'marriage can last a dear long time, and with the wrong man 'twould seem a cruel sentence indeed. Or with a woman hankering after another.' So said Lizzie, doing her best too for Henry Carrington, to whom she had taken an instant dislike.

Alice half smiled. 'I have already decided that I will not marry with Colonel Carrington, Lizzie. So 'tis not three lives, but one. My own. For it is apparent to me that Master Chris feels only affection for me.' She sat on the bed to put on her shoes, so did not see Lizzie's amazed expression.

So that is what she thinks, is it? Lizzie thought pityingly. And the young man coming out of that grim space behind the hall ready to kill because a stranger had shown her some attention! And them bickering the day long like an old married couple. But what could you tell young things? Lizzie had had her share of joy before she was sixteen years old, and the man she had set her heart on had turned out to be a dud. But that did not prevent her from remembering it fondly and recognising the same condition in others. She was in her middle-age now and had seen a lot of lovers, some happy, some not, but always the disease was the same, and if her poor pretty Alice had contracted it, then Lizzie would swear blind that Chris Rokesby was in the same state. She said carefully, 'You haven't told him, then, what it is you feel for him?'

'No, indeed! How could I? I have *told* you, Lizzie, he thinks I am committed to his friend! And even if he thought I were not, he thinks of me only as *his* friend.'

Lizzie hesitated a moment longer. 'I see the way it is, and would only say this: let him go to war, my dear, for he will not be content until he sees the end, but when he comes home—— When he comes home, be sure you are not of any entanglement. And be you rid of that red-haired, cold-hearted man without delay!' Lizzie opened the door and was gone before she could say anything she might regret, leaving Alice to complete her toilette and ponder on her desire to return to Gull's Nest at some later date. It might be possible.

Although Parliament now effectively ruled the west, Cornwall and Devon, local government had not really changed. Fervent Royalists still continued to function in the roles of justices and sat on county committees. Those landowners who had had their property and land sequestered by Parliament until mammoth fines were paid were few—most had taken advantage of the sleight of hand of signing over their property to friends among the opposition. Besides, the west had always been for the King, and even the so-called rebels were used to it.

Alice thought that it would not be that way at all when she returned to Kent, and upon this thought she took out the covenant which gave her possession of Oaks. She must persuade Chris to sign it before she left.

She knew from the ubiquitous newsletters lately that most of England's Royalists did not lie easy under the new rule. Many of the great families who had chosen to back the throne now found themselves homeless or dwelling in poor shelter while their inferiors—men who in the past would not have been welcome in the poorest part of their great mansions—had, usually on the flimsiest pretext, gained possession of the beauty of Welbeck and Raglan.

Chris was even stronger today and radiated a hopefulness of spirit. Alice, while being happy to see it, knew also what it meant. He had risen early and was already at the table when she came down. He rose and held her chair for her as Lizzie hurried in with hot food. He filled her ale mug.

'You are looking very wan this morning, little Alice,' he said cheerfully. 'Is it that you did not sleep well, or is it the effects of the wine last night?'

'I slept well enough, and please do not speak as if I were a habitual wine-bibber,' she said sharply.

'I would not dream of doing so,' he teased her. 'Particularly since those whom you describe seldom show signs of distress after heavy drinking. It is to your credit that you are less than well this morning.'

She broke the crust from the bread and began to crumble it. 'I don't know why you are so cheerful—inappropriate, I would have thought, for a man under sentence of death.'

'If Henry had had any such thing in mind, he would have done something last night. I know him well enough for that.'

'I feel I don't know him at all. Or you, or myself, come to that.'

He removed the crumbs from under her fingers and cut a fresh piece of bread and buttered it. 'Here—eat properly. I suppose we are all changed—small wonder when our lives are in such disarray. You will feel more at peace when you get back to Ashley.'

'Knowing you are riding for Bristol with all haste? There will be little peace for me thinking of that.'

He could have been surprised at the bleak tone in her voice, but for some reason was not. He turned his head and looked out into the blowy day. The seasons were more advanced here in the west, he thought. Already summer was waning, autumn showing herself in small ways. The winter campaign had been hard enough last year with few supplies and loss of men; the coming months would obviously be worse. He said, 'Alice, I hope you won't think me interfering, but what you said to Hal last night—about neither forgiving nor forgetting his quite reasonable request for you to go back to your family—will be a poor sentiment to take to your new marriage.'

'I won't be doing that, for there will be no marriage.'

'But—— Surely not because of what happened last night?'

'No. I had decided before that.'

'But you are betrothed, legally and morally. It is a serious business to change your mind.'

She stopped trying to eat. The last time Chris had played advocate she had been both amused and annoyed. This time she was neither, felt only how ironical it was for the man she loved to argue for her to marry another. She shrugged and said, 'I should not have spoken of it to you. I should have declared myself to Henry first. Please, forget I spoke.' She stood up and went quickly to the open door and was out into the sunlight before he could move.

He was still slow in walking and judged that the muscle in his thigh had been badly damaged and that it would be some time before he regained the swift-moving grace he was accustomed to—if he ever did. At the door he surveyed the gardens and caught a flash of Alice's white dress among the shrubbery overlooking the cliff. He limped over the ground and called to her as she was descending the steep path. 'Alice!'

She did not turn, but continued on down to a plateau of grassy stubble which jutted out over the sea. With difficulty he negotiated the slope and lowered himself to the ground at her feet. He stretched his injured leg cautiously and winced.

'Damn! I shall be useless unless mounted.'

She looked down at his bare head, then back at the restless sea—blue on the surface where it took colour from the sky, a rich turquoise beneath. White froth capped the waves breaking on the sand at the foot of the cliff. He reached up and caught her hand.

'Sit down and talk to me.'

She knelt reluctantly, spreading her skirts among the sea campion growing in clumps around them. 'I shouldn't have said anything to you about my marriage,' she repeated. 'And I don't wish to discuss it now.'

'You must have a reason for throwing up a year and more of certainty, Alice.' He tried to see her expression, but she was pleating her skirt between her fingers, her bright hair hiding her face. 'I know Hal has annoyed you—he annoys me often enough—but you must learn to laugh at his funny ways. That is what marriage is, I imagine, putting up with the bad as well as the good.'

'I don't find his ways amusing. I don't like them. I don't think I like *him*. Also,' she added in a rush, 'he frightens me now——'

He gave a shout of laughter. 'Frightens you? Hal? Dear Alice, you are being foolish. You have known him all your life!'

'I haven't! Why does everyone always say that? I

didn't begin to know anything about either of you until the war.'

'And I? Do I frighten you now that you have this sudden knowledge of us both?'

'No,' she muttered. 'But you do annoy me.'

He laughed again, and yet. . .memories were tugging at the back of his mind. Small differences he had had with Henry over the years—their opposite views of poaching, for instance. Chris, like every country gentleman, took a poor view of the game on his estate being filched—such was inbred in any man of his class. But he always turned a blind eye if possible—if crops were poor and food scarce one year, he had no real objection to the odd bird or animal being taken for a cottage pot where a man was trying to feed a hungry family. Henry was a stickler for the rules—men had been hanged or transported for such an infringement at Fox. . . He said thoughtfully, 'You haven't known many men. Only really your uncle and, very charming though Uncle Richard is, he is not typical, and Henry and myself—three males is not enough to make you any kind of authority.' Another memory surfaced in his unwilling mind. The year before the war one of the maids at Fox had become pregnant without benefit of a suitable bridegroom. Government laws on this were rarely enforced—most households got around the Puritan insistence that 'twas a grievous sin and worthy of the severest punishment and cared for the girls. Walter and Mary Carrington would have done the same on this occasion, for the maid was but fourteen, but Henry had allowed little Phoebe to be whipped through the village in sore distress and forbidden any of his tenants to take her in after. Chris had been appalled by such inhumanity and a swift message to Molly Judd had ensured a home and care for the child.

'I know that.' Alice lifted her head and looked at him.

'You know I had never even been kissed before you said goodbye to me at Oaks that day.'

His mind faltered; he had been guilty of something he could not quite analyse that day, and did not choose to remember it now. 'Did I do that? I had forgotten,' he lied.

'Had you? Really?' During the night she had not slept well, but tossed and turned thinking of the revelation she had had about him and what it meant to her. Towards dawn she had almost believed that it was impossible that what she felt would not be returned. But this morning brought reality. He could not remember even holding her in his arms. . . There was no change, either, in his attitude towards her.

It might have been that their thoughts crossed in the pure air on the windy cliff, for he was suddenly uncomfortable and all too aware of their isolation in this place, hidden from the house with nothing by the rolling water before them. 'I am sorry if I took advantage of you last year,' he said stiffly. 'I had no wish to upset you.' He thought, If this were any other girl I would kiss her again now, and probably say all sorts of things we would both regret.

They fell silent, the only sound the seagulls crying overhead and the gentle thunder of the surf on the shore, then she said slowly, 'If I asked you to read something, would you do it—to please me?'

'You know I hate to read.' Somehow it was not what he had expected her to say, with that look on her face. 'When do you expect me to have time to read?'

'I have heard that there is more boring time to be filled for a soldier than in any other occupation. You could take it with you and while away some hours.' She got to her feet with one of her swift free movements. 'Oh, never mind, 'twas a silly idea of mine. Shall we go back to the house?'

'Help me up, then.' She took his hand and leaned

backwards as he got painfully up. 'Give me whatever it is and I'll look at it,' he said when he was upright. 'But can you not just tell me what it is about?'

'No, I can't, for I do not have ten years.'

'What do you mean?' He staggered and she kept her grip on his hand until he was steady. It was the fever he had endured over the past month which made him so weak, he thought. A few days more rest and good food would give him back his strength—a strength needed for the last stubborn twilight of a glorious adventure.

Chris knew now that there was no longer any hope for the Royalist cause, but he was determined to be there at the end. Perhaps he would lose his life in that end but he did not fear death, for it had been his constant companion in the last two years. This lack of fear had enabled him to be in the thick of every fight, to play a significant part in each violent skirmish, to rally and encourage less courageous men. But perhaps, he thought suddenly, those men had had more to lose. Perhaps they had had a woman like Alice Ashley waiting for them in some distant manor house, or on some small farm. Children, too, made and raised by that woman.

Alice watched his face, always expressive. Once it had been vulnerable too, showing all his thoughts, but those days were gone. He is holding my hand, she thought, but he is already gone from me. Gone back to the mysterious land men inhabited when they fought together in the destructive business of war. She said, 'You will be careful, won't you, Chris? When you are gone to Bristol?' There, she had said it. In the open, and he did not deny it.

'I am always careful,' he returned lightly. 'And now will be the more so. You have risked much to preserve my life and limbs. I feel I owe it to you to bring the one and the other four safely home.'

It was something, anyway, she thought dully, something to take out and treasure in the months to come. She released his hand and turned to look out again over the playful sea. 'You have not yet signed the deed of tenure on Oaks that I drew up.'

'I have been indisposed. Also——'

'Also?'

'I feel such a gesture on your part must raise a barrier between you and Henry that I should not wish to be responsible for.'

She could have said again that such a barrier already existed, insisted again that she had no intention of marrying, but instead she said consideringly, 'You should do it, you know, if only for your cousin Margaret. When all is over and the country—the government—takes stock, those who supported the losing side will be in jeopardy. By association, your cousin will be in that unhappy state. This way, even if everyone knows of your convictions, she cannot be deprived of her home.'

He sighed. 'Yes, of course I have thought of that. But——'

'There can be no buts,' Alice said decisively. 'If I am the owner of Oaks, all will be well.'

At noon Alice left Bude for Kent. Henry had kept his word and sent a dour-looking man to escort her. Sergeant Black introduced himself, then remounted his horse and waited at the end of the drive. Alice and Chris said their farewells before the house under brilliant azure skies.

'You know that you must be gone from Gull's Nest within the week,' she said anxiously as Jack saddled her horse.

'Yes, I know that.'

'And must keep close to the house before you go?'

'Yes, yes.' Chris took her mare's bridle from Jack,

who moved tactfully away. 'I do thank you for giving me the extra mount for my own use.'

'Oh, that is nothing.' Alice was rearranging her hair beneath her hat; the wind kept trying to take the gleaming strands. 'Although, I do wish 'twere Jenny I was leaving for you,' she added wistfully.

'Yes, I know. . .' Chris had had the truth about Jenny's demise out of Jack the day before. Another debt he owed to the slim girl by his side, he thought, putting an arm around her waist to help her to mount. She looked up at him.

'Will you kiss me goodbye as you did all those months ago?'

'If you wish.' He pressed his lips to her forehead, but she lifted her chin and her mouth sought his. A primitive desire to deny the imminent departure, to carry her instead back into the house, gripped him. My God, he thought, just as well she is leaving. . . He lifted her into the saddle and stood with the bridle in his hands.

'Time we were away, Master Chris,' Jack said quietly.

'Yes, indeed.'

Alice held her reins with one hand and touched Chris's bare head with the other; the black hair seemed to have a life and vitality of its own. 'When you have done what you must, come home, Chris. Promise me you will.'

He hesitated. Her mare, disliking the restraint, danced on the dusty cobbles. Alice resisted her attempt to move away. '*Promise* me, Chris.'

'Very well. I promise.'

She looked at him, trying to imprint this last sight of his face on her mind forever. Perhaps it was for the last time. But then he had given her his promise, and he had never lied to her. 'So,' she said, 'at Oaks when it is over.'

Chris stepped back and the two riders moved down the drive to join their escort.

* * *

It was not a difficult journey home. Under the stal-
wart—if morose—wing of Sergeant Black, who carried
papers signed by his master, the Roundhead Colonel
Carrington, Jack and Alice knew no danger or hardship.
The sergeant had little to say of the war's progress, but
Alice kept her ears open and gathered as much information as she could in the hostelries they patronised on
the way. It did not cheer her.

In military terms the Royalists were now hopelessly
outnumbered. Naseby had left only four thousand horse
to the King. He had scraped together another three
thousand foot, reinforced by about three thousand from
Wales. The seven thousand strong western army, under
Goring, had been defeated some weeks before when
Fairfax had laid siege to, and taken, Taunton. In the last
month private letters from the King to the Queen in
Paris had revealed negotiations to solicit men and
finance from foreign powers, particularly France, and
the King's intention to invite Irish Papists into the fray.
These published letters had greatly incensed many of
the throne's supporters.

Almost the whole of England was now under the
control of the Roundheads, saving Wales, a small part
of the west, the country around Oxford and a little of
Northamptonshire, centred in Newark.

Hardly surprising, thought Alice, lying in the attic
room of a small inn the night before they would enter
Kent, that the Prince Rupert had been so desperate to
sue for peace. How she wished he had succeeded in
persuading his royal uncle, and then perhaps Chris
Rokesby would be under this same roof on his way
home. As it was, Rupert was now in Bristol, trying to
hold it, knowing that Fairfax would undoubtedly come
there when he had done mopping up the rest of
the west.

* * *

Back at Ashley, Alice continued to read anything about the conflict that she could lay hands on, went regularly to the local towns to garner any news she could and, as Christmas came and went with no word from Chris, looked onwards to her nineteenth year with sadness and despair. Then one day, in the year of 1646, one week before her nineteenth birthday, Chris came home.

CHAPTER EIGHT

ALICE was taking tea with her aunt and uncle at the time the news came, supplied by Betty who had brought in the steaming pot. She had had it from Jack Madesley.

'Well, now!' Emma Ashley exclaimed delightedly. 'I am that glad! Since Will died, Margaret has been sorely depressed. She will be so happy he is home.'

'Indeed,' agreed Richard, his eyes on his niece. 'Shall you ride over to welcome him back, Alice?'

'I may,' Alice said, lifting her cup with trembling fingers. Not a word had she heard about, or from, Chris, since their parting outside Gull's Nest eleven months ago. And not a day or night had passed without her thinking of him. Thinking of him dead on some muddy field, his blue eyes open to the sky, or his dear body swinging from some hastily erected gibbet. The Ironsides had not been kind in the last weeks of the war. She put down her cup.

'We must pray that all our friends will shortly be restored to us,' Richard said gently.

'Oh, of course,' Emma agreed fervently. 'When Henry comes home, Alice, we shall see your wedding!' Alice had decided not to confide in her relatives of her intentions. . .

Henry had written punctiliously correct letters at regular intervals. Dated, but not headed with any clue as to where he was. Alice rose. The sun, slipping down the sky now, but still July-hot, turned her hair to gold, enhanced the cream and carnation of her skin. She said breathlessly, 'I think I will ride over to Oaks and see if Margaret has—has——'

'Coped with the returning soldier?' suggested Richard mildly.

She found Chris in the stable-yard. Slipping down from her horse, she joined him at the paddock rails. He did not turn his head when he heard her footsteps, but continued to stare out over the grass paddock. Alice looped her reins over a post and waited for him to speak.

'Well,' he said, 'I have come home, as promised, Alice.'

'Yes. . .' She wanted to touch him, to hold him, but the expression on his face, his rigid stance, prevented her.

'Why I have done so,' he continued, 'I have no idea. The place is a ruin now.'

It was a slap in the face for her. She had tried so hard to keep Oaks up, neglecting her own house to ride over every day. She had even spent days behind a borrowed plough-horse. . . She said painfully, 'I know. I have tried to find men to work it for you, but——'

'But no man wishes to work the land of a known Royalist,' he supplied.

'That, yes, but also the whole county is in chaos at present. Since we heard of the. . .surrender, men have been coming home expecting the reward that they were promised. Such has not been forthcoming and we are all confused. Still, I have done my best, and Margaret has not suffered, I think.'

He looked at her now. Impossible, he thought, that she should be even more beautiful than when he saw her last. Beautiful and. . .somehow untouched by the privations he knew she must have endured. With nothing constant in his life now, Chris unaccountably resented her beauty. After what he had seen in the last months, it was. . .unnatural for Alice Ashley to remain unscathed. 'Without Alice,' his cousin Margaret had declared, 'I would be *destitute*. Without her I would have *starved*.'

Bitter words for him to hear on his return, on a flagging horse, shabby and thin and so tired. . . He said with an effort, 'I know that. Margaret has nothing but praise for your efforts. I do thank you for all you have done for her,' he added politely.

'Don't thank me, Chris. What I did, I did for you. For our. . .friendship.' She touched his arm timidly. 'Was it bad—the end?'

His eyes were stormy. Bad? Yes, it had been. . .bad! Roundhead troops had attacked Bristol in September. Chris had barely had time to cover the miles from Bude to rejoin his regiment, where he had been greeted with joy, but also a degree of consternation, by Prince Rupert. It had been a miracle that Rokesby had got into the beleaguered city at all, for there had been violent skirmishes on the outskirts for days before. The Prince had made what preparations were possible, laying in supplies enough for a lengthy siege, and fortifying the boundaries with all the men he could muster. But he knew the concentration of troops available to the enemy; his was but a last valiant effort. . .

Chris had seized his opportunity at nightfall; his likeness to the King's nephew had often been remarked and he had had no trouble from the sentries, or in being presented to his general without delay.

'Good God, Rokesby!' Rupert had dismissed the accompanying sentry and given Chris a glass of wine. 'I thought you away to some safe place! How is your injury?'

'What injury?' Chris had asked, dropping into a chair. Actually, his leg still pained him considerably and without the dark medicine Lizzie Mote had thoughtfully packed in his kit he could not have ridden so hard. The mixture still induced a hallucinatory state—he had had some vivid dreams during both the past nights and days—but perhaps that particular condition might be an advantage in the days to come, for this was obviously a doomed enterprise. He gave Rupert a brief account of what enemy activity he had seen in the vicinity of Bristol and the prince shrugged.

'I know all there is to know, my friend.'

'Then why pursue it? Fairfax is a just man—and a compassionate one. Admit the situation is hopeless for us and offer him terms.'

'What terms?'

'Terms which will mean no more unnecessary loss of life.'

Rupert considered him. No candles were in use in the fort, only fat flares with their noisome stench and fitful light, but even had he been semi-blind he would have sensed the great change in his friend. Rokesby counselling caution when there was even a faint chance? No need to think long and hard on why that should be so; women were usually at the root of any man's metamorphosis, and where a woman like Alice Ashley was concerned. . . He said, 'The terms—any terms—would compromise honour too severely, Chris.'

'Well, honour is usually a casualty of war.' He had said those words to Alice. . .

'Not mine,' the Prince said swiftly, 'or, I think, yours. Why else have you come?'

Chris grinned. 'I would have thought it obvious; you need every man, do you not?'

Rupert laughed. 'Very well, now you have offered me your common sense advice, give me now your valuable military opinion.'

Chris's face sobered. 'It is the same. We cannot possibly hold this place. We are outmanned, outgunned, outflanked, and—'

Rupert raised his hand. 'Enough! Did your mother never impress upon you that if you cannot utter any pleasant word, keep quiet?'

'Seriously, though,' Chris said, smiling.

'Seriously. . . I am commanded to do this thing,

however *impossible*. And we are as ready as we will ever be. Now, let me fill your glass and we can await events and while away the time in a little conversation. Tell me about Mistress Alice.'

'Alice?' The smile left Chris's face. 'I have nothing to say about her.'

Rupert raised his eyebrows. Had he touched a nerve?

'She is affianced to my best friend,' Chris went on.

'Ah, yes, I see.' Rupert tipped more wine into his own glass and held out the bottle to Chris, who refused it. The combination of opium, Oporto wine and talk of Alice was too explosive a combination on this night.

Rupert made himself comfortable in his chair. He leaned back and closed his eyes. It was the mark of an experienced soldier that he could. Having done all possible towards the coming confrontation, he was able to think and speak of other matters. He said thoughtfully, 'There is a full moon tonight. 'Tis a state said to promote madness. In that vein, love—they say—is the purest form of madness.'

'I know little of that, sir,' Chris said.

'Do you not? Do you not? For myself I have never been in love, but can imagine the condition from romantic literature.'

'I am sure you can't.'

'So you do have some thoughts on the subject?' He waited for Chris to speak. When he said nothing, he went on, 'Well, here are mine for what they are worth. If a man should meet the woman who appears to embody all that man admires most, then he would be a fool to pass her up, whatever the circumstances.'

Chris said nothing.

'Well, anyway——' the Prince refilled his glass, thinking Rokesby unusually silent on this particular subject '—tell me about her betrothed. He is a man you approve of?'

'As I have said, he is my firmest friend. As to

approve? As a Royalist, I suppose I should not really approve of Colonel Henry Carrington.'

'Carrington, eh?' Rupert tapped a fingernail against his full glass. 'One might almost say that it is your duty to rescue her, then. I have heard of this man, and cold-blooded was the most complimentary thing said of him.'

'I may not criticise your choice of words, sir,' Chris said. 'But do not have to listen to them either.' He rose. 'If you will excuse me.'

'Oh, stay, Rokesby!' Rupert said hastily. He appeared to have discovered two subjects on which his friend was unusually touchy—or was it just the one? 'Very well, no more talk of the dreary Colonel Carrington. Come, fill your glass.'

Fairfax had made his move at two a.m., signalling the opening of hostilities by lighting a beacon on a nearby hill and firing four great guns at Pryers-fort. Rupert's guns returned the compliment and a mighty storm broke over Bristol. With only a half-hour's engagement, the Roundheads broke through Royalist defences in two places and flooded into the town.

For the first time during enemy action Chris was inactive physically, Rupert having refused him permission to add his number to one of the outlying forts which ringed the city, where the fighting was hottest. He spent the hours in the council chamber with the other commanders, attempting to work out tactical moves, knowing—as they did—that when any force was so severely outnumbered—particularly in the area of artillery—no tactic could be successful.

One by one the forts fell to the Roundheads, and at daybreak the Prince, having been forced to withdraw to the castle, thereby cutting himself off from those who still defended the perimeter of the city, ordered the surrender. Fairfax, true to his reputation, was generous. Rupert and his men would be permitted to march out of

Bristol with colours, pikes and drums, bag and baggage. Horses and swords they could keep, but firearms—except in the case of the Prince's Lifeguard—they could not. The wounded were to be left unmolested in the city, its innocent citizens and their property left free from plunder. He personally escorted the defeated army for two miles across the downs. . .

Alice knew some of this, but not all, and guessed that it would be some time, if ever, before Chris found himself able to talk about it. She said, 'You are home now, and must put such remembrance behind you.'

'Yes, indeed,' he agreed, 'home. . . As a hired hand on my own land. That is what I am now—a servant, where once I was the young master.'

'No,' she protested. 'That is not so, and you know it.'

'Oh, but it is, my dear. Jonas Spragg has informed me of that in no uncertain terms this very day.'

Her heart sank. She had had to produce the deed for Oaks, made over to herself, to show the commissar to prevent Margaret Rokesby being turned out of the manor. Margaret, desolate and confused since her husband's death, had been more than glad to hand the whole business over to Alice and had scarcely taken in that her young neighbour now owned Oaks. Alice had hoped that the whole affair might remain similarly obscure to others. Damn Jonas Spragg for coming here to taunt Chris with it.

'What did he say? How did he treat you?'

'He appeared to enjoy his work. He probably remembered my treatment of him during his last visit.' Chris returned to staring out over the paddock and the fields beyond. 'Was it necessary to sell quite so much stock, Alice? And the horses? There is not even a hack in the stables now.'

'They were not sold,' she told him patiently, 'but requisitioned by the government army. They needed mounts and food, as we were constantly told.'

'No wonder we had no chance, then. Fed and mounted as they were by the good folk of England.' He glanced at her. 'I should have gone with Rupert; there is nothing for me here.'

She had removed her gloves on dismounting, now she put them back on, smoothing the patched doeskin over her fingers. 'Did he ask you to?'

He did not answer her directly. 'He was cashiered, you know, after we failed to hold Bristol for His Majesty—who chose to forget his nephew's past brave victories. A fine reward, eh? And not only that,' he went on bitterly, 'but suspected of being capable of mutiny, of aspiring to the English throne, and ordered into immediate exile! After all those years of loyalty. . .'

'But he was cleared of any crime, was he not? I seem to remember reading——'

'In one of the newsletters you devour so avidly? I can imagine the delight Parliament had in printing that particular news. The "Royalist Robber Prince" brought so low as to have to defend himself before the very men he had risked his life so many times for. . . But yes, he was eventually vindicated, though only after we had pursued the King across half England to demand it!'

A disgraceful affair, some felt, with Charles already humiliated by Rupert's publishing of a declaration detailing the whole of his part in the siege of Bristol—a declaration which had unequivocally relieved him of any blame attached to the fall of that fair city to the enemy, and which by implication criticised the monarch's action in cashiering his general-in-chief. Chris had been with Rupert and his brother, the Prince Maurice, when they had literally stood over their royal uncle until he granted them court martial, at which time Rupert was completely absolved. There was little more of the German Prince's involvement in the civil war to remark. When Oxford fell the Prince was ordered to leave English shores within six months and Chris had left him the month before he sailed for Holland.

'I would ask you to go with me, Chris,' Rupert had said during their last private conversation. 'But feel you should first go home and see how your estate fares.'

'I would have done that anyway, but after I have seen for my cousin. . .?'

The Prince had laid a hand on his shoulder, an unusual gesture for he who normally disliked any physical show of affection. 'After, write to me. But I know you, my friend. You are no mercenary, to fight under a foreign flag. You are an Englishman, a Kentish man and, as I have found out to my cost, England's ways are incalculable except to the native-born.'

'There is little of the England I know left these days.'

The Prince had been slightly wounded at Oxford and his shoulder was still stiff and painful. He had eased it thoughtfully, looking for the words he wanted. 'I think it is still there,' he had said at last. 'Swept at present by the strong wind blown by the fanatics. In time this will blow itself out and then men like you will be needed to restore the rightful heir to rule over it.'

Chris had looked incredulous. 'You think His Majesty will ever be. . .restored?'

'Not he, no, for I fear his stiff-necked ways will bring him to ruin.' Only complete disillusionment could have wrung this comment out of Rupert. 'But his son will rule in a country which favours a monarchy. Now, let us not waste our last evening on dry politics.'

Riding home on his flagging horse, Chris had not doubted his friend's words, thought them almost a prophecy, but not those regarding himself. He was done with a country which could so pervert his pleasant life.

'Why didn't you go with him, then?' Alice asked.

'And leave Margaret to survive alone? Thank you for thinking me capable of that!'

She turned abruptly and freed her horse. With one

foot in the stirrup she kept hold of her temper and said, 'Well, I came only to welcome you back, Chris. I'll go now.' She mounted without his help. He leaned back, his arms over the rails of the fence.

'Not to give me your first instructions, mistress? As to the running of your fine new property?'

She carried only a light whip; she could have wished for a heavier one to bring down on his head. She turned her horse. It was a recent acquisition and had been badly used in the past—hence its affordable price. Now it sensed her anger and showed its unpredictable nature. Chris watched her struggling for a few seconds, half ashamed by his recent comments, then stepped forward and reached for the bridle. The mare snapped at him and reared. Chris ducked and stepped aside and the mare dashed past him across the yard and out under the stone arch.

Two weeks passed by, during which Alice had troubles which took her mind off her main concern. Kentish men were coming home now, singly or in bands, back to their manors and farms. Few who had upheld the Royalist cause came back at all. Many were dead, an equal number imprisoned awaiting trial, some were sold into slavery and others—the nobility—had gone into voluntary exile with their young Prince Charles. Those of the working class who came back to Ashley and Fox Hall had been on the winning side and fully expected their just deserts for being so. At Fox they were in luck: they found their land flourishing and their acres belonging to their families. Others were swiftly disillusioned. With so few Royalist estates in the area to be taken and cut up piecemeal to honour the promises made by recruiting officials, they had to come cap in hand to their former masters and request employment. Alice was at her wits' end to keep the peace on her land.

Those Ashley families who had been left on their

farms to eke out a living while their breadwinners went
to war had been well looked after by Richard and Alice,
and were grateful. Their returning men were not.
Instead they were truculent and disappointed and made
trouble at every opportunity. One such man was with
Alice in the library when Christopher Rokesby made an
unexpected visit.

Seth Blake was a young man with a downtrodden wife
and four children under six. He had left at the beginning
of the hostilities and Alice had provided his abandoned
family with food and kept their cottage mended and
weatherproof for four long years. She was therefore
taken aback by the attitude of the ex-soldier.

'I only want my rights, miss,' Seth said belligerently.
'I was promised my own bit o' land—to own, not rent—
and now I come home to find I'm still nothing more'n a
labourer for the Ashleys.'

'But my uncle and I never promised you that,' Alice
protested. 'You chose to believe Jonas Spragg, who had
no earthly right——'

'He tole me that Larks would be mine when I came
back,' Seth said stubbornly. 'So I'm here today to get
the bit o' paper which say it is.'

'But,' Alice said patiently, 'you cannot have what
does not exist. Many farms, I know, were. . .bought by
the government and have now been given to returning
soldiers. Larks is not one of them. It is part of the estate,
and——'

Seth had been sitting in Richard's old hide chair. Now
he came and stood over her. 'I want that bit of paper,
miss. Or you must give me the money for its worth. One
or t'other.'

'I have no money, Seth,' Alice said quietly. 'Nearly
all my livestock and horseflesh have been taken long
since. I have been forced even to sell most of the
furnishings of the manor in order to replace some, and

buy other necessities. Anyway, there is no way I would ever part with any of Ashley.'

'I want what's mine,' Seth said menacingly. Alice was suddenly afraid. Her uncle was away for the day, her aunt up in her bedroom. . .

The door opened and Chris stood in the doorway.

'What is this?' he enquired, his blue eyes on Seth.

Alice stood up. 'Oh, Chris—er, this is Seth Blake—he is a little confused about the matter of his farm.'

'I ain't confused.' Seth swung round to meet this new challenge.

'Lower your voice, man,' Chris said, coming further into the room. 'And don't contradict a lady—where are your manners?'

'I come here in good faith,' Seth said angrily. 'And she deny me——'

'This interview is ended,' Chris said politely. He pulled open the door. 'Out.'

Seth assessed the opposition. This was Rokesby of Oaks, who had fought with Prince Rupert. Seth, veteran of a dozen battles, had come up against the Bluecoats on several never-to-be-forgotten occasions. He came slowly to the door.

'Royalist scum!' he hissed. Chris smiled.

'I shall be happy to trade insults, or fists, or cold steel at any time in the future. But not now, not before this lady.'

'I'm not finished here. There'll be another time.'

'Not so,' Chris said casually. 'Come within six feet of Mistress Ashley in the future and you'll answer to me.'

There was a deadly pause, then Seth said, 'You *lost*, my young sir. Do you forget that?'

'No. We lost, and I have, therefore, nothing further *to* lose. Think about that before you speak again.'

Seth thought about it, then passed through the door. Chris closed it behind him with exaggerated calm. He took Richard's chair and said genially, 'So this is how you spend your days, Alice.'

Alice smoothed damp hands over her skirt. 'That was most unwise. Seth Blake has a loose tongue, and the ears of the men who are powerful in this area are long.'

Chris looked around the room, noting that various objects of value were missing now. 'Richard used to keep a supply of wine here, is it still in the cupboard beneath the volumes of Shakespeare's plays?'

Alice went to the cupboard and took out a bottle of wine and two glasses. As she poured she asked, 'Why have you come? For your instructions, as you put it a fortnight ago?'

Chris put a shabby booted foot up on the stool before him. He accepted the wine and drank. 'No, to apologise. For treating you so abominably a fortnight ago, when I should have been on bended knee kissing your hand for what you have done for me.'

'You are always apologising,' she said stonily. 'Such a performance coming after the many occasions of your bullying is becoming monotonous.'

'Then I won't do it any more. Either, I mean. I am reformed—aren't you glad? You must be, you have tried so hard on my behalf. Saving my unworthy skin, nursing me back to health, then coming here to care for my kin.'

She tried her own wine. She drank very seldom these days; she associated wine with happier times. 'I always feel you're laughing at me when you are kind.'

'Do you? Then I'm sorry. Perhaps I am not the kind of man who can accept favours without resentment.'

She was silent. There was a summer storm brewing outside—lightning flashed across the sky.

'Do you accept my apology?' he asked.

'Certainly. Why not? Is that all?'

'No, I also came to return this.' He put a hand in his pocket and took out her grandmother's journal. He held it up for her to see, then laid it gently on the table by his chair.

'Did you read it?' The sight of the diary, with its worn covering, set her heart racing, reminded her of the nights she had spent deciphering it by flickering candle-light while Chris hovered between life and death. She could hear again the sound of the rough Cornish seas beyond the windows, feel again the pity she had felt for its author, and her own strong identification with its words.

'Yes, I read it.' Chris reached for the bottle and refilled his glass. 'In the quite inappropriate places that a soldier finds himself in. It moved me very much.'

'Did it?' She searched his face for any indication that he had felt the journal had any special relevance for him, any special meaning, but he was not looking at her.

'Is Henry back?' he asked abruptly.

'Henry? No. No. . . I believe he is in London.'

'Ah, yes, he would be. He has excelled in his duties over the past two years and will be rewarded for it.'

The mention of Henry left her unmoved, although she was aware that when he returned she would have to face an unpleasant scene. But what else came her way these days?

'Have you heard from him since the surrender?'

'Yes. He does not know when he will be free to come home.'

There was a sharp rapping on the door, then it was opened by Jack Madesley. He had been Alice's strong right arm in every crisis she had faced lately, and now his face was full of consternation. He had come in haste from one of the far pastures and was out of breath. 'Oh, beg pardon, miss. I saw Seth Blake riding away from the house and thought—— I thought you was alone.'

Chris stood up to shake his hand. 'Good day, Jack. How is it with you?'

'Well enough, sir. And I am glad to see you looking so well.'

'Compared to the last time we met, I am. . . Well, I must go, Alice.'

'It is beginning to rain. Won't you take lunch with us? I know my aunt would like it.'

'Thank you, but Margaret will be expecting me back. Jack, walk me to my horse if you please.'

'Chris.' Alice followed him to the door. 'Thank you for what you did, although I fear it was foolish.'

'The day it is foolish for me to stand between you and rough words, Alice, is the day I shall wish myself long-dead on some battlefield.'

'Hush, don't say such things. Before you went away you knew how things stood hereabouts; now it is much worse. So many are discontented, filled with malice that the rosy future they were promised has not come about. They are looking for any excuse to take it out on someone.'

He grinned. '*They* will be welcome at Oaks for that purpose any time they choose.'

Knowing that he had survived the war, that he was but a few short miles away, knowing that she could—if she could bear his careless remarks—ride over and see him, had given her a strange joy, but she could not prevent the irritation creeping into her voice as she said sharply, 'Perhaps you don't know how lucky you are to have escaped retribution at the ceasefire. Some of my uncle's friends declare that while the King lives no Royalist can be trusted. 'Tis the reason why so many have been executed.'

'Perhaps I was not important enough to hang alongside those brave men.'

Jack cleared his throat from the hall and Alice turned back into the library.

The two young men walked in the gathering downpour to the stables. As Chris reclaimed his horse Jack said tentatively, ''Twas not a question of importance, you know, sir. It would have been a pleasure to them to hang you for all the country to see.'

Chris ran a kind hand over his horse. The poor animal was failing more each day; it broke Chris's heart that he could not be turned out to pasture to live out his days in peace. He looked at Jack, his eyes shining blue through the veil of rain. 'I know that, Jack. But a King's man beaten and humiliated upon his own acres is a far more valuable lesson to any backward-lookers than a pile of bones.'

'What will happen now? With His Majesty, I mean?'

Chris swung into the saddle. 'My common sense—of which I have a share, despite my reputation—tells me that there can only be one eventual end. As Alice said, while the King lives there will always be those prepared to trouble our new and insecure masters.'

Jack's plain face crinkled with disbelief. 'Surely you can't mean—— Why, what men would dare to take such an act upon their souls? The Lord would strike them dead where they stood!'

Chris chuckled sardonically. 'These men are in close communication with the Lord, Jack, did you not know? However, I believe that time to be some way into the future. . . Meanwhile, we lesser mortals have to try to rearrange our lives into some semblance of order.' He turned the reins loosely in his fingers. 'You are loyal to Mistress Ashley, I think?' he asked suddenly.

'I would be racked to save her a moment's pain,' Jack declared.

'So I thought. What happened today with Blake must not happen again.'

Jack reddened. 'It wouldn't ha' done today, sir, but I was having to see to something beyond the house—we are desperately short-handed here——'

'You are doing the work of ten men around here, I know that,' Chris said, with the easy charm which had made him so loved by the men in his command, both above and below. 'But stick close to the manor until things settle a little. When Master Carrington comes home I imagine no one will dare to be so disrespectful to your mistress.'

Jack turned up his coat against the driving rain. He had little faith in these words. When Master Henry came back to Kent Jack thought that Alice would send him about his business. He was surprised that Rokesby did not know this, could not see the way the lass came to life in his presence, did not suspect the reason for it. He muttered, 'Mebbe so, sir. I hope you won't mind me saying that it might be a good thing for her if you were not—not—'

'Not in evidence here? Yes, I take your point. But know this: if you need me, you may send for me and I shall come. At a moment's notice.'

'Yes, sir.' Jack stepped back, and Chris rode out of the yard and was soon lost from sight in the teeming rain.

Henry came back a month later. It had been a gratifying few months since the surrender. His contribution—of money, of men, of personal effort—to the war had been noted, remarked upon and duly rewarded. He had taken part in Parliament's verbal deliberations at Westminster, and fancied he had played a valuable part. He came back to his home county assured of an important place in the new order, and was well-satisfied. He was pleased to find that his uncle's estate flourished, his relatives as well-fed and apparently well-founded as in the past.

Riding across the country, Henry had seen much deprivation. No country could go to war without hardship; a civil war demanded even more of its people, and England had suffered greatly. But here at Fox Hall little had changed. He sat down to the good supper Mary had joyfully provided, but was almost immediately displeased by the conversation. He laid down his knife.

'You say you have not been to Ashley lately?'

Walter Carrington glanced at his wife. 'It is this way, Henry. I was used to riding over once or twice a week to see how Alice fared. You asked me to do this and I was more than happy with the arrangement. But lately. . . since the end of the war, and even before that, she has been rather. . .rather disinclined to take my advice on any matter. Indeed, she has positively discouraged me from offering it. Hrrumph! Of course, Richard is still master there, but as you know he is. . . Anyway, Alice now has the reins and will brook no interference.'

'Your help and advice can hardly be seen as interference,' Henry said coldly. 'I cannot think what Alice is about.'

'Yes, well. . . Now you are here and I am sure it will all be easier.' Walter helped himself to another portion of beef and sought to change the subject. 'Chris Rokesby is back at Oaks, you know.'

Henry pushed back his plate.

'I rode over to see how he was getting along and was sorely distressed. The estate—never very prosperous—is now in a very poor way. Most of his tenants—er—followed him to—er—well. . . Few have returned safely, I believe.'

'Has Chris been much at Ashley since his return?' Henry asked abruptly. He fingered his water-glass. He imagined that the lack of wine on the table had been decided upon for his benefit, but would have welcomed a drink.

'No, no, I have not heard that,' Walter said consideringly. 'Although a man called Seth Blake has been shouting it about that he was turned off the place a month ago. Claimed Chris had threatened him. But, no, I think the Rokesbys have seen little of Alice lately.' He sighed. 'Shame, really, we are such old friends—the

Ashleys, the Carringtons and the Rokesbys, but . . .'
The table conversation then moved on into safer
channels.

Henry approached Ashley Manor the next morning with
trepidation. He had no idea what would be his reception
there. He had recalled the evening at Gull's Nest at odd
times over the last year—Alice's part, Chris's part—and
could not calculate how his fiancée would receive him.

He noticed as he rode over Ashley land how desolate
it looked. Only one field in ten was cultivated, and
although the farms were reasonably well cared for and
their few animals healthy enough, there was a general
air of neglect. In the stables he dismounted and looked
about him. In the old days a score of thoroughbreds had
been housed here; now only a wild-looking mare was
loose in the paddock, and a couple of toothless old
animals within the stalls. A tall, tow-headed youth came
to take his mount. 'Jack Madesley? I am happy to see
you well.'

'Master Carrington.' Jack ignored the proffered
hand. 'I will inform Mistress Ashley that you are here.'

'I'll do that,' Henry said. 'Do you take care of my
horse.'

Henry entered the manor by the back door. Betty
Mote detained him in the kitchen. 'If you will go into
the winter parlour, sir, I'll tell Miss Alice ye're here.'
Unused to such formality—he had been used to coming
in and out of Ashley for so many years—Henry allowed
himself to be led into the parlour.

Alice was in her bedchamber. She had been puzzling
over the tax demand she had received a week ago. It
seemed that the new government felt entitled to one-
third of her revenue from the estate. Since most of the
profits Ashley gleaned from the sale of crops and other
monies obtained from the sale of livestock was immediately put to use among its dependents, Alice was in

some straits to discover how to come up with enough hard cash to meet this bill.

'Master Henry is below,' Betty announced. She might well have said, There is a wild tiger in the parlour, missus, to judge from her tone. She and Alice had become even firmer friends since her mistress had returned from Cornwall. Alice had told her of her mother, of her old home, and Betty had been entranced by the romantic tale of Chris Rokesby's rescue. Alice had encouraged her to write to her mother and had been shown the joyful reply.

Alice had said nothing to her maid of her personal feelings for Chris, but that had not prevented Betty sensing the unspoken words, knowing that something tumultous had overtaken Alice in regard to Rokesby and asking Jack for his opinion. Jack had been reluctant to voice it. It was now common knowledge in the village that Chris appeared to have renewed his old relationship with Molly Judd. Her father had died the year before, and Molly had been swift to trim her sails to the prevailing wind. She had changed the outward face of the Evening Sun almost overnight, pressing forward its role as respectable hostelry for travellers, exchanging its alcoholic beverages for more acceptable dishes of tay, and tall glasses of elderberry wine. After hours, when darkness came, no one seemed to know what went on with Molly and her now demurely clad sisters, or at least no one was saying. Chris Rokesby spent a great many of his evenings there.

Alice dropped the bill. 'But— Have you told my uncle and aunt? I am sure Henry would like to see them.'

'It's you he's come to see, Miss Alice,' Betty said flatly. 'Anyway, the master's over to Applewood, and your aunt is lying down with one of her heads.'

Alice rose and looked in her mirror. Henry could not, she thought, disapprove of her gown today as he had so

plainly at Gull's Nest, for she looked no more fancy than
Betty in her untrimmed buff-coloured dress and linen
coif hiding her hair. She went slowly down the stairs and
into the hall. Henry came out of the parlour and greeted
her by the open windows opposite the hearth. It was
cool today, but the fire was unlit—another small econ-
omy. She said, 'Good morning, Henry. Welcome back.'
She curtsied with these words and surveyed him on
rising. 'You look very well, positively blooming.' The
edge to her voice was explained by his contrast with
Chris. They were of similar build, both tall and slim, but
Chris had not regained the supple flesh which had been
stripped from him after Naseby. Henry had added to
his—was there not a suspicion of a paunch beneath his
finely tooled leather belt?

'Alice!' He kissed her cheek, then reached to close
the windows. 'Do you mind? And perhaps Betty could
set a match to the fire—it is uncommon cold today.'
Alice nodded to Betty, who had remained in the hall.

'Will you take a glass of wine, Henry? Or do you not
drink these days?'

'Wine would be most pleasant. Shall we sit down?'

She took the chair furthest from the window. No
special word of affection, he noticed, sitting with the
light from the windows behind him.

'When did you get back?' she asked.

'Last night. I would have come immediately to Ashley
to see you but my uncle and aunt were so delighted to
have me home again that I felt I could not leave them.'

'Oh.'

Betty came in with the wine and then went to the
hearth to coax the sparse kindling to a timid blaze.
When she had gone Henry cast about for something to
say. What their reunion would be like he had had no
idea, but knew now that he felt acutely uncomfortable—
an unusual and unwelcome feeling for him these days.

'Uncle Walter tells me you have not been anxious for his help with Ashley in the past year,' he said at length.

'He does not understand how things are here,' she said. 'His answer to every problem is, "Well, your tenants must pay more rent, do more work, Alice." These people have suffered enough during the war, Henry. Hardly a day passed without their produce, their animals, their stores being plundered by your army. They work hard to survive now, and I *will* not ask them for their poor profit.'

Her vehement tone was very unbecoming, he thought, but said mildly, 'Hmm. Well, naturally, our fighting men needed the support of England's farmers.'

'I am sure, but it was not your pigs and poultry they took, Henry,' she returned with asperity. 'Fox Hall was apparently sacrosanct. Ashley and Oaks were not, and we are now trying to find our feet again. If Uncle Walter thinks Ashley in need of his good advice, he ought to ride a little further to Oaks. There, they barely have food to put on the table.'

Henry blinked. He had thought Alice sharp-tongued at Gull's Nest; now there was a cutting force to what she said. He still tried a placating tone. 'I will do all I can for you and Richard and Emma—you know that. And for Margaret Rokesby too. But for Chris—he made his choice and must now take his punishment. He is fortunate that he still retains his property.'

'*My* property,' she said bluntly. 'Chris signed Oaks over to me while we were together in Bude.'

There was a taut silence. 'He did what?' Henry asked carefully.

'I believe you heard.' Alice rose and went to the fire. She was a creature who liked to be warm; blazing fires in every room had been a feature at Ashley in the days when there had been a man whose sole duty it had been to replenish the wood.

'How dare he ask you for such a favour?' Henry

remained seated, but with a quickened pace of her heart Alice recognised the cold anger in him that had so frightened her at Gull's Nest.

'It had to be done to safeguard his cousin Margaret's interests, and he didn't ask me to do it, I insisted.'

'You must reverse the deed immediately.'

She reached out her hands to the pathetic heat. 'I can't do that,' she said reasonably. 'If I do Margaret will be turned out, for the all-seeing commissary will seize the estate.'

'Uncle Walter will offer her a home at Fox Hall.'

'And Chris?'

'He should never have come back. The Prince Rupert, I believe, has now joined the French fighting force. Chris should have gone with him.'

'But he came back to care for his cousin! Do you think it is happy for him to work Oaks knowing that it no longer belongs to him? Do you know that not one of the local gentry has called upon him since his return? Saving my Uncle Walter, of course, who only upbraided him for leaving in the first place! He is now an outcast among the men and women he grew up with. You spoke of punishment a moment ago; well here is punishment indeed!'

'You are very passionate on his behalf.'

Alice bit her lip. In the past all three of the young people from Fox and Ashley and Oaks had been passionate on one subject or another, but united in their support of each other. Henry's cool words reminded her that life had moved on, circumstances had changed. Chris would never again get support from this man.

Henry stood up and refilled his glass. The wine was inferior and he would normally not drink such stuff, but this interview was very upsetting. . . 'I did not come here to discuss the problem at Oaks, but to see you and to ascertain—now I am home and my future assured—what date will be our marriage.'

She had known this moment must come, had tried to prepare for it, and she now gave the little speech which had come to her during one of the long nights she had spent without sleep. 'Henry, of course you have every right to ask that question. And I must answer it. But I never gave you a definite date and cannot do so now.' It sounded well enough, but she saw his face harden.

'Why so? You do intend to honour your promise?'

Outside the day had darkened; another storm was on its way—it must surely be the wettest summer in history. She went to a small table and began to fumble with the tinderbox. Succeeding in lighting one candle, she took it and went slowly around the hall igniting the others. It took several minutes, then she turned to face him.

'No, I do not. Please do not be angry, Henry. You must see how everything has changed since I accepted your betrothal ring.'

'Nothing has changed for me. If it has for you, then pray explain it. Is there, perhaps, another man?' It was a thrust in the dark, and he did not expect the sudden flush of colour in her face. The stub of candle she still held tilted and warm wax ran down over her fingers but she appeared not to heed this.

'Who is it, Alice?' he asked quietly.

'I—— This is very difficult for me. I wish—— But, well you see. . . Chris——'

'Chris Rokesby! I knew it!' Henry put down his glass so forcefully that the stem shattered, and they both looked at the little pile of glass glittering in the clouded light through the windows. 'He swore to me that no such relationship existed between you! And I believed him,' he added bitterly.

'He spoke the truth,' she said helplessly. 'This is a thing entirely in my own mind.'

'In your own mind,' he repeated harshly. 'And he the foremost rake in the countryside. You know, of course, that he has resumed his scandalous conduct with the slut from the Evening Sun?'

'No,' she said painfully, 'I did not know. But I have stated the case as I see it, and you will just have to accept it.'

On entering the hall he had laid his cloak across the back of one of the settles. Now he got up from his chair and lifted it, replacing it over his shoulders. He bowed.

'I said about Chris that he had chosen his way and must accept the consequences. I do not feel that you must do the same, Alice, and will inform you now that I will not give you up.'

'That sounds like a threat. . .'

He gave his chilly smile. 'A Christian gentleman does not issue threats, my dear. As I said, I do not hold you to blame for this situation, but I do Chris, and shall tell him so without delay.'

Emma Ashley, descending the stairs after a painful few hours nursing a sick headache, saw them at the door and hurried down.

'Henry! How delightful to see you back and looking so well.' She kissed him affectionately. 'And your coming now is most opportune. This morning I sent an invitation to Margaret and Chris Rokesby to dine with us tonight, and was about to do the same to your uncle and aunt! Now we can all be together again after such a long time.' She looked from Henry's frozen face to her niece's. 'Will that not be nice?' she pressed on, aware from their expressions that it appeared to be the reverse. . .

'So now you can have those words without delay,' Alice said to Henry maliciously. She had been frightened a moment ago; now the thought of seeing Chris gave her courage. But how he would react to her foolish disclosure of her secret when Henry accused him, she could not think. He had not been near her since the morning she had interviewed Seth Blake, and had sent no word even on her birthday, which had fallen some weeks since. She asked her aunt, 'Have the Rokesbys accepted?'

'Indeed, they have. Now, Henry dear, wait a moment while I pen a little note to your aunt. . . I know she will not be offended by the short notice.' The other two waited in silence while she did so. Henry took the folded sheet with a bow and, replacing his tall hat, went out with a brief nod to the women.

'There,' Emma said. 'Now, what shall we put on for them tonight, my dear?' She touched her niece's arm, unable to account for the atmosphere she sensed between the two young people. 'You are not angry with me for arranging the little party without consulting you?' It had been a sudden whim on her part—she was a woman who liked a little gaiety and there had been precious little of that lately. Also, well, she loved Alice dearly, and knew that her strength had carried the little family through hazardous times for several years, but after all it was her house. . .

'No, of course I am not,' Alice sighed. 'I suppose I must order the little pigs killed, although I was saving them to grow up and be salted and smoked to see us through the winter.'

'Ah, well,' Emma said vaguely, 'I will leave all that in your capable hands.'

Yes, you always do, thought Alice, but could not bear to spoil her aunt's pleasure in the coming supper by saying so. 'Are we celebrating anything in particular?'

'Apart from both the boys being home now? Yes, for your birthday passed almost unremarked, you know, and it is a tradition for us all to be together. William, of course, will not be here.' She sighed a little, then brightened. 'But I think Margaret would welcome a little pleasure, as we all will.'

Alice patted her hand. 'Yes, indeed, a little pleasure,'

she agreed, wondering how pleasurable it would be to have two young men who had just fought a war on opposite sides, and who now might be at daggers drawn again over a domestic matter, under one roof. . .

CHAPTER NINE

EVENING came. The nights were still light until quite late and Alice usually stayed out in the fields until dusk, overseeing what work could be done for the coming harvest, which would obviously be poor again this year. But today's rain had driven her in early and she could not regret having a little party to look forward to. She ordered the fires lit and new candles substituted for the misshapen stubs. She and Betty polished and tidied the hall, both mourning the lack of silver now to be set upon the cupboards and tables, and the bare look of the walls which had been denuded of their hangings.

'Never mind, Miss Alice,' Betty said comfortingly, 'the pork is tender and savoury and I have made marigold eggs for dessert. To begin we are having some of our own carp with a sharp sauce. It will all be very good. And I've pressed your brown dress and the vinegar rinse has made your hair shine so. In a moment I'll help you put it up.' The dress was the one Alice had worn for her sixteenth birthday three years ago. It was in good condition but Betty had taken it upon herself to adjust the waist seams, for Alice was even more slender these days. 'Miss Alice?'

'Mmm?' Alice looked over the table, rearranged the little posies she had set on the court cupboard shelves.

'P'raps now is not the time, but. . . Jack have spoken to me today. He wants to wed me.'

Alice turned with a smile. 'And you have said yes? I am so glad for you, Betty. But I had no idea that, well, that you thought of each other in that way.'

'No, 'twas never like that between us,' Betty agreed. 'Until one day last week. We was just netting over the raspberries together and one of the brambles pricked my wrist. Jack took my hand to have a look, and. . .all of a sudden we just *knew*—— But there, I don't s'pose you can imagine what it was like.'

Oh, but I can, thought Alice wryly. I can imagine it very well. She said, 'You shall have the best wedding we can manage, dear Betty. Take any one of my gowns you like for the ceremony; we will have a little breakfast here to celebrate, and—and I shall give you two new golden guineas to begin your married life.' I'll sell my pearls, she thought impulsively; there was still a market for good plain stuff.

Betty clasped her hands before her. 'You would do all that? Why, miss, you are the best mistress a girl ever had! And don't think anything will change with Jack and me wed—we'll carry on just as usual, except——' she blushed furiously '—I'll be going home with him o' nights.'

Going home with him o' nights, repeated Alice to herself enviously. How I wish I could say those words about another man.

I'm glad someone at Ashley is happy, Alice thought later, as washed and dressed she came down to the hall to await her guests. Her uncle had returned and was pottering about the cellars, tutting about the lack of good wine he had to offer that evening. Her aunt was still in her bedchamber, no doubt regretting allowing her niece to sell most of her fine jewellery. Hearing hoofbeats outside, Richard came into the hall and opened the door.

'It is the Carringtons,' he said, advancing out into the porch.

Alice stayed by the fire, watching the arrivals but not going forward to greet them. Walter came bustling in and managed to slip Richard a couple of bottles under cover of his hearty greeting. Mary came to Alice.

'Well, well, my dear, we are to celebrate your birthday this year after all.' She took a chair and eased her feet in their tight slippers. Emma came hurrying down and the five sat around the blaze, making small talk.

A little later Chris and his cousin arrived. Margaret was tearful, remembering that the last time they had all been together her beloved husband had been alive. Alice looked Chris over hungrily. She saw that he had made an effort to be dressed for the occasion; his thick black hair was smooth and tied back, his linen sparkling white. An incongruous note was struck by his choice of coat—the distinctive sky-blue coat of Prince Rupert's cavalry, shabby, but clean and neatly darned. Alice noted Henry's sharp eyes observe it.

There was an awkward moment when the two young men met.

'Well, Henry,' Chris said, offering his hand. 'You are looking prosperous.'

'And you are. . .tidy, at least,' Henry returned, extending his own hand briefly.

'A glass of wine, boys,' Richard said, hurrying into the breach.

'Sit here, Christopher,' Emma said, patting the chair beside her. They all sat down and looked at each other.

Good heavens, thought Alice, amused despite herself. I wonder how often this scene has repeated itself the length and breadth of England recently as Royalist neighbour met Roundhead neighbour after four years of mayhem.

Chris carried the honours tonight. He had a light touch in any assembly and was at his best on a social occasion, even with antagonism in the air. But as they sat down to eat he could not resist saying, 'The latest from London is that the new government is unable to agree about anything at all. One recalls Astley's words.'

The last senior commander to make a stand for the

crown had been the grand old man, Lord Astley. When he had eventually surrendered at Stow-on-the-Wold he had addressed his captors from a seat on a warm cannon barrel. 'You have done your work, and may go now to play—unless you fall out among yourselves.' What he had implied had come about. Two main factions split Parliament: the Presbyterians and the Independents, with sub-groups within both a trial. The Presbyterians wanted the whole of England under their ecclesiastical rule; the Independents thought that each man had the right to worship as he wished. The country remained in disorder as they endlessly debated this one point.

'The right to argue is what we fought for,' Henry said repressively. 'And——'

'I think we want no politics tonight,' Richard said uneasily.

'No, indeed,' Chris agreed. 'For I am sure that their politics are as dull as the rest of their philosophy.'

Henry sent Chris a glance down the table. Before he could speak Alice said, 'I do hope you will enjoy the fish, Uncle Walter. Our pond has been overstocked lately, with no one to fish it, and according to Jack these on the table now practically leaped from the water to oblige him.'

Walter sampled the dish before him. '*Very* good. You boys must get out your rods again—'twas a favourite pastime of yours, I remember, the taking part in which involved being disgracefully late for meals and the need of dry clothing when you did come home.'

Chris raised his eyebrows. 'I fear I have more pressing duties now, sir. The wet clothing, I recall, was mostly Henry's—he had a tendency to swim the water, rather than fish it.'

'On your insistence,' Henry said. 'You found it amusing to tip me in at the slightest provocation. You always did have a strange sense of humour.'

'I still have.' Chris picked up his glass and tried the

wine, guessing that it was from the Carrington cellars. 'If you wish to take a walk down memory lane, I can accommodate you.'

'You would not find it so easy to get me wet these days.'

'I am sure of that. I would be no match for a man who has been full-fed and soft-quartered for the last two years.'

'Boys, boys,' Richard murmured pacifyingly. 'We do not wish to fight old battles tonight. This is Alice's night, after all.'

'Perhaps we could find something new to wrangle over,' Henry said, his cold eyes resting on Alice.

'We have a present for Alice tonight,' Mary said hastily. 'I wonder if you can guess what it is, my dear.'

'A present?' Alice looked up. 'How very kind. No, I cannot guess.'

'When we have concluded this excellent meal we will take you and show you,' Walter smiled. Alice pleased him tonight. For a while now he had been uneasy about the prospective match between his nephew and the brisk, argumentative girl his betrothed had become. But this evening the softer Alice had appeared, as pretty and suitable—fussing over her guests with charming solicitude—as ever. Walter, who was no fool when it came to human relations, hoped that she would show this side most often to Henry, for the boy was greatly changed. He had gone away a straitlaced, rather dogmatic but essentially kindly boy, but come back with the gentle part of his nature overruled by. . . Well, Walter admitted it regretfully, a certain narrow-mindedness.

Chris Rokesby, on the other hand, Walter thought scarcely changed at all by his experiences, perhaps because he had always been the impulsive, headlong one of the pair. That wildness was still there, partially concealed by a control he had obviously had to learn in the discipline of military life, but ready to break surface at any time. Henry, Walter decided, would do very well in the society prevalent in England now; Chris would find it much harder.

Walter had always had a soft spot for Chris Rokesby; he had always been the sort of boy he had sympathy for. In spite of his apparent support of Parliament in the last two years—which had actually been no more than a form of neutrality—Walter had been prepared to help Margaret Rokesby if the need arose. But Alice had done such a determinedly good job that there had been no such need. Now that Chris was home he was prepared to extend that facility to him—albeit surreptitiously.

After supper the company trooped out to the stables and Walter led out the grey mare which was Alice's gift. She fell instantly in love with the pretty animal.

'She has good blood, as you can see,' Walter said happily. 'A fitting replacement for Jenny. What happened to her, by the way?'

A shadow crossed Alice's face and she glanced at Chris, who was looking the mare over with appreciative eyes. Her instinctive reaction was seen by Henry, who set his teeth. Anger had been growing in him all night, and as the mare was led away to her stall and the party moved to go back into the house he put a hand on Chris's arm to detain him.

'Walk with me a moment,' he said in his new peremptory manner.

'To the fish pond?' Chris asked, grinning.

'I have something serious to discuss with you.'

Both men watched the others hurry back into the warmth of the hall, Alice with a swift look over her shoulder at them. When the door had closed, Henry said, 'Let us go into the gardens.'

Chris followed him. He did not take his friend's new manner very seriously. He did not like what Henry had been in the last two years, but a man's convictions were personal and no other's business. Now that it was over, Chris felt happy enough to put it behind him. Of course, that did not mean he was not amused to tease Hal a little.

'Is this new sobriety of yours here to stay?' he enquired as they approached the rose garden. 'Sobriety of manner, that is, not of temperance. I notice you bend your own rules a little in the matter of good liquor.'

Henry made a sharp gesture with his hand. 'I have said I wish to be serious—is that too hard a thing for you?'

'No, indeed, for all evening you have been sending me sharper glances than thrown swords. Truly Hal, if looks could kill, I would be cold stone-dead.'

'Perhaps that will be reality if you cannot give me a straight answer to what I will ask you now. About Alice.'

The teasing smile left Chris's face. 'What of Alice?'

'She has broken our betrothal. When I pressed her for an explanation she insisted 'twas because of you.'

'Because of me?' Chris repeated slowly. All evening he had been aware of Alice. Aware in a different way. They had spent weeks together last summer, virtually alone, and he had felt then, he believed, the normal attraction of a man for a pretty girl. He had also admired her as always, for her courage and straightforwardness. When she had come to see him on his return to Oaks he had been angry with her because he was in her debt, and when he had come upon the disagreeable scene with Seth Blake he had felt an angry desire to defend her. All these feelings had crystallised tonight as he had observed her, so gallant in her old gown, moving about a home stripped of its comfort, but as gracious and unaware of any pathos as any princess in a luxurious castle. He very much appreciated the strong woman the remembered girl had become.

'You have nothing to say?' demanded Henry. He

must be careful, he thought, not to be deflected from his intent. He had always been peculiarly susceptible to Chris Rokesby's personal charisma, an attribute he knew he did not possess himself. 'Charm the birds off the trees, and get 'em to trill for him,' Walter Carrington had once said of Chris. No doubt he had used this ability on Alice, as he did on other more dubious women. . .

'About myself and Alice?' Chris turned up the collar of his coat; the night was chill and he hated the cold and damp. All the nights he had spent in the open lately, often in wet clothing, in anticipation of a morrow which would bring if not oblivion then almost certainly pain and the death of some friend or other, had made him associate such discomfort with a deeper emotion. He said, 'You have asked me that question twice before. Each time I have said to you that there is nothing between us. Must I really say it again? Has *she* declared that I have something to confess to?'

'No,' Henry grudgingly admitted. 'She has only said that the feeling is entirely her own. But I find it hard to believe she would feel such without encouragement from you. You do have a way with women, Chris.'

Chris laughed, then sobered. 'Hal,' he said seriously, 'you know Alice as well as I. Know how instantly her heart is caught by a creature under duress. That is what I was, you will appreciate, after the débâcle of Naseby— sick and tired in spirit. As I said to you in Bude, had it been yourself in similar straits it would have been *you* she felt such tenderness for. She is a very soft-hearted girl,' he added thoughtfully.

Henry considered. He could not disbelieve what Chris said, for the man was no liar.

'What are you doing out here?' Alice had come out of the house in search of them. Not knowing what to expect, she approached warily, but saw only two old friends apparently engaged in amicable conversation.

'Nothing,' Chris said. 'Where is your cloak? It is freezing tonight.'

'I am used to the cold.'

Henry put an arm around her. 'Let us go in. Chris is right; it's too cold out here for you.'

She moved away from him. 'Don't fuss, Henry! If you knew what I have endured in the past months you would think a little cold the least of it!'

Chris frowned. 'Well, don't scratch his eyes out for showing you some concern. You are not the only one to have—endured, you know.'

'I know.' She turned to Henry. 'Please, Henry, I would like to have a few private words with Chris. There is something I must discuss with him.'

He leaped to the acceptable conclusion for this. 'About Oaks?'

'Oaks. . .? Yes, yes, about Oaks.'

'Very well. I believe we are to end the evening with a game of cards. Don't stay out here too long.' He left them.

'We'll go into the vinery,' Alice said. Chris followed her in.

'Close the door,' she said, 'any slight cold can affect the grapes—and I have a market for them when they are to fruition.'

He laughed. 'Are you going into trade, Alice?'

'No,' she said shortly. 'But from the small profits I can pay some bill or other. . . What did Henry say to you just then?'

He sighed. 'You both are always asking me what the other has said, or what I have said. Why don't you talk to each other?'

'Please, just tell me.'

'Hal accused me of trifling with your affections—as my cousin Margaret's romantic stories print—and consequently making you wish to break off your engagement.'

'And what did you say?'

'I denied the charge, of course. Said that I thought you were merely sorry for a poor cavalier broken on the battlefield and then disenfranchised of his heritage.'

'This is not a joke, Chris, to me or to Henry.' She sat down abruptly on the stone bench.

'Well. . .no, my dear, but did you really use me as an excuse for not wanting to marry Henry? I can't say I appreciate that.'

'An excuse? No. What I told him was the truth.' Since her conversation with Henry that afternoon, she had been feeling. . .ashamed. It was not right for her to have brought Chris into the matter when he was totally unaware of how she felt. Not *fair* that he should be taken to task by Henry about it while in ignorance of how she felt. Her straightforward nature rebelled that he should be involved without knowing *why*. 'It was the truth, Chris,' she repeated.

He looked astounded. 'But── What are you saying? You told me at Gull's Nest that you wished not to marry him—not that you were going to blacken my name to get out of it!'

'I didn't blacken your name! But── Did you not read the diary I gave you? You said you did.'

'Alice Ashley's diary? Yes, I read it. But what has it to do with this? Certainly I read it, and was, as I said, moved by it—moved to scorn that a silly woman could cause so much trouble for two good men!'

'It was not like that! She changed her mind, that is all.'

'Changed her *mind*? After ten years of marriage? To a good man—your grandfather, after all. But what has it to do with us? You and me and Hal?'

'It was a way of telling you what I felt,' she said slowly. Why had she started this conversation? She felt that Chris would shortly be moved to scorn by what she had to say. . .

'You and I have never before needed any kind of go-between for what we have to say to each other,' he said quietly. There was a tension he could not explain present here in this quiet place.

She stood up. 'Very well, then! *I* have also changed my mind about a marriage. Because I love you, Chris. Perhaps I always have done. Perhaps it grew upon me gradually over those years of our shared past. Perhaps I was struck by lightning on the road from Naseby! Howsoever it came about, that is what I feel.'

There was a moment's silence, then he said, 'I don't believe you. What game are you playing, Alice?'

'It is no game.' She came to his side.

It was ghostly in the vinery; in the strange greenish light Alice appeared as a ghost to him, her face above the dark of her costume a pale oval suspended, its expression half remembered from dreams he had had. Then she was in his arms and he was kissing her.

They had kissed before, but not like this. As if nothing and no one else in the world existed, only they two—suspended in time. He had kissed other women, but not like this, for her lips were at once familiar and excitingly different. Her response, even to a reasonably experienced man, unbelievably passionate. The timeless moment stretched on into eternity then, abruptly, he released her. What am I doing? he asked himself. What are *we* doing? My God, and I have just sworn to Hal that there is nothing between us!

Dragged back from a place she had not dreamed even existed, she said breathlessly, 'Now you see how it is for me, why I cannot marry Henry.'

'Yes, I see how it is,' he repeated.

'And you. . .want me, too. . .'

'Want? Yes, that is the word.'

'What do you mean?'

Confusion made him cruel. 'What I say. Yes, I want

you, Alice—in this moment. What normal man would not?'

It took her a moment to understand his words, then she protested, 'It is more than that!'

'Is it? I don't think so.' He had taken several steps away from her, but she could see the moonlight choosing the shine of his eyes. 'If you won't marry Hal, you won't,' he said quietly, 'and perhaps that is for the best. I would not wish my friend to take a wanton to wife.'

She flushed brilliantly, but anger braced her. 'You *know* that is not true! You are a liar! And worse, a coward, too. And it is Henry you are afraid of!'

'I fear no man,' he was boyish enough to retaliate. 'And feel I may have proved it over the last two years!'

'Fighting an army which you despised and hated! But you don't despise or hate Henry, do you? You love him, and that is what makes you the coward.'

His mind, used now to analysing facts swiftly and acting on them, immediately acknowledged what she said to be true. He was afraid—of hurting Henry, his friend, and also of what he had felt a few moments ago. Did that make him a coward? If so, then that was what he was. Certainly he felt almost fearful of Alice, standing so straight and accusing him of something his heart wished to deny. In an attempt to defuse the explosive situation, he fell back on reason.

'We are both overwrought, I think. The first time all together after so many years, and your birthday——'

'I shall certainly remember your gift to me this year! Frank insult!'

'I regret what I have just said. It was just. . .just. . . Come, Alice, we are old friends. We must not—either of us—confuse the feeling into something it is not.' There, that is the truth of it, surely, he thought. At least——

'Friends!' she said scornfully. 'Friends do not speak to each other as you have just done!' She scarcely knew what she was saying, she was so humiliated, so hurt. To throw herself at him, and be turned away so absolutely! 'And friends do not take advantage of each other. If I was. . .wanton, you did not dislike it!'

No, he thought, on the contrary. And his heart turned over knowing he had hurt her—Alice, whom he cared for.

The door of the vinery was pushed sharply open and Walter Carrington peered in. 'Alice? Chris? We are awaiting your company for the cards.'

'I am coming now,' Alice said stiffly. She went past him and out into the night; her footsteps receded down the path.

'Is aught wrong?' Walter asked as he and Chris followed.

'We have had a slight disagreement.'

Walter chuckled. 'What is unusual about that? It seems to me that you and Alice are permanently in disagreement.'

'Yes. . .'

Walter paused to smell one of the rose blooms. Alice had had no time to give to her garden recently, but the roses had flowered extravagantly anyway, although their leaves showed signs of blight from neglect. 'My boy,' he said to Chris, 'Henry tells me that you have signed Oaks to Alice?'

'That is so. It seemed politic in the current climate.'

'Hrrmph, you are right of course. However, I don't think Henry thinks it quite seemly for his—er—intended, to be the paper owner of a—er——'

'Royalist stronghold?' Chris lifted his eyes to the sky; the moonlight was more constant now and the wind was blowing the rainclouds away. 'No, I am sure he does not. However, if I had not done so, Margaret and I might now be homeless.'

'I wonder if you might persuade her to re-sign it to me?'

Chris looked surprised. 'To you? But surely, would Henry think that. . .seemly? Also, what if——?'

'What if I should die, and he inherit?' Walter asked. 'Don't be so quick to shovel me under, Chris! But, yes, I accept your point. I will put it to Henry that 'tis but a business arrangement, and be assured that there will be definite instructions in my will as to Oaks—that it pass to another. . .neutral owner, in trust for you.'

'My home,' murmured Chris, 'passed around like a parcel. . . Still, 'tis kind of you, Walter, to concern yourself in my affairs.'

'Kind!' Walter snorted. 'Nonsense! All three of you young people are like my own. It grieves me that this country's bad patch has come between you.'

'Bad patch?' Chris had to smile. 'You call this a bad patch?'

'That is what it is,' Walter said solidly. 'I have lived considerably longer than you have, my boy, and have seen all manner of strange events. Kept quiet, too, knowing that sense would eventually prevail.'

'What do you see as the eventual good sense in this?'

Walter lowered his usually vibrant voice. 'Can't last, Chris. This government. Too. . .' He fumbled for the right word. 'Too un-English. God-fearing we are, as a breed, but Bible-thumping we are not. Stands to reason that there must come in time a reverse. I believe it is begun already.'

Chris thought about it. Walter was only saying in different words what Rupert had said. Whether they were right or wrong, he felt it would come too late for him.

Walter put a heavy arm about his shoulders. 'Listen, my boy, have you thought of cutting your losses and leaving Kent? Not forever, of course, but just for a time. You have friends, good and powerful friends, I have heard. Would it not be sensible to seek shelter with them?'

Chris gave him a swift glance. 'What exactly are you saying, sir?'

'It is not for me to interfere, and I don't want to see you gone. Never think that. But this race will not be to the swift, to the bold, but to the careful. You are not careful, Chris, 'tis not in your nature to be so. Sooner or later you'll do or say something. . .regrettable, and then you'll answer for it. Probably with your life. You should not have come back.'

'I came back to fulfil my obligations to my cousin,' Chris said formally. And because I promised Alice, he added to himself. Well, Margaret obviously did not need him—would, in fact, be far happier to accept the charity of the Carringtons. It had been very hard for her, he knew, to be ostracised with him, for she had always been one of the mainsprings of the community. If she left Oaks she could slip back into that life. But Oaks—Oaks was dying now, its fields lying fallow and fast becoming reclaimed by the woods. . .

'I would, of course, see to the upkeep of Oaks,' Walter said, reading those thoughts. 'No one would think it strange, for it would be—to all intents and purposes—my own property. Whenever it would be. . . safe for you to come back, you could do so knowing you would find it in fair order.'

A generous offer, thought Chris, from a generous man. And tempting, too, to leave this place where he had always been so happy, but now no longer was. Running away—he subdued a part of him which protested—was often the better part of valour. . . He said, 'I will think on it, sir, and do thank you again for your interest.'

'Good, good.' Walter left it at that, hoping that the boy would see the advice as good, but fearing he would not.

When they returned to the house they found the card game abandoned and the ladies donning their cloaks.

Chris thanked Emma and Richard for their hospitality and bowed to Alice, who tried to ignore him but found herself going out to say goodbye to her guests just behind him. He had almost conquered his limp, but seemed to find it again in that moment. The others left them behind. Just before they entered the yard, he turned and said, 'I apologise again for what I said earlier, Alice.'

'You said you would not apologise again,' she said, trying to get past him. He did not touch her, but blocked her path. She could not look at him, but fixed her eyes on the ground. He put a finger under her chin and looked directly down into her eyes.

'Perhaps you should apologise to me, then. I am only a weak male after all, and your onslaught was enough to turn any man's head.'

'Haven't you tormented me enough for one night?' she asked, giving him back his glance. 'I wish you would just go now.'

He hesitated, then said, 'I don't want to part from you in this way. I ask you to pretend that what happened in the vinery. . .had not happened.'

Pretend it had not happened? Humiliated and furious though she was, she could never pretend that. Would not want to. 'A taste of paradise,' her grandmother had written of her embrace with Charles Rokesby. Now Alice knew exactly what those words meant.

'Why should I do that?' she muttered. 'I learned a valuable lesson—not to believe my instincts. For they are not infallible, it seems. But, if it makes you happy, *you* pretend it never happened.'

He shrugged impatiently. 'I want to ask you a favour.'

'Do so, then.'

'Not now. When you are in a more receptive mood.' She managed to get past him and walked away. 'Alice!' She turned at the gate.

'I wonder when I will be in a more receptive mood.

Perhaps I will write you when I am.' She continued on into the stables, where Henry was waiting for her, holding his impatient horse. She could have struck him, as she so desired to strike his friend. 'Well?' she demanded.

'I notice you do not wear my betrothal ring,' he said mildly.

'Are you afraid I have sold it?'

'No, I am not. Any more than I am afraid that you meant what you said this morning.' He mounted. 'When you are a little calmer I shall come to see you, Alice, and we will talk again. Write me, please, when you feel this could happen.' He clucked to his horse and joined the party waiting at the gate. She watched Chris spring up on his horse, then walked slowly back to the house. Two men awaiting two letters I shall never write, she thought, going in to help Betty clear up.

Chris Rokesby waited two weeks for Alice to write to him, then decided he could wait no longer. If he was to take Walter Carrington's advice he must begin to make plans—for Margaret and for himself. His own were already in train. He had written to Rupert in France, and as soon as a reply was received he would take the first available ship sailing for Calais. As for Margaret, tentative words with her had produced the expected response.

'Why, Chris——' She had been unable to keep the delight from her voice. 'I believe I could be very happy to make my home with Mary and Walter. But what will you do? And what of Oaks?'

'I shall be well enough, Cousin—I am sure you must have realised that it has been hard for me to settle again to a rural life when I seem to be cut from the cloth of a soldier.'

'I *have* thought that,' Margaret had said happily.

'And no wonder—you are a young man and young men always crave adventure. Where will you go?'

'I have decided nothing definite,' he had said evasively. 'But as to Oaks—Walter Carrington has generously offered to keep it safe for me. For when—or if—I return.'

'Oh, you will return! But, meanwhile, I do see that it would be better for you to seek a home elsewhere.' Margaret had then gone happily to her bedroom to contemplate her unexpected reprieve.

But now I must persuade Alice how much better it would be, Chris had thought wryly. The next day he completed his chores around the farm, ate a hasty meal at noon, washed and shaved and changed into his less disreputable clothes. On horseback, he had a sudden fancy to take his time riding over to Ashley, and so took a circuitous route which covered all his land.

I have to leave all this, he thought, almost in wonder that such a circumstance had come about. Not for any conviction, as when I went away to war, but because it no longer really belongs to me. *I* feel that it no longer belongs to me. . . The sun was already dipping in the sky when he trotted up the drive to Ashley Manor. There he found Richard and Emma away for a little holiday, and Betty Mote strangely reluctant to allow him to see Alice. Her mistress was in her room, she said, not so well today.

'Not so well? But what ails her?' Chris had never known Alice sick for a single day of her life. Even with childhood complaints she had always been up and about.

Betty wandered restlessly about the hall, picking up this object and that.

'Stand still, woman!' Chris said irritably. 'And answer me. What ails her?'

'Well, you see. . .' Betty looked into the bowl she had in her hands. It was the only remaining piece of silver—

a shallow pierced container, which Alice used for dried
rose petals to sweeten the room. It was sadly in need of
polishing; Betty thought she would gather some ashes
from the hearth and give it a good rubbing. . .

'Out with it!' Chris said.

''Tis this way. Master Henry came yesterday. . .'

'Henry? And that has upset her so much she has
taken to her bed?'

'Yes. . .'

'Nonsense!' Chris began to climb the stairs two at a
time, but Betty was faster. She barred his way at the top.

'She don't want no visitors,' she said breathlessly.

He put his hands around her waist and lifted her
aside. 'Stop being a fool, Bet, and go and find me
something to drink! There's not a drop of liquor at Oaks
these days.' He went lightly along the gallery and
drummed his knuckles on Alice's door. She called
faintly from within and he pushed open the door.

The room was in semi-darkness, the drapes pulled
closely over the windows. He advanced to the bed.
Alice drew up the covers defensively. 'What do you
want?'

'That favour I told you about. What's wrong with
you? Are you having an attack of the vapours? Why is it
so dark in here?' He strode to the window.

'Leave the drapes!' she said. 'I am ill, and don't want
to be bothered.'

'Very well, but you can listen, can't you?' He came
back to the bed and looked down at her. She looked
very small under the embroidered coverlet, and her eyes
were dark and frightened in her pale face. 'Alice,' he
said gently. 'What is amiss?'

'Nothing.' Tears rose in her eyes and trembled on her
lashes. 'But I do think I might be allowed a little peace
in my own bedroom.'

'You shall have it.' He lifted a chair and placed it

beside the bed. 'Do you have a pain? Have you called the doctor? Where are Richard and Emma?'

She sniffed. 'No, I don't have a pain. No, I have not called the doctor, and my uncle and aunt are visiting their cousins in Canterbury. You know that.'

'Oh, yes. . .' Each year at this time Emma and Richard made a pilgrimage to an ancient relative in Canterbury. It had been spoken of at the Ashley supper two weeks ago.

'Tell me the favour,' she said, 'then go away.'

Chris grimaced. This was not the receptive mood he had hoped for. But he must settle it soon. . . 'Uncle Walter has pointed out to me that it was not a sound idea for you to hold the deeds of Oaks. He suggests he hold them instead. I have come here to ask you to agree to this.'

'Good. Yes. I agree.'

'You. . .agree?'

'Yes. Arrange it all and I will sign the necessary papers.'

He stared at her. Until this moment he had not known how much he had wanted—needed her to raise objection. . .

There was a sound in the doorway and Betty came timidly in, bearing a tray with wine and glasses. Chris jumped up and took it from her, holding the door as she went out again. He placed the tray on the table by the bed.

'Have some wine, Alice. It will hearten you.'

'I don't want it! You have got what you came for, now leave, please.'

'A glass of wine will do us both good. But first let us see what we are doing. . .' He found flint and tinderbox and soon the room was softly illuminated. He poured wine into both glasses and held one out. 'Sit up, girl.'

'No.' She shrank back into the feather mattress. He

put down the glass and, leaning, lifted her against the pillows. The covers fell back and he stared. Her lawn nightgown exposed her arms to the elbows; her wrists and forearms were black with bruising, the marks livid in the shadowy light.

'My God,' he said. 'What has happened to you?'

'It's nothing.' She tried to raise the covers again, but he prevented her.

'Who did this to you?' he asked, with deadly clarity.

'I fell over,' she said faintly.

'Fell over? Someone has done this to you, Alice. Now, tell me who.' A dreadful thought came to him. 'Was it. . . Henry?'

'I annoyed him,' she said, tears falling now.

'*Annoyed* him?' Chris was white. The killing rages he had experienced in the heat of a dozen battles were nothing compared to what he felt now. The world turned red before his eyes. He fought for control. He lifted the glass again and held it to Alice's lips. 'Drink now, darling, then tell me what brought this about.'

She swallowed a mouthful of wine. She had had nothing to eat for forty-eight hours and the brew went straight to her head. She pushed away the empty glass.

'Oh, Chris. Oh, Chris. . .it was terrible. He came the day before yesterday and tried to make me set a wedding-date. I told him—I *told* him I did not want it, but he could not—would not—accept it. He said that I had promised, and I had, of course, but that was before I knew. . .' She was crying so hard that he could scarcely make out what she was saying. 'I tried to leave the room. . .he seized me. . . Uncle Richard and Aunt Emma were not here and Betty and Jack were out. . . I was so afraid. I thought he would surely kill me, he was so angry——'

Chris took her in his arms. His tenderness was such that she could hardly think. His lips caressed her face; his arms were a haven. And all the time the rage within

him was white-hot. He laid her gently back on the bed.
'Now, sweetheart, that was very unpleasant. But I will
deal with it. How long since you slept?'

'I couldn't close my eyes last night, and the night
before—it hurt so much——'

'Then sleep is the thing,' he said calmly.

'Will you stay until I sleep?' she asked, like a child
afraid of the dark.

'I will.'

The minutes passed until sleep closed Alice's frightened eyes and Chris got up. As he quietly left the room
he noticed Henry's ring on the dressing-table, winking
coldly in the dim light. He picked it up and put it in his
pocket.

In the hall Betty was waiting for him. 'Give her food
when she wakes,' he said, going to the door.

'Master Chris.' He turned, his hand on the latch.
'Don't do anything hasty,' Betty said. 'Remember who
and what he is now. For your own safety remember
that.'

'*My* safety? Have you seen your lady's bruises,
Betty?'

Betty coloured. 'I was not here, Master Chris. There
was no one to help her.'

'Well, there is now.' Chris pulled open the door and
went out into the dying sunlight. The miles to Fox Hall
were five, but did nothing to dispel the anger within
him. Master Henry was not in the manor, a liveried
servant assured him, but could be found in the south
pasture. Chris remounted his horse and, wheeling it
about, took the extra mile at a wild speed.

Henry had just dismissed his labourers for the day.
He was well-satisfied with the harvest that Fox would
reap this fall—the corn in the fields behind him was
upright and thick under the darkening sky. He came
across to the boundary and greeted his unexpected
visitor.

'Well, Chris, you are a stranger here nowadays.'

Chris quieted his tired horse. He dismounted and let it stand. Vaulting over the low fence, he stood a few feet from Henry.

'I have come from Ashley, Henry.'

'Indeed?'

'From Alice, Henry. In her bed, with marks upon her body that I looked upon with extreme prejudice.'

'Ah. . .I see.' Henry glanced over his shoulder. His men were now mere toy-sized figures as they made their way home; there would be no help from them. 'You are come to remonstrate with me, then?'

'Remonstrate? Too mild a word, Hal. I believe I am come to beat you, as you chose to beat her.'

'You have not the right, Chris,' Henry said coolly.

'The *right*? What right have you to lay rough hands on her?'

'I am her future husband. Would you come between a husband and wife?'

'If that husband were you, and the wife Alice, then yes, I would. How could you, Hal? With *Alice*! So small, so defenceless!'

Henry summoned his authority. The authority which had granted him great favour in the new order. Here before him was a man who was renounced by that new order—surely he could deal with this small opposition? He said reasonably, 'Now, Chris, you have said yourself that she needed a firm hand. In the past you have often remarked that her aunt and uncle were too lenient with her. . . That is all I applied: a firm hand.'

'A firm——' Chris stared across the few feet which separated them.

'She was most recalcitrant,' Henry went on, still in the reasonable tone. 'Now, surely you and I are not going to fall out over so small a thing?'

So small a thing? thought Chris, bemused. Why, the man is a stranger to me. A heartless, icy stranger. And

Alice, sweet Alice, with her kind and generous ways, had been committed to him, with his connivance. He said slowly, 'I have said in the past that I had no special feeling for Alice. I have promised, and meant it, that I would inform you should that change. Well, now it has. I am come here today to tell you that you may have no further claim on Alice Ashley. She and I are to be married.'

Henry narrowed his eyes. 'Such a move on your part would be most unwise, Chris.'

'Why so?'

'Because I will not give up my claim to Alice, and you are hardly in a position to contest it.'

Chris let his eyes wander over the empty fields. Above them the swallows darted and lent their individual presence to the deserted landscape. 'We can contest it now,' he said softly. 'We could do that now, Hal.'

Henry considered. They could do as Chris suggested, but there would be only one outcome to that. Chris might pretend to be weakened by the past two years, certainly he had lacked good food and adequate care, but he was a born fighter, whatever the odds. Better, Henry thought, for them to come to grips in a more civilised situation. A situation of his choosing. He said, 'No, Chris. No, I do not agree to that. Go home now. If we must, we will speak of this another time. But go home now.' He waited to see the result of his calm words.

Chris, too, was considering. His impulsive words had appalled him. He was set to leave Kent. He had spent two weeks deciding this. Now, in a moment, he had thrown away that option. Instead, he had put himself in harm's way. For that was where he was; he made no mistake about that. Henry Carrington was all-powerful now, in this small part of the world. And he would not forgive this affront to his new position. And Alice? Her behaviour in the vinery two weeks ago had not convinced Chris that she loved him. Rather, that she was confused, and her instinctive fear of the man Henry had become had led her to seek a way out. Chris wanted very much to give her a breathing space, but his hasty words might have provided a trap for them both. But need it be so?

He could still leave Kent, he could still keep Oaks, and he could keep Alice safe by formally betrothing himself to her before he left. No definite date of marriage need be set, and it would be an arrangement of convenience only, to be broken immediately should either wish it. It seemed to Chris the sensible, the only course of action. But to follow this course he must forgo an immediate confrontation with Henry, and Chris badly wanted that confrontation, felt that nothing else could satisfy the fuse lit within him by the sight of Alice's delicate flesh marked by this man's fingers.

As so often before in his life, he stood at dual crossroads. One path indicated clearly the practical and rational, the other disaster. Chris struggled with his passionate nature under the sky, turning rose purple now as the sun began to set.

'Well?' Henry judged it safe to speak. He had seen Chris in too many similar situations not to know him to be a man who acted on the instant, or not at all. This whole tangle, Henry decided, could be sorted out with reason. He bent to pick up his hat. 'We have had many a disagreement in the past, Chris, and I don't think you want to make more of this than it warrants.'

'What I want,' Chris said slowly, 'is to give you a taste of what you inflicted upon Alice.'

Henry adjusted his hat. 'Not the words of a gentleman,' he remarked.

'They were not intended for the ears of one.'

Henry flushed, but said stolidly, 'I admit that I might have been in error to. . .to be quite so. . .harsh with Alice, but you know better than most how difficult she can be. Now—come up with me to the house and take a drink.'

'To celebrate my betrothal?'

Henry frowned. 'I don't think you meant what you said concerning that. Naturally, you were at pains to take me to task over my behaviour, but——'

'I meant it. You will just have to resign yourself to that, Hal.'

'I cannot do so. She has my ring——'

'*I* have your ring, and now you may have it back.' Chris took the bauble from his pocket and tossed it over the ground separating them. Henry made no attempt to catch it, and it fell on to the dusty ground and bounced, its glittering stones reflecting the fiery light. Both men looked down upon it.

'You *cannot* be serious in this,' Henry said. 'Cannot be intent on making such a foolish and dangerous move. Why? Just to best me?'

'Alice is not someone I would ever use to *best* another in argument,' Chris said quietly.

'Do you know how precarious your position is at present?'

'I have a fair idea.'

'And yet you exacerbate that situation, by *this*?'

Chris turned and put a foot up on the fence and climbed it. He sprang on to his horse. 'Friendship, Hal,' he said gently, 'is something I would have sworn you knew all about. I was wrong.' He chirruped to his horse and moved off down the lane.

Henry stared after him a moment, then knelt to retrieve the discarded ring. If Chris had chosen to beat him bloody, Henry felt that he would have remembered it more kindly than his contemptuous gesture with the Carrington betrothal ring and his words a half-second ago.

Riding back towards Oaks, Chris pondered his next move. He had surprised himself by his self-restraint.

One of Richard Ashley's favourite expressions came into his mind. 'Sooner or later, Chris, every man has to grow up.' Perhaps that was what he had done in the twenty short minutes it had taken him to get from Ashley to Fox. Grown up. If so, he thought ruefully, it was a damned uncomfortable experience, apparently involving letting his best friend be treated roughly, without her assailant being called to account.

He must, of course, go soon and confess to Alice what he had done. But not now, for she was safe asleep under the watchful eye of Betty Mote, and he was in need of a large drink. He turned towards Larkspur and the lights of the Evening Sun.

Molly Judd was in the taproom when he ducked his head under the low beam and came in. She came to him immediately with her swaying, suggestive step.

'Master Chris, I'm glad to see you. Will you come into the parlour for your glass?'

'I will if it be on the house, Molly,' Chris said. 'for I have not a penny-piece to my name.'

Seated in the cosy room, a full glass in his hand, he smiled at her. There had been nothing intimate between them since he had returned from Oxford. This was a source of grief to her, but she was not displeased by the easy friendship which had taken its place. Times had changed now and the men who came into the inn were all the same kind: stolid, worthy farmers and merchants. One of them had become more than a casual visitor and last week had invited her to become his wife. He was a widower with three young children and a prosperous business in Canterbury. Molly thought she would accept him soon—she would like children of her own and a home and a respectable life. But her heart, rather brittle and worn long before she reached her twenties, would always belong to Chris Rokesby and she would have it no other way. Now she said, 'What have you been up to, Chris?'

He tossed off his wine and held out his glass for another. 'Getting myself betrothed,' he said cheerfully.

'Betrothed! Who is the lucky girl?'

'Alice Ashley.'

'Ah, yes, Mistress Ashley. But what will the gallant colonel have to say to that?' Henry Carrington was notorious in Larkspur now. Since returning he had waged war on the community with regard to what he called 'following Christian rules'. He had been trying to bring about the closure of the Evening Sun for weeks. No use to remember the gangling red-haired youth of five years ago, the local people said, for times had changed. . .

'He doesn't like it,' Chris said.

Molly placed the bottle conveniently to her guest's hand. She shook her head. 'Haven't you had enough of dispute, Chris? Why take this on?'

'I must.'

'Hmm.' Molly opened the door and called the pot-boy to order food. 'Some of the fresh pig, and pan-fry a couple of those fat herring.' She closed the door. 'If you need help, you know you'll find it here.' She laid a plump hand on Chris's black head. He took it and raised it to his lips.

'You have always been kind to me, Molly.'

Kind? One of her sisters had once laughingly referred to Chris Rokesby as Molly's Beautiful Boy. Well, he had been that all those years ago, but also much more. Molly had set her mind to taking for husband her desiccated widower, but no one could take away from her all those sweet-scented nights in Chris Rokesby's arms. Now it seemed that the little Ashley girl was to inherit all that sensuous delight, and Molly was fair-minded enough to think that that would be quite fitting. Alice Ashley was a likely girl—brave and loyal, and somehow the feminine twin of the young man getting quietly drunk tonight. If all went well they would find themselves with a happier marriage than most.

'Mistress Ashley is prepared to weather the storm she'll raise breaking her engagement to Master Carrington and taking a Royalist outlaw instead?' she enquired.

'She doesn't know of it yet,' Chris admitted. 'About our betrothal, I mean, although she has said she loves me.' Chris got up and paced about the room. He could never remain for long in any passive state. 'I don't believe she does, though, Molly. I think she was just looking for a way out of her present liaison, and I was conveniently to hand. We go back a long way, she and I.'

Molly smiled sceptically. The girl she had interviewed two years back, in this very parlour, had not seemed to her a girl who did not know her own mind. Young, yes, and inexperienced, but the essential core of resolve had been there when she had chosen to take on a task which might have daunted a grown man. If Alice Ashley had decided that she loved Chris then she did, and Molly put her mind to making her path easier if she could. 'Why don't you tell me *all* about it, Chris? From the beginning.'

It was late when Chris left the Evening Sun. The inn had been closed for some hours, respectable citizens gone home or up into the spotless bedrooms to get a good night's sleep. He and Molly had sat talking beside the dying fire. When he finally—and unsteadily—mounted his horse, a plan of campaign had been worked out.

Molly would take charge of any communication with old friends; she had already despatched the letter to Prince Rupert for Chris. She was well-qualified for this. England was now officially at peace, the so-called rebels subdued, but many young men who had cast their dice on the losing side had come home to find a hostile reception. Those young men had been spirited across the Channel before disaster could befall them. Molly Judd knew how to accomplish this, and if necessary would do it for Chris Rokesby. She also had powerful friends among the gentry of Kent. Walter Carrington was not alone in feeling that the new order could not last. They had not liked the old ways, these practical men, but the new were not entirely to their liking either.

But about Henry Carrington, she had warned Chris several times during the evening, she could do nothing at all; he was heart and soul for the ethics he had fought for. 'Forget your association with him,' had been Molly's advice, 'for it can count for nothing now.' When Chris had gone Molly locked the door behind him thoughtfully. She had the feeling that none of the arrangements they had talked of would, in the end, be necessary. . . .

CHAPTER TEN

CHRIS opened his eyes the next morning with no memory of how he had got home. But somehow he had, for he was in his own bed, in his own nightshirt. He sat up.

'Chris?' Margaret came into the room, bearing a glass of milk and bread and butter. Chris looked at both with disfavour.

Margaret perched on the bed. 'Now, eat and drink, my dear. I gather you were less than well last night.'

Chris drank some of the milk; the liquid was cool and soothing to his parched throat. He drained the glass.

'Good, good,' Margaret said sympathetically. 'Jack Madesley brought you home, you know. Said he had encountered you in the lanes and thought that he would see you safely to Oaks. He stabled your horse and put you to bed.' She got up and drew the curtains. Chris winced as the sunlight poured into the room. 'I am invited to Fox Hall today,' she said. 'What will you do?'

'I am going to Ashley,' Chris mumbled.

'Are you? Well, that will be nice. Now, my horse is at the door—can I do anything for you before I go?'

'No. . .yes. At least, Cousin, do you remember once telling me that my mother left in trust for me her betrothal ring?'

Margaret paused at the door. 'Why, yes. . . It is among her things in the study. Do you wish me to find it?' Oh, dear, she thought, has it come to that? That the poor boy must sell his mother's ring?

'If you would; I don't wish to delay you.'

'No delay, for I know exactly where it is. I will put it on the table in the hall for you.' Margaret disappeared.

Chris got up, trying to ignore his whirling head, washed and dressed. In the hall he found the velvet pouch containing his mother's marriage ring. He tipped it out and held it in his palm. It was a pearl, dull from being so long in the dim softness of the case, but the setting was finest Italian gold and the surrounding diamonds large and imposing. He slipped it back into its case and tucked it into his pocket.

Alice was in the hall when he arrived. Jack Madesley was with her and they were discussing his and Betty's wedding; he stood politely aside as they greeted each other warily. Chris gave him a sheepish glance.

'Well, Jack, you brought me home last night, I hear. In the most shameful condition.'

'You were a bit under the weather,' Jack conceded.

'What is this?' asked Alice.

Chris took a chair by the open window. 'I was inebriated, Alice.'

'Had you been to the Evening Sun?'

'Yes.'

'I see. Jack, I think we have everything arranged— perhaps you will continue in the orchards and I will join you later.' When Jack had gone she said to Chris, 'I won't offer you wine, as you have had a surfeit of it in the last few hours.' She sat on the window-seat, within an arm's length, but could have been out in the yard her manner was so distant. She was wearing a dress with close-fitting sleeves; the narrow lace at the cuffs did not quite conceal her wrists with their yellowing marks.

'I went to see Henry yesterday,' he said.

'Indeed?' She took a folded paper from her belt and handed it to him. 'This arrived this morning.'

He read it aloud. '"Dear Alice, It constrains me to make my apologies for the unpleasant circumstances we found ourselves in during our last meeting. I believe we both regret the incident, and must try to forgive equally.

Henry."' Chris refolded the letter. 'He manages to put you neatly in the wrong along with him,' he remarked.

'Why did you go to see him?'

'To return the ring he gave you.' She gave him a nervous look. 'Don't look like that. 'Twould be less than honest to keep it, you know.'

'I did not intend to keep it. . . But what did you say to him?'

'I told him that I intended to give you my own ring to take its place.' There really was no better way to tell her, at least none that he could think of.

'Is this some joke of yours?' she asked, her breath coming quickly. He reached out and took one of her hands.

'Listen, Alice, we have found ourselves in rather a difficult position here. If I stay at Oaks sooner or later one of my neighbours will find a reason to have me arrested. Listen, now——' She was trying to take her hand back; he moved closer and held it pressed between the two of his. 'I cannot go and leave you at odds with Henry. While you are free I believe he will not give up trying to make you wed him.' He wished he did not have to have this conversation now, with his head banging and a sick stomach. 'So I told Henry that I intended asking you to marry me.' She jumped up. 'Now, don't explode, Alice.'

'So ask me!' she said.

He sighed. 'Don't make this more awkward than it already is.'

'Awkward? You wish me to be your wife, so ask me!'

'Very well. Will you marry me, Alice?'

'No.'

He was getting angry himself now, but made an effort to be calm. 'Please, sit down again and discuss this sensibly. It is for your protection.'

'I do not need your protection.'

He pushed the window wider and a current of cool air

flowed in, but he still felt stifled. 'Could Betty find me a cool drink, do you suppose?'

Alice ran to the door and, opening it, shouted for Betty, who arrived at a run. 'Yes, miss?' She saw Chris and bobbed. 'Good day, Master Chris.'

'I had not noticed that it was. Do you have anything cold I can drink, Betty? I am parched.'

'An excess of wine has that effect,' Alice said. 'Also the activity you were probably engaged in last night at the Evening Sun. Well, don't just stand there, Betty, go and get something.' She closed the door in the startled maid's face.

Jack was in the kitchen, making himself a little lunch to take out into the orchards. 'What's happening in there?' he asked as Betty took tall beakers from a cupboard.

'I'm sure I don't know. What happened last night? Old Madge was here from Oaks this morning and said you had put Master Chris to bed.'

'I did, and no easy job it was. I met him in Honey Lane a-reeling about on that old horse of his'n. I offered to take him home to Oaks but he was all for going to Fox Hall to drag Master Henry from his bed and "give him what I should have done earlier".'

'Hold on a minute——' Betty ran out to the well to draw up the keg of ale she had lowered into its cool depths. She extracted the peg, tilted the keg, and let the ale foam into the beakers. 'Go on.'

'Well, I'll vow we were a comic sight—him so strong, despite his looks, and me trying to keep a-hold of him and two horses, and a-feared that the special constables would come along at any moment and take him to the bridewell for being so disorderly.'

'So how did you manage to get him home?' Betty's eyes were wide.

'He took a sudden fancy for his sword. "Fists too good for him," he was a-shouting. "Cold steel is the thing for vermin." So I said to him that his sword was in the hall at Oaks and we'd best go there and find it. When I got him there 'twas all over. I carried him up to his room bodily and put him into his bed. He was out like a rushlight and I had no trouble stripping him off and covering him up. He looks awful young when he's asleep,' Jack added thoughtfully.

'He is young,' Betty said. 'Just one and twenty last birthday. I'll get these into them now.' She carried the two beakers carefully into the hall and gave one to Chris. He downed the ale without pausing for breath. Alice took hers but did not drink it, and Betty tiptoed out again.

'She and Jack are to be married, did you know?' Alice put down her beaker without tasting it.

'If you don't want that, may I have it. . . .? Yes, I know—Jack came over last week and asked me to stand up with him. At least, I think that is what he wanted. He was so tongue-tied that he couldn't get the words out. Isn't he rather young to be taking on a wife?'

'He is older than you are, and you are preparing to do just that.'

'Are you ready to talk quietly now about the solution to your problem?'

'I don't have a problem.'

'You did yesterday.'

She swallowed. 'Yes, I admit I was. . .worried then, but on thinking it over perhaps I did bring it upon myself. I was very brusque with him.' Worried was too inadequate a word for what she had felt, she thought. Terrified was more apt. It had begun so innocuously, the nightmare, that she still could hardly think how it had developed the way it had. One moment she had been telling Henry that she was so busy she had no time to discuss something which was already settled, the next he had been across the room and staring down at her. Even then she had not thought to fear him, although part of her brain had registered that she was alone in the house. She had turned to open the door and then he had seized her around the wrists. Annoyed, she had twisted in his grasp, and then had come the really horrible part, for he had pinioned her arms to her side, twisting and wrenching and all the time looking down into her eyes. In this position she could hardly take in what he said— that she had promised to marry him, that he had come this day to ascertain a date, and would not leave without it. Her resistance, far from deterring him, had seemed to inspire him to further violence. . .

To prevent himself from getting angry all over again at the bewildered expression on her face Chris jumped up and took the ring from his pocket. He took her hand and slipped it on to her finger.

Her mind slid back to the evening three years ago when she had refused to allow Henry to do the same. . . Unaccountably her eyes filled with tears.

'What? You don't like it?' Chris asked. 'I think it pretty, and my mother wore it with pride, I believe.'

She lifted her hand to examine it. ''Tis not that. . . Of course it is lovely, but. . . Oh, Chris, it is not what I imagined.' Night-dreams, daydreams, always the same. That some miracle would happen and the all-consuming love she had for him would be returned. . .

'What ever is?' he asked quietly.

'I mean. . . I have told you that I love you, and I do. So much that it hurts me to have to do this for reasons other than the return of that love.'

'But, sweetheart, I do love you, have always done so. Are you not my best friend?'

She blinked back the tears. 'It is not the same.'

'Listen.' He put his arms around her. He held her so gently—he was always so gentle. 'You must understand why I am doing this thing. I cannot leave you, knowing that what happened lately may happen again. Do you think I would have a moment's rest thinking of that?'

'But why must you go? If you could only be a little more. . .practical. If you could stop. . .stop arguing for a cause well-lost, you could stay.'

He drew back. 'I do no *arguing* these days. My energy is exclusively reserved in trying to find enough food on my estate for both human and animal consumption!'

'Oh, you know what I am talking about! Isn't it true that several gentlemen have called upon you recently and seemed prepared to be. . .friendly?'

Chris was silent, for what Alice said was only the truth. Kent was settling down now, and its citizens were eager to restore normality. Men like Walter Carrington, powerful in their way, had pointed the road, and others were set to follow. Rokesby was an old and valued name among the landed gentry. They felt that the young master of Oaks had made a mistake, but that that mistake could be recouped. His cousin William had been a local magistrate, Master of the Hunt, and had held all manner of other titles. His heir could inherit these duties, but. . . Chris had been obdurate in his refusals, and that did not enhance his status among men who thought that he should be grateful for their overtures.

'I cannot be other than I am,' he said slowly. 'They choose to ignore four years of conflict, very well, but I am apparently cast in a different metal.'

'Then where will you go?' She had dried her tears now. This was following the course now of their traditional conversations; he had always brought his ambitions and aspirations to her. She tried to put aside what she felt inwardly and help him.

'I am for France,' he said without hesitation—evidence that he trusted her completely. 'I will join Prince Rupert in this.'

Alice raised a hand to her disordered hair—the breeze through the windows teased and pulled at the shining curls. 'To go a-soldiering in a foreign country might satisfy your hankering for something definite to do, and I can quite see that you would be happy to join forces again with your friend, but had you thought that *we* might need you? Your neighbours in Kent, I mean. This county is being reformed now, and I would—and I am not the only one—that there was a tempering voice among the zealots.'

Chris thought about it. He could understand Alice's point.

'You are an *Englishman*, after all,' Alice went on resolutely. 'Would you leave your country to be divided among religious fanatics, many of whom belong across the border?' The Scots, having helped English Puritans to victory, had now showed that they expected a say in the government.

'I am not the stuff that politicians are made of. Besides, Henry would never allow it.'

'He is but one voice among many.'

'Even so—I would take no part in any company he is in.'

How ironic it was to have to take Henry's part after his treatment of her, and against the man who had been ready to defend her! She said lightly, 'It is not so long since you were inclined to manhandle me yourself, Chris. I remember vividly an occasion where you pushed me so hard that I fell down the river bank and cut my leg.'

He half laughed. 'I was nine and you *seven*—and, as I recall, you jumped up and dealt me so hard a blow with a handy stick that I bore the mark for a sennight.'

'Yes, well. . .'

'And you must know that it is quite different for a grown man to treat a woman in that way,' he said seriously.

'It still seems a little drastic to put your neck in the yoke to save me from him.' There, she could be as light in tone as he.

Chris finished his ale and rose. He could not say to her, for she was too innocent in that way, that a man who could do what Henry Carrington had could not be trusted in other areas. 'I must go. Margaret will have a dozen problems when I return.'

'Have you told her of your plans to leave?'

'I have, and she is delighted. Hardly surprising—I am poor entertainment for her these days. She will be happy to make her home with the Carringtons.'

'With Walter and Mary? Then 'tis all arranged. . .'

'As I have told you.' Chris looked around for his battered hat and retrieved it from the settle. 'When Richard has returned please let me know, for I must discuss the matter with him as he is your guardian.'

Alice turned the ring on her finger. 'This all seems so cold-blooded, Chris. What if——? Well, you are going to a foreign country, maybe for some years, you may well meet a lady who. . .who attracts you, but you will have made this contract with me.'

'The same applies to you. So it must be clear between us from the onset that our bond may be broken at any time.'

She could have wept again! Her comment had turned the knife in her heart, and he would agree it! The arrangement was designed to protect her, she knew that, but—— She said, 'What do you intend saying to my uncle?'

'Only that we have discovered a mutual attraction and wish to consolidate it in a formal engagement. Of the rest—I will say nothing. I cannot feel he will object.'

'Then you cannot know how rumour breeds in this close community! He will ask you why—if you are so set on me for a wife—your conduct with Molly Judd is the talk of the countryside!'

'Molly Judd?' He was both annoyed and puzzled by her attack. 'There has been nothing between Molly and

myself which will not bear the scrutiny of. . .of the
Puritans since I returned from the war.'

'Is it so?' she asked, turning to look at him. 'Is it *truly*
so?'

'Why, yes.' He felt she should have known this, but
thought that feeling obviously quite irrational. He put
on his hat and came to her.

'Why?' she asked, with her candid look.

Why? He could not really have said, except that
Molly no longer held that sort of attraction for him.

'But you still go regularly to the Evening Sun?' she
persisted. 'It can be misconstrued, you know.'

'By whom? Men whose opinion I do not value? Molly
Judd is my friend, Alice, and has been for some years.
That does not change because we no longer have a. . .
closer relationship.' He would have defended this stance
with no other person, yet it was important to him to
know that Alice Ashley understood it. He looked for
that understanding in her face, but she was looking over
his shoulder through the open window, at her roses
losing their last petals in the wind driving up from the
Medway.

She was thinking, if only I could go back! To being
twelve again, with no more pressing worry on my mind
than how to whiten my hands, to subdue my hair
beneath its lace cap, to persuade Uncle Richard that I
really *can* ride the latest spirited addition to the stables.
To know I can rely on Henry to help me and always take
my side in any small argument, on Chris to—— Well, to
provide amusing company, to know the latest dance
figures and what the fashionable lady is wearing, even if
he is so reluctant to look respectable himself. Now she
knew that she could never trust Henry again, and Chris
had become that unknown quantity—the man she
loved.

'What are you thinking of?' he asked, going to the
door and opening it.

'Of how happy we all were before the war. Don't you ever think of that?'

He unlooped his reins from the rail beyond the porch and climbed into the saddle. 'I certainly do—each time I ease my aching bones into bed at night. In those days I had fifty men to do the work I'm trying to do at Oaks.'

'Has none of them come back?'

His face hardened. 'Many were killed, some paid another price and some are in gaol.'

She smoothed the velvet face of his old horse. The poor thing should have been out to pasture long ago, and would have been if Chris had had any other animal to ride. 'If you stayed and fought a different fight, perhaps you could get some of those men released.'

'Perhaps you should do that—now that you are the official owner of Oaks, they are *your* men.'

She looked up. 'My property becomes yours when you become my husband. Before that, in theory, you own what I own now we are betrothed.'

He grinned. 'I hadn't thought of that. How everything does turn full circle, if one waits long enough.'

She moved back into the shadow of the stone porch. 'Think about what I said earlier, Chris. You once thought it worthwhile to risk your death for a way of life, now perhaps you should consider putting your life into the arena for the same cause.'

Chris hesitated. His horse dropped its head and longed for the peace of its stall; another flurry of leaves was gently torn from the trees by the wind. How annoying Alice could be, he thought, when she applied her intelligent mind to good use. However much he tried to persuade himself that he no longer owned Oaks, that the women and children on the estate were not his responsibility, in his secret heart he knew that they were. He had encouraged no one of his tenants to join in his enterprise, but they had rallied just the same. Over the two years he had served he had often met up with them—brave men and valiant in their efforts. Their families, too, were not convinced that Master Chris was not now their squire, and it was to him that they brought their troubles and queries. And he was about to betray them, leave them. . .

'Think about it,' Alice said. She turned into the house.

Richard and Emma Ashley returned three weeks later. They had enjoyed their break from the routine at Ashley and had had an eventful time towards the end of their visit. The elderly cousin they had been staying with had been taken suddenly ill, and had died within twenty-four hours, leaving Richard Ashley as his sole heir. Richard now found himself possessed of an imposing house in Canterbury, plus the hoarded monies of a lifetime, and considerable revenue from the various business concerns his cousin had had interest in. The unexpected windfall would be the saving of Ashley, Richard told his niece during their first chance to have a private conversation.

'It will mean a great difference here, Alice,' Richard said. 'I can now employ a competent foreman and you will be free to go to your marriage without feeling that you are leaving your aunt and me in difficult straits.'

'My marriage to Henry, you mean?'

'Why—of course.'

They were in the library. Richard had brought back a dozen bottles of fine French wine with him and they had enjoyed one at supper and were sampling another now.

'It is off,' Alice said bluntly.

'Off?' Richard looked bewildered. 'But surely he has not let you down, my dear? Why, I never would have supposed——'

'No, I broke the engagement,' she said, 'and am now betrothed to Chris Rokesby.' It was really a shame, she thought, to spring this on her uncle, who looked even more confused.

'Perhaps you ought to explain from the beginning,' Richard said resentfully. All the way home he had been speculating upon how pleasant it would be to have a little gold now, to give Alice what she should have as a young bride, to buy what he knew Ashley needed most: a replacement for his dutiful and brave young relative.

'We found we were not suited—Henry and I,' Alice said soothingly. 'At least, 'twas that on my side. He is having a little. . .difficulty in accepting it.'

'Yes, he would. . . . However, Chris has not applied to me,' Richard added sternly.

'He was but waiting for your return. You will have no objection, I presume?'

'Well. . .no. . .except——'

'If you are thinking of his reputation with such as Molly Judd, then all that is over with him.' She held up her left hand. 'And I am wearing evidence of his good intentions.'

Richard blinked as he recognised the ring. He had seen it last on the hand of Chris Rokesby's mother, Elinor, whom he had met briefly in his youth but never forgotten. She had died young, and her husband soon after, but what a lovely woman she had been! As fair as Chris was dark, as small as he was tall, but her son had inherited her shining blue eyes and her charming manner. Elinor Rokesby had had the knack of endearing every human being within her near vicinity.

'I don't expect you to be pleased with the arrangement, Uncle.'

'Why should I not be?' Richard demanded, showing a side he never usually did. 'The Cornish Rokesbys were, in their time, honoured by every king to sit the English throne, and the Kentish branch fine, upstanding gentlemen!'

Alice looked astonished. 'But you were so pleased about the match with Henry Carrington!'

'Certainly I was. But the Carringtons are. . .well, dull fellows, you know, and Henry the dullest of all.'

'Why, Uncle Richard!' Alice came across the room and kissed him. 'You should be talking me out of such folly!'

'Don't want to,' Richard said stubbornly. 'To tell the truth, I have always thought Henry a bit of a wolf in sheep's clothing. I'm a poor excuse for a guardian these days, I often accuse myself, but in the past I've seen a bit of life, and if I'm honest I've always had my doubts. There! Now you'll be wondering why I never raised my voice before.' Alice knelt by his chair and kissed him again. 'You say Henry cannot accept what you have told him?' he asked, looking at her in appreciation. The hardship of the last years did not seem to have affected her beauty at all, he thought. If anything it had enhanced the unusual lustre of her eyes and the strength in the contours of her face. A challenge suits her, Richard thought, and that is exactly what she will get if she takes on Chris Rokesby.

'No, he can't seem to,' she answered.

'Hmm. Still. . . If Chris is now involved, Henry will find it hard to stand against him,' Richard said thoughtfully.

Involved? Chris? He had not been to Ashley again since he had brought Alice his ring. As arranged, Alice had given Jack a note to take to Oaks informing the master that her uncle was now back home. No doubt he would arrive at some time to talk to him. But, involved? Alice thought there was little involvement on his part. Betty, who always seemed to know the neighbourhood gossip, had told her that Margaret Rokesby had removed lock, stock and barrel to Fox Hall, so that piece of his plan was now complete. Alice assumed that

Chris was only waiting to talk to Richard Ashley before following his own course.

In thinking this she was wrong. Chris came the following morning to speak with Richard, hardly knowing himself how the radical change in his future had come about. It had begun with Rupert. Chris had received—via Molly Judd—an acknowledgement of his own communication from Rupert, though unsigned.

My dear Friend, How happy I was to hear from you! How happy I would be to have you with me now in this new enterprise, but must urge you to wait awhile.

There followed a detailed description of the Prince's adventures in the French army, and the information— relevant only to another soldier—of a pause now in the fighting and the reasons, then Rupert continued in his distinctive black script.

It would be better, therefore, for you to wait to hear again from me. Meanwhile, I have heard that life is awkward for the returning Royalist soldier in England just now and consequently know you will not be offended if I offer a little practical help. I enclose a draft, to be drawn on any English bank, for monies to facilitate this help. It is, of course, guaranteed by a name not my own! But good, just the same. Use it, dear Chris, in any way you think proper. After all, my comrade, 'tis only arrears of a soldier's pay. . . And know that I remember our friendship always.

Chris had tentatively proffered the draft at a bank in Canterbury, and learned that it *was* good. He was now possessed of a quite extraordinary amount of cash.

The second unusual occurrence—in the same week— had been a visit from Walter Carrington. He had wandered about the bare hall at Oaks, obviously in

some state of indecision. Eventually he had managed to
get out a few words.

'Margaret is all set to come to us? Good, good, we are
ready for her and Mary much looking forward to her
arrival. . . Henry tells me that Alice has broken her
contract with him and thinks you to be his successor?'

'That is so,' agreed Chris. He was embarrassed that
he could offer neither wine nor cakes to his visitor. He
had not yet got around to stocking his cellar with his
new money, and Margaret had been in such a fever of
packing that she had ordered no baking. He did invite
Walter to sit down, though.

'Thank you, I will.' Walter disposed his bulk into a
chair and looked pensively at his hands. 'Henry has not
vouchsafed any details of the affair, but I gather 'twas
Alice who set the terms. That being so, I cannot
presume to argue with a lady on her choice. But seems
to me that you have made an enemy, Chris.'

'I know that. But also know I could take no other
way.'

'Hrumph! Quite so, quite so—as I say, I don't know
the details, and 'twas not about that that I have come. I
have come to. . .to offer you a position, my boy.'
Walter ceased examining his hands and looked up. The
object of his scrutiny was not prepossessing. Chris was
dressed for the fields, in old shirt and breeches, his black
hair ruffled, a defensive expression on his handsome
face. 'Yes, a position of some quality. . .' Walter continued. 'Various of the local dignitaries have got
together and proposed you for magistrate.'

'Me? A magistrate?' Chris could have laughed,
remembering his harum-scarum youth—a youth which
was not quite overlaid by his responsibilities, both
recent and present—but the deliberate tone of the other
man's voice sobered him. 'But, sir, I am no magistrate
in the making!' Magistrates, he thought, were dry and
elderly. Wearing wigs and a sanctimonious manner,

they dispensed lectures and fines—or worse—to men such as. . .well, himself!

'They don't feel that. And nor do I.' Walter could be very straightforward when the occasion demanded, and now he said firmly, 'You are as fair-minded as any man I know, my boy. Also, you will have a certain knowledge of the men who come before you—all the villagers have your acquaintance. Your heritage, too, lends itself to authority. I would, myself, be happy to know you wore the justices' robes at the county sessions.'

'A great compliment, sir,' Chris said sincerely.

'Then, how say you? I am empowered to take your answer back to those who have sanctioned the proposal.'

'I think you may say. . .I agree,' Chris said consideringly. With those seven words he was aware that he was changing his life; this offer would be the first of many such. . . Oddly, he had no desire to take the words back.

Armed with this new appointment, plus his unexpected bounty of gold, Chris rode up the drive to Ashley. Richard received him in the library.

'Sit down, I have wine here.' He poured the glasses and both men sipped.

'Excellent,' Chris pronounced. 'I must congratulate you on your recent good fortune—it is the talk of the village.'

'Hmm, yes, it is a blessing,' Richard acknowledged. 'Now, to business. Alice has told me of your proposal. I was surprised, but not unduly so.'

'Not, sir?'

Richard smiled. 'You were always good friends, you and Alice. I have been thinking of you both since yesterday and can see now that there have—over the years—been a dozen signposts to your present condition.'

Chris thought, Dear, kind, Richard—he must always

find a reasonable explanation for all that happens. He was probably convinced that all the scraps Chris and Alice had had in the past had masked some fatal attraction. Before he could pursue this startling thought, he said determinedly, 'I am come here today with various inducements to make you look favourably on me, Uncle Richard. I have been asked to sit on the bench of the justices, and have accepted.'

Richard raised his eyebrows.

'An unlikely honour, I am sure you are thinking,' Chris said, smiling. 'But one I find I am growing to look kindly upon. Such an appointment might well lead to others, and perhaps I am ready now to take on the responsibilities my cousin William was always trying to encourage me towards.'

Richard refilled their glasses. 'I see. . . But, forgive me, Chris, if I have been listening to idle rumour, but 'tis said that you plan to leave us soon. How does that gossip fit in with what you are telling me?'

'That was my intention, certainly, but I have changed my mind. At least until I see how things turn out. . .'

'But Margaret has already left you, I understand.'

'Indeed. As you will appreciate, Oaks has not been the most comfortable place recently, and I thought she deserved better.'

'So you have no woman to see for you?' Richard asked, raised in a time where a 'woman to see for you' was the right and essential for every man.

'I have old Madge. She has not been paid for her work for a long time, but——' he grinned '—refused to go when given the chance.' Also, since Margaret had left, several of his tenants' wives had come regularly to the manor, bringing home-baked food and dairy produce, and it was not unusual for him to come in from the fields to discover one or other of them briskly cleaning his home under the martial eye of Madge. 'I am really managing very well.'

'I come now to the main problem of the whole matter,' Richard said uncomfortably. 'That of Henry. You have not, according to Alice, set any firm date for your marriage and I don't think he will feel his own suit entirely rejected until you do.'

Chris wondered exactly how much Richard knew. Not much, he decided, as Alice would hesitate to put her gentle uncle in the position of having to tax his neighbour's son in any way. He said easily, 'Frankly, sir, I would give Alice a little time to be quite sure of her mind. Her last engagement was—without mincing words—always a thing encouraged by you and Mistress Emma, as well as the Carringtons and. . .the Rokesbys. Almost a foregone conclusion, one might say. Well, it didn't work out, and Alice changed her mind. Better, I think, for her to be absolutely sure this time.'

Richard contemplated the young man before him. He had always found Chris Rokesby a very attractive creature, and his sense of rightness made him anticipate a match between him and Alice as a beautiful thing. 'A lovely pair' was a well-worn phrase, but apt in this case. But there was something not quite right about this, Richard thought anxiously. Nothing he could put his finger on, but. . . Perhaps it was the way Alice looked when she spoke of Chris—that look was not in this young man's face when he spoke of her. . . But what could he do—or anyone else? It must be resolved between the couple. He said slowly, 'Yes, there is reason in that, I agree. So—on to other matters. How is Oaks faring? With my sudden solvency I have been able to set Ashley straight again. Say the word and I will be more than happy to do the same for Oaks.'

Chris smiled again. Old friends, he thought, were a valuable currency. And Kentish men were geared to solidarity. Chris knew quite well that Walter Carrington must have been the main proposer in his offer of position within the community. And Jack Madesley and

Betty, and all the loyal souls of Ashley and Oaks, had played their part in the attempt to reinstate him. . . . Yet he had been prepared to desert them all! He said, 'I do thank you for that, sir. But—in confidence—I have a little money of my own. Enough to put Oaks on the right road, enough to lay a little aside for my forthcoming wedding.' It was the first time he had actually thought in those terms. My wedding. To Alice. Something vital moved in his heart as he heard himself utter the words.

'Indeed? I am very happy for you. Do you wish to tell me where this bounty came from?'

'In confidence, as I said, it is in the nature of payment owed.'

'I understand.' Richard rose and put out his hand. 'Thank you for coming, my boy, and for being so candid. We will leave all as it lies for the moment.'

In the passage outside Chris found Alice waiting for him. He closed the library door and she said, 'Well? What happened?'

'Weren't you listening at the door?' he teased her.

'Certainly not,' she said, affronted. 'Tell me, what did my uncle say?'

He walked into the hall with her. Some of Richard Ashley's new-found prosperity was evident here. He had brought back with him new wall-hangings and rugs, a great fire was blazing in the hearth, pure white candles—also purchased in Canterbury—were lit, their flames reflected in the newly acquired silver on the tables. I will do the same for Oaks, Chris thought, with a sudden and exultant feeling of joy. He said, 'Richard did not object to the arrangement we have made.'

'Did you explain that you will be leaving soon?'

He took her arm and steered her out into the porch. October was well under way now, and had declared the fast-encroaching winter in a hard frost the night before.

The day was cold and rime still patterned the almost bare branches of the trees lining the drive.

'The summer is over,' Chris said thoughtfully.

'As I was saying— Did you tell Uncle Richard you are going to France?'

'No, I did not. For I have changed my mind over that.'

'Changed your mind?' She looked at him, noticing that in some subtle way he had changed since last they met. She could see no sign of the bitter young cavalier who had relinquished his dream and come home, beaten, to work on an estate no longer his own and impoverished to boot. No evidence, either, of the man resigned to leaving that estate. He had the look now of the old Chris—the free spirit who was unconventional enough to choose his own way, but had somehow come to terms. She wondered what could have happened to cause this new maturity. 'What do you mean?' she asked.

'I mean just that. I had thought my only course to seek a place elsewhere, now I have changed my mind.'

'But what of our. . .agreement?'

'It will remain the same.'

'The *same*? How can it? You made it to protect me— or so you said—from Henry while you were away. If you are not going——' Not going. The words resounded in her heart. But what difference to her if he stayed or went? 'Well, there seems little point in that. You are not anxious to marry me, and I. . .I shall soon be old enough to be that despised thing, an old maid.'

He laughed. There was even a different tone to *that*, she thought. Her frustration turned to anger. If he could be so light-hearted about something that meant *everything* to her. . . She went on bitingly, 'You may laugh, but I would like to have children before I am old enough to be their grandmother!'

A child, he thought, with the same feeling he had had

when he had thought of restoring Oaks. . . A boy, maybe, with her brave ways and frank honesty; a girl, perhaps, with her glinting hair and unexpected femininity. . .

'So?' she said, pulling at the ring on her finger. His mother had been a very small-boned woman—the circle of gold and pearl and diamonds refused to come off.

He said mildly, 'Really, Alice, I think another broken engagement would be rather. . .odd, to say the least. There is a new substance I have heard of. Come out of the New World, it has properties which enable it to bounce back and forth endlessly. . .'

'Don't mock me!'

'I would never do that.' The wind was sharp today, with a suspicion of sleet, and she was lightly clad. It hurt him to see her shivering in the blast while tugging at his ring on her finger. He tried to draw her into the shelter of his arms, but she pushed him away.

At the door, she said, 'Go away, Chris. I think all is plain between us.'

'Not at all,' he said deliberately. 'Now calm yourself. I said to your uncle earlier that I want you to have time to decide, rationally, what it is you want. I meant that. My going to France or not does not affect that which I believe to be true.'

'I *have* decided—'tis you who cannot do so. You speak of this. . .substance, and of bouncing back and forth. Isn't that what you are doing? You bounce away to support the King; you bounce back and sit around tables with the very men who had deposed him. Treason used to be your word for that, Chris.'

He went white around the lips, but held on to his temper, saying calmly, 'Perhaps you are entitled to that comment, perhaps not—but I can't say that I like hearing it, or like you for making it.' Their eyes clashed. But—already regretting her outburst—she must just say one more thing.

'But none of that is what this is about, is it? It's all about *Henry*! You might not like what he did to me, you might have hastened over to Fox to perform your grand gesture with his ring, you might even have considered knocking him down. But you didn't, did you? Instead you are now wondering if he was, after all, in the right.'

'That is not true!'

'Is it not? Then pray explain why you are now his valued *collaborator*! Why you and he and other *traitors* sit at council meetings in perfect amity.'

He was horrified by her accusations. Did she think it had been easy for him? God knew, it had not! Naturally combative, inherently honest, Chris Rokesby had been persuaded to these meetings of the Kentish gentry by Walter Carrington with the greatest misgivings. The members were almost entirely composed of Parliamentarians, some young enough to have fought in the war. But since sitting around tables with them, as Alice had so scathingly put it, he had achieved valuable results. Four of his men had been returned to Ashley, released from foul gaols in the shadow of the hangman's gibbet—reprieved by his efforts. Their womenfolk had come with tears in their eyes to thank him. . .and Alice spoke of treason.

And what she said of Henry was not true. Chris would never forgive or forget his affront to Alice, any more than Henry would forget Chris's part in the outcome. But Chris remembered his former friend's words at Bude. 'There are more ways of winning a war than taking sword in hand.' Surely Alice herself had counselled this a short time ago; now she flung his attempt at diplomacy in his face.

'You seem to be at a loss for words,' she said, trying to read his face and failing.

'A pity we are both not in that state,' he returned. Much of what she said was true; he could not bring himself to argue with her. 'I think you ought to go in; it is very cold now.'

He turned and she said angrily, 'We have not yet settled anything.'

He swung back to her. 'I have told you, Alice. Our agreement still stands. At Christmas——'

'Yes? At Christmas?'

'We'll speak of it again.'

CHAPTER ELEVEN

THE year seemed to run downhill rapidly when autumn was done and true winter set in. Kent was assailed by storms which even the Ancients could not recall experiencing before. For weeks on end rough winds blew and rain fell in torrents. In the first week in December there were two days of hailstones thundering down, then an abrupt pause during which great purple clouds lowered over the countryside. This strange, unearthly state, when it was hard to decide whether it was day or night whatever the clocks said, continued until two weeks before Christmas Eve, then the leaden skies released their burden of snow. At first only a polite frosting coated the bare branches of the trees and hedgerows, then prolonged flurries drifted this way and that, and there fell an endless curtain of white.

Ten days before Christmas Eve the Ashleys received an invitation from Mary Carrington—brought by a youth, half frozen, whom Alice set to thaw before the blazing fire in her hearth—inviting them to join the festivities at Fox Hall for the duration of Yuletide.

'Please, do come,' Mary wrote, 'Chris Rokesby has already accepted, and of course Margaret is already here, and I think it would be so delightful for us all to see in the New Year together.'

Richard waited until after supper that day to show the letter to Alice. Her lot had been considerably improved lately. She no longer had to pinch every penny, or wake in the night and wonder if there would be enough food for those within the manor, let alone in the farmhouses. She had tactfully taken over the administration of the new wealth and used it well. For the past few years

Ashley had limped painfully along, barely keeping its head above the tide of poverty engulfing post-war England. Now Alice laid plans that would ensure the coming year of 1647 would be a return to safety for all at Ashley.

'What do you think to this idea?' Richard asked, rising from the table and going to the fire.

Alice read the invitation again, her brow puckered. ''Tis kind of Uncle Walter and Aunt Mary, but might it not be a little embarrassing? I mean for Chris and Henry and myself to be all together?'

Richard tapped his long-stemmed pipe against the hearthstone. 'I don't think so. After all, we are all such old friends. And Henry appears to have accepted his loss now.'

Alice was silent. She looked out over the glittering scene beyond the windows. No snow had fallen that day and the candlelight from the hall joined the pale moonbeams radiating from a clear sky to turn her gardens into a fairy-land. Henry had not been over in person to Ashley Manor lately, no, but he had written, and his carefully phrased letters had seemed to her to hold some kind of threat. Chris had visited once a week without fail, until the poor weather deterred him, and had held stiff conversations with his betrothed which had torn at her heart.

Each time she saw him riding up the drive, dismounting before the door with his black head exposed to the sleet, a pale sun reflecting off the hard brightness of new snow, she had thought, This time—this time 'twill be different. But it never was. At nights she managed to convince herself that she was wasting her life, and her love, waiting for him to fall into the same state as she continued to be in. But, in the mornings, she thought it better to be contracted to the man she loved without response rather than free to find second-best. For that was what any other man would be to her—second-best.

Now came this prospective added flick to the wounds on her heart. They were invited for a fortnight, for that was how long the season of jollity lasted even in these austere times. They would sit for long hours at a festive table, eating and drinking and making merry. Then they would dance, play games, open gifts each night—and all to be done in the company of two young men. One who bore a grudge against her and would do her harm if he could, the other protecting her against this harm, but for all the wrong reasons.

'So?' Richard enquired. 'What will be our answer?'

Emma had left the table to go out into the kitchens to talk to her maids, but Alice had received an eloquent and pleading glance before she left the table. She said slowly, 'I think my aunt would like to go.'

'Indeed she would,' Richard said. 'And so would I.'

'Very well, then,' Alice said resignedly. She knew as well as any other how dull it could be in rural areas when poor weather set in. She simply could not deprive her aunt and uncle of this pleasure.

In the next few days Alice tried very hard not to be half-hearted about the forthcoming visit, to respond to Emma's chatter over what gifts to take and what offerings of food and wine would be needed, and the urgent message to the village dressmaker—'We must have at least two new gowns apiece, Alice!'—but she began to dread the coming time. It was all too *civilised*, and she thought that at least three of the party could not be so described. . .

Christmas Eve came with a fresh avalanche of snow. Alice woke to a world of white and silver shadows. She dressed and stayed at her window, admiring the dazzling sweep of white—rosy where the rising sun touched it, purple in the shadows. Each tree and shrub had its covering of cream velvet; icicles a foot in length hung from the eaves of the house. As she watched Jack

Madesley came ploughing across the yard beneath her window carrying milk-pails. One of the new grooms stooped to pack a ball of snow in his mittened hands and Jack set down his churns as the snowball caught him square in the chest. The two men had a pitched battle there and then, laughing so hard between volleys that Alice smiled too. She opened her window and leaned out.

'Shame on you, Jack Madesley! On your wedding-day too! Do you think Betty will welcome a bridegroom covered in bruises?' The festivities would begin today with a wedding. Jack and Betty would be joined together at noon in the village church.

Jack brushed the melting snow from his face and grinned. The groom touched his cap. 'Do you want for me to take Julia out for a little exercise, Miss Alice?' Julia was the pretty mare that the Carringtons had given her for her birthday gift. She had proved an excellent riding horse, and was a constant source of delight to her mistress.

'No. . . Yes, perhaps you had better, Joe, for goodness knows I will not have time today, and will not get to her until we ride for Fox Hall.'

'Really, Alice!' Emma came into the bedroom. 'Talking to the men from your bedroom window!' She closed the window. 'I hope you will show more grace at the Carringtons'—'tis already a little scandalous that you be under the same roof as your betrothed without benefit of ceremony. And no prospect of such!' She plumped down on the bed, puffing. She had been up since cock-crow, supervising the packing into baskets of the good cakes and pies she intended taking to Fox. In another basket were delicacies of marchpane and gingerbread, and the sugar-coated fruits which were a special favourite of Walter's. 'If you and Chris would but set the date it would make it more seemly, you know.'

'I know,' sighed Alice. And if it were up to me

'twould be tomorrow—today—this very hour, she
added silently.

'Yes, well. . .' Emma removed her mind from this
aggravating subject and said cheerfully, 'I have put in
with the luggage your gift to Chris, although I still think
it rather personal to be respectable.' Alice's Christmas
present to Chris was a pair of gleaming leather boots—
finest softened hide, fashioned and stitched by the best
cobbler in Canterbury. It was something of a private
joke, for the boots she had carried to him at Naseby had
been an improvement on those he had purloined from
the dead Roundhead soldier but still too small, and—
along with all his other rambling grievances—on the
road to Cornwall there had been a constant litany on the
discomfort of his feet. She had made sure of an exact fit
this time. Old Madge had seen to that by drawing
around a pair of his old shoes on to a piece of paper and
smuggling the result out to Ashley.

'Is there anything I can do, Aunt?' Alice asked.

'No, I don't think so. Betty and I have laid out the
wedding-breakfast in the hall. Richard is attending to
the ale and wine, and Betty is just now putting on her
marriage-gown.' Emma gave her niece an approving
glance. 'You look very pretty, my dear; that new dress
suits you.' Alice was wearing one of the new gowns
made hurriedly for her, and had chosen this material
because it matched her eyes. The other was a honey-
coloured velvet and more formal, in anticipation of the
evenings at Fox Hall to come.

'Thank you, Aunt. I am ready for the wedding and
think we should be in the church just before midday.'

'Plenty of time, but I believe I will change now.'
Emma bustled out.

Alice surveyed herself in the tall glass. Pretty? Yes,
she thought she was in her dove-grey silk, which
appeared blue in the brilliant light. She turned the pearl
ring on her white finger, slid it up and down, reflecting

that perhaps she had lost weight, for in October, when she had wanted to remove it and throw it into the giver's face, it would not budge.

The tiny church was packed to the beams when the Ashleys arrived with Betty. So that the bride could walk with her attendants in some comfort, Jack's friends had been up since dawn, clearing a path through the snow to the little stone building which was fortunately situated not far from the manor. Betty hovered in the porch while Alice peeped inside to make sure that the groom was there. He was, red-faced and nervous-looking, Chris standing by his side, elegantly dressed; Alice was not the only one to have acquired new clothes. He looked over one shoulder and saw her at the door and winked. She withdrew her head and said to Betty, 'I will just alert Master Moran, and then Uncle Richard will take you up the aisle.' Betty gulped. 'Don't be silly now, Betty. 'Tis no more than a little stroll and at the end of it—Jack.' She tiptoed into the church and caught the eye of the organist. He began to play and Alice stood back for Betty to make her stately progress.

It was all over in a quarter-hour. The old days of long drawn-out ceremonies was long gone now—the current religious thinking forbade any pomp and even the exchange of gold rings was a little unorthodox, but Betty had wanted it and so marched triumphantly back down the narrow aisle, the ring on her third finger shining. As they paused outside Chris kissed her on the cheek and pressed an envelope into her hands. 'Read it later, sweetheart.' Betty tucked it into her sleeve and Jack lifted her on to his horse and everyone made their way back to Ashley.

'What did you give her?' Alice asked curiously when every guest had a drink—either a fruit distillation or something more heartening, according to their convictions—and business was brisk around the groaning table.

'A letter from her mother,' Chris said, accepting wine from Richard.

'From Lizzie?' Alice asked guiltily. She had not thought of Lizzie Mote for months.

'Indeed. Would any girl be happy on her marriage-day without greetings from her mother?'

'No. . .'

'Betty wrote to tell of forthcoming events and received her approval. Lizzie wrote separately to me and enclosed something to give to Betty on the great day. She would, of course, have dearly liked to be present but felt that her first duty lay at Gull's Nest.'

'How is it there? Do you know?'

'I do. Really, Alice, you are a poor mistress to your estate.'

'I have had a great many other concerns,' Alice protested. She had, of course, considered Gull's Nest, and Richard had agreed that when Ashley prospered again she could give it more consideration.

'Haven't we all?' Chris said mildly. 'However, everything goes well there. Lizzie seemed to be a little constrained for ready money so I took the liberty of forwarding her a little cash.'

'You sent her money? To use at Gull's Nest, and didn't tell me?'

'As you say, you had other concerns. . . I was glad to help her. The woman nursed me tenderly when I should have been the business of the gravedigger; I don't forget that.'

Later, the company, having eaten and drunk well, became lively. Old country dances were in progress and Betty, blushing, was led out by her new husband in the first.

'Shall we try our luck at this?' Chris asked Alice. 'It looks to me more frightening than an infantry charge, but I am game if you are.'

When the interval came he took Alice and set her in a

chair and brought her wine. He took the seat beside her and said casually, 'I am told you will be at Fox Hall for Yuletide.'

'Yes. You are going and so my aunt and uncle thought——'

'I am sure they did. Walter asked me personally to attend because he thought that Margaret would not enjoy herself if I were alone at Oaks, but I must say I am a little surprised that you accepted.'

'Why? We will be all old friends together, isn't that the idea?'

'Old friends?' Chris raised an eyebrow. 'Do you still regard Henry as an old friend?'

Alice folded her hands in her lap. This very morning had brought another missive from Henry. It was couched in reasonable terms, but conveyed the message that if they were both to be together at Fox in the coming days it would be a chance for their differences to be resolved. She gave Chris a nervous look.

She said quietly, 'I would not wish for there to be any. . .trouble while we are there.'

His glass was empty; he set it down by his chair and took one of her hands. She experienced again the uprush of courage that his presence—his touch—always gave her. He ran one long finger over her palm. 'Don't worry, little Alice. There will be no trouble.'

'But if things should become awkward I would not wish you to jeopardise your new position over it.'

'My treacherous new position, you mean?'

She flushed. 'I should not have said that.'

'An apology? How unusual——'

'I didn't mean what I said, you should know that.'

'And you should know that I would throw my new. . . position over the cliffs of Dover rather than have you discomfited for a moment.'

'Do I know that?' she asked quickly. 'If so——'

Betty was standing before them, her face bright with emotion.

'Oh, Miss Alice, Master Chris!'

'What is it, Betty?' Chris let go of the hand he held.

Betty was holding her letter in her hand. 'This letter from my mam—and this——' She held out her other hand and showed them the small ring on her finger. 'The old mistress gave it her when she was a girl, now she give it to me for my marriage-day.' Alice looked at the ring which her grandmother had given to this girl's mother.

'What are you thinking?' Chris asked as Betty danced away.

'Of this and that. . . . As to Christmas, perhaps it will not take place. There are rumours about that the Long Parliament wishes to ban all such celebrations and Yuletide among them.'

'They have been trying for years to do just that but the English are tenacious about their old ways—especially country folk. I was in Canterbury recently and there were riots in the streets—the working men were playing football in the town square in open defiance of the Mayor's attempts to open the market. It got quite out of hand, with a mob rampaging about and even releasing prisoners from the gaol. 'Twas said that ten-thousand Kentish men have signed a resolution that if they could not have their Christmas Day, they would have the King back on his throne.' He laughed. 'Men like Walter Carrington are finding it increasing tedious being done out of their pleasures and I think you'll find that Fox Hall will keep to the usual traditions, even with Henry as a death's head at the feast.'

'I think it is Henry I am most worried about,' she said quietly. 'That he will provoke you in some way and you will retaliate.'

'He's been provoking me for years and I have not done him injury yet. Besides, you were at pains to point out to me that I had failed in my duty recently in *not* allowing him to provoke me.'

'I shouldn't have said that either.'

He rose and bowed. 'I think with two apologies from you in one day I will leave you while I am ahead in the game. I believe we leave at four?'

In the late afternoon the Ashleys, and Chris with them, set off for Fox Hall. Jack and Betty were to have a little holiday, but join them in three days. The four rode together, their horses picking their way slowly in the snow-filled lanes. Emma kept her eyes anxiously on the groom and the pack pony carrying the provender. The journey, so swift in good conditions, took a lengthy time to accomplish, as the party kept finding their way blocked by drifts too deep for horses and riders, but eventually they were on Carrington land. When the imposing manor was in sight they drew aside to allow a group of men dragging a huge log to pass by. Ten men, up to their thighs in snow, held the ropes and several children sat astride the log. Baritone and high tenor voices floated on the crystal air—'Come, bring with a noise, my merrie, merrie boyes, the Christmas log to the firing. While my good dame, she bids ye all be free and drink to your hearts desiring. . .'

A quiet navy dusk had fallen as they rode up the drive to Fox Hall, Walter came out of his house to bid them welcome and they trooped inside to discard their damp cloaks and be ushered to the fire in the hall. The Yule log had been rolled into place in the great hearth; already orange and blue flames licked its solid weight. It must burn from now until Twelfth Night—a body of servants would take turn to watch its progress, for it boded the poorest luck for this particular fire to go out. When it was done, its ashes, which were said to possess magical properties, would be scattered into the farmland to give added fertility and to protect the house from fire and ill fortune.

Henry was standing by the fireplace. He raised Emma's hand to his lips, then Alice's. He shook hands with Richard and Chris, but the clasp he gave Chris was brief. The visitors sat down, and Mary supervised the handing of pewter mugs of toasted crabs in ale. The crabs were not to be found on any seashore, but were sweet, wild apples served in warm beer, the origin of their appearance in this season as old as the Roman tiles at Oaks.

Alice sat down and linked her fingers around the hot mug. Chris chose to stand behind her chair, Richard and Emma Ashley were together with Margaret Rokesby and the Carringtons on the vast settle.

'Mmm,' Margaret said, sipping her brew. 'Could anything be more pleasant than us eight together at this time?'

'No, indeed,' agreed Walter. 'Tomorrow we will welcome other guests—outsiders—but tonight 'tis just us. Now, what comes first?'

Mary jumped up. 'The Christmas candle!' She went to her cupboard and took out the fat white candle—layer upon layer of beeswax, made with old incantations to an ancient receipt of her grandmother's. She set it on the table before the window, beside a bowl of pot-pourri, and Chris came with his easy graceful stride to light it. 'Do you know the old prayer?' she asked him, her head tilted up to his tallness.

'I do.' He watched the candle-wick curl and straighten to send the flame up to the rafters. He turned to face the assembly. 'Candle light, candle bright, burn with God's grace. Candle light, candle bright, burn with our hopes for the future. Amen.'

'Amen,' agreed the others.

'And now we will eat,' declared Mary.

It was a full meal: brawn and mustard, pike stuffed

with erbage, lamprey and other assorted fish, including halibut, sturgeon and whelks and several fresh-water species, followed by marchpane with almonds, plum and raspberry pies and roasted nuts. When all this had been consumed there came the first game—Snap-dragon. Raisins, currants and other dried fruit were heaped on to a shallow dish. Brandy was poured upon the blue-black mass and set alight. The idea was for the diners to attempt to snatch the fruit from the flames, puff out the fire and eat the fruit. A song accompanied the exercise: 'Here comes the flaming bowl! Don't be mean to take the toll! Snip! Snap! Dragon!'

When the red-hot dish was set before Alice, Chris, seated beside her, caught her hand to prevent her plunging it into the flames. He coolly thrust his own hand in and laid the glistening result upon her plate. She turned her head to look at him and there was an unexpected timeless moment. What she knew about her love for him was an absolute, written in stone, and could never be reversed or changed. Now, amazingly, she thought she saw an answering emotion in his eyes.

He was thinking, My God, I love her! He was stunned by what he felt. As the Christmas candle burned brightly away before the black windowpanes an equally bright light fell upon his soul. Perhaps I have loved her for years, he thought wonderingly, but there has always been some irrelevant obstacle to prevent my admitting it. First our abrasive childhood together, then Henry's prior claim. How unimportant any barrier seemed now. . . For nothing could stop him from having Alice. As they had come to Alice at Gull's Nest, looking across the winter parlour and knowing that she loved him, so the words from the journal surfaced in his mind. Yet it was not quite like that, he thought, not for him. A remembered love? No. Remembered affection and friendship, maybe, but what he was experiencing now was newly born, almost painful in its intensity and force.

The revelation took his breath away; he could only stare dumbly into her blue-grey eyes and feel a heat like a forest-fire run through his veins.

'What is it?' she whispered, half knowing, half disbelieving. 'You look as if you saw ghosts.'

'Perhaps I have. The ghosts of Alice Ashley and Charles Rokesby.'

It was enough for her. She understood, or thought she did. 'So what happens now?' she breathed.

He covered her hand with his. 'Now we play the game, Alice. The old game of pretence.'

'As with King Richard and Blondel?'

'Certainly. The sex of your character is all wrong, but did he not rescue his master from a dark and hopeless place? So have you done for me. For, darling, not to feel what I do now would be to be in just such a place. Now I am out in the light—can you ever forgive me for being so dense?'

She was almost in tears. 'I knew in the moment I came into your sickroom at Gull's Nest. I tried to tell you in the vinery at Ashley. . . Why here? Why now?'

'Who can explain these things?' If he had been alone with her he could have demonstrated exactly these things. Instead he was seated at a table with a chattering group of people, and a cold-eyed devil opposite who was watching their every move. He said, 'We must be careful, my love.'

'Am I your love? Truly?'

'Yes. Have I *ever* lied to you?'

'No. . .'

The meal continued, everyone could eat just a little more, and fresh wine was opened and poured. After supper Walter insisted they play cards. Alice laid down the brightly coloured plaques without thought. She wished that she and Chris were quite alone to discuss their magical state. She still could not quite believe it. Yet in another way she could. The looked for, longed

for expression to mirror her own was now in his eyes
and on his handsome face. Often she found him staring
at her, a little puzzled, a little rueful, but always with a
sort of joy he could not hide.

Henry, too, looked constantly her way. He was sitting
next to Chris at the card table and, knowing him so well,
had immediately detected the vibrations. As the days
had passed each encounter with Rokesby had angered
him more.

He had been astounded by his boyhood friend's
presence in the council chamber of the Guildhall and his
appointment to the justices' ranks. He understood,
naturally, the need for a token representation of the old
guard—the 'named' gentry who had fought on the
'wrong' side, but had not expected Chris to be one of
them. The scene at Fox that he had had with Chris over
Alice was clear-cut in his memory. He knew he had
handled it wisely, but came away with the feeling that—
as usual—Chris had got the better of him. No blows had
been struck, yet his dignity had been deeply offended
because he knew that had not been his choice. Then he
had been confronted by Chris being treated in deferential fashion by his fellow council members. Like Seth
Blake, Henry, in his heart, thought that a beaten man
should know it and act like one. Also, from somewhere,
Chris now had what appeared to be a comfortable
amount of money. Henry had made discreet enquiries
regarding this, but had only been able to ascertain that
it had been paid into the Canterbury bank in the name
of John Smith. Even putting pressure on the owners of
the bank had not elicited the real identity of the donor.

He had tried to strike at Chris over his campaign to
get Ashley Royalists released, but there again Chris had
defeated him. Henry had expected his volatile friend
soon to lose his temper at the debates, to use his nimble
tongue to alienate the stolid members. Instead he had
used all his charm and ability with words to put a

convincing case for these men. But most of all, at the root of all Henry's smouldering hatred, was the question of Alice. She refused to see him still and her uncle—in his mild way—appeared to support her in this, although he obviously had not been told any facts. Richard Ashley appeared to take the view that his niece should not be told her duty but should decide for herself. His own uncle, annoyingly, took the same stand. It was all very frustrating, and Henry badly wanted some sort of revenge.

The evening wore on. Chris, stretching his legs after some hours, went to the window and parted the drapes a little, remarking that another blizzard was in progress and that if it continued they would find themselves snowed in.

Alice, about to take the hand with her queen, paused. Snowed in? The words reminded her. . . Reminded her of the dramatic account of Grandmother Alice's journal, when she too had been snowed in over Yuletide. And the tragic outcome. A rough finger touched Alice's heart. Foolishness! That had been over forty years ago—a different house, different people. . . But what had Uncle Richard often used to say when he had tutored her in history? 'We know the future because we know the past. . .'

'Alice,' Walter said jovially. 'Get your triumph over with, my girl. We all know you have the winning card. Why, what is amiss? You look as if you see ghosts.'

Chris turned from the window and came swiftly to her side. 'What is it?' he asked gently. 'Are you unwell?'

'No. No, but I am tired.' She let fall the Queen of Hearts.

'We all are,' Mary said. 'So let us find our beds, for we have a great many days of merrymaking ahead. Alice, you are in the little room above the porch. Richard and Emma, the best bedchamber——' Mary detailed her guests to their quarters. She had a great deal to do before she could go up; her maids were still working in the kitchens. She and Margaret Rokesby went to see what they were doing and came back to kiss everyone goodnight.

'The maids are baking their Dumb Cakes,' she chuckled to Chris. 'Although who they think will come on a night like this——!'

One Christmas tradition taken seriously by every spinster in the parish was the making of a little cake, which they pricked with their initials and placed in the oven. The belief was that when the cakes were removed the initials of their future husbands would be etched beside their own. In every household, large and small, throughout England a great many naughty pages and stable-boys had a deal of fun with this superstition.

'Have you not prepared one of these offerings?' Chris asked Alice as he kissed her lightly on the forehead at the foot of the stairs.

'No,' she said, giving her radiant smile. 'For I already know your initials, Chris.' The moment of foreboding had gone; she was so happy again that she could have scandalised her aunt and the other ladies by running to the top of the stairs and sliding back down the curving banisters as she had used to do at eight years old.

Days of fun followed days of fun. Walter's other guests were not deterred by the weather and arrived as invited on Christmas Day. Alice manoeuvred so that she could give Chris his special gift alone. She waited on the landing windowseat until he came in search of her, then made him sit down and drew the curtains across before them. She watched him remove the boots from their wrapping. 'Well? Do you like them?'

'Who would not?' He ran his fingers over their shining length, turned them about to admire the stitching, felt inside the lining of soft lambswool. 'Thank you, thank you.' He looked at her.

'Have you nothing for me?' she asked. His eyes held hers.

'You are getting me — is that not enough for you?'

'Yes. It is enough,' she breathed. Being near to him when all the love between them came from her had been tormenting enough, now their desire for each other was almost a tangible thing to be touched and tasted.

'However,' he said, 'I have done my duty.' He put a square box in her hands. She opened it and discovered the creamy pearls nestling on dark blue velvet.

'Oh! They are beautiful.'

'Betty told me that you sold yours to give her her dowry.'

'But these are much finer. . .' She fastened them around her throat, her fingers lingering on the smooth flushed beads. 'Do they suit me?'

'Everything suits you.' He bent his black head to kiss her. It was a restrained salute, but she valued it more than his passionate response in the vinery six months ago.

The curtains were pulled roughly open and Henry looked down on them.

'If you have no care for Alice's reputation, Chris,' he said softly, 'please remember that she is a guest in my house and as such under my protection.'

Chris sprang up. 'I have seen evidence of your protection!' he returned in equally soft tones, but with a chilling edge to his voice.

Alice quickly got up. The two men were standing at the head of the long flight of stairs — a dangerous place to argue. 'Please, let us go down to the others,' she said, putting a timid hand on Henry's arm.

Chris looked at Henry, then at her hand, perhaps debating whether he would snatch it away and throw his host down the steps. Instead, he took Alice's arm and they all turned and descended the stairs together.

'You promised,' she said to him as they took their

seats around the table. The plump geese, their succulent
flesh hardly able to contain the rich stuffing, were
already before Walter for carving, and Mary had dishes
of the best from her vegetable garden for dispensing.
Servants moved to and fro carrying platters of more
food than twice the assembly could consume. Each glass
had been filled to the brim with ruby wine.

'I did no promising about this,' Chris answered.

'Please, please,' she begged. 'If anything should
happen to you——'

'Nothing will happen,' he assured her, but he kept his
blue eyes on his plate so she would not see the storm in
them. He had thought himself capable of spending this
time with Henry without incident. But had not bar-
gained for his heightened senses regarding Alice. Could
not have foreseen that his fury in the autumn would be a
pale shadow of what he felt now on recalling the dark
marks of assault. . . 'I will avoid the occasion for sin, as
the clerics used to say.'

New Year's Eve came and the ladies retired early to
their bedchambers to put on their best gowns and
prepare for the long night of revelry. Alice removed her
velvet dress from its tissue and put it on, turning this
way and that before the glass. Betty, back to her duties
after an ecstatic 'honeymoon', had agreed to act as maid
to several of the other ladies, but before going to them
she had brushed and put up her own lady's hair.
Gathered in a little bun at the back of the head, the knot
of hair was fitted into a jewelled coif then its curls pulled
out again to frame the face; Alice was pleased with her
coiffure. The dress, too, delighted her, although she was
a little doubtful of its neck—rather lower than was
decorous, even with its lace collar. Still, the other
visiting ladies had defied the conventions frequently in
the last week, and how well Chris's pearls looked lying

above the warm swell of her bosom just discernible through the smooth velvet.

Coming down the stairs, she saw Chris waiting at the foot, one arm casually over the carved newel post. He looked up and saw her, and she slowed her pace while his eyes travelled over her. He took her hand and led her into the hall.

Good Lord, he thought wryly, as he saw the other men assess her appreciatively. I hope I am not going to turn out to be the kind of husband who cannot bear another man to look at his wife. If so, I am going to be unhappy for a long time. Had she always been so beautiful? He supposed yes; it was the added ingredient of being in love with her that made him notice also how desirable she was.

Over supper one of the ladies said, 'Now, Walter, do tell us if we are to appoint a Lord of Misrule for this special night!'

Walter eased his clothing surreptitiously, to allow for all the food he had eaten. 'Hrrumph!' He glanced uneasily at Henry. 'We think it not quite appropriate in the—er—circumstances to—er—lend ourselves to too much—er——'

There was a murmur of disappointment, but all present understood what he meant. The Puritans had fought long and hard over every religious festival since gaining power. Their insistence that most were rooted in paganism was quite true, of course, although their main objection was over the amount of drinking and dancing and gambling—the other immoral revelry— associated with the occasions. Christmas had been harder to get rid of because, although surrounded in practices descended from older religions than Christianity, its real purpose was to celebrate the birth of Christ, and English people felt entitled to mark *that*.

Henry, in his discussions with Walter about the

forthcoming festivities, had managed to whittle away at the more outlandish Christmas practices—for they were, he had pointed out, mainly Popish in their origins. Since Walter was first and foremost a strong Protestant he had not argued against Henry's suggestion that they have no mince pies topped with pastry 'babies' representing the Christ child, or the Nativity Feast with its definitely Roman Catholic prayers, or the burning of the holly bush to honour Moses' role. . . Henry's list of prohibition had been lengthy, but Walter had managed to make it clear that he would have his good food and wine and jolly games and had wanted to have one of the gentlemen take the part of the naughty Lord of Misrule, whose lightest command everyone must obey. But Henry had been adamant about this point and Walter, who had in the past spent this season in other—grander—houses than his own, and knew that such rule events could become rather bawdy, had given way.

The meal concluded, the village orchestra of fiddles and lutes and pipes struck up and everyone danced. A great many gentlemen would have liked to partner Alice, and thought it rather unsporting that her betrothed always seemed to be there to deny them. Despite enjoying her popularity Alice had no wish to be in any other arms, but wondered what Chris would say if Henry came to claim her. He did not, however. In fact he did not join the dancing at all, but stood drinking at the hearth.

Midnight came and went, and again certain gentlemen were disappointed in their efforts to kiss pretty Miss Ashley, due to Master Rokesby's adroit manoeuvring, and the company, slightly exhausted now, settled down to a few games to round off the evening. At the last they played Hot Cockles.

No one seemed to know where this odd game had come from, but it was played thus: one person knelt with his back turned to the rest of the company. He—or she—was then blindfolded and must hold out his hands behind him, palms upwards. Then someone from the watching assembly must be appointed the 'bandit'. The person kneeling shouted, 'Hot Cockles! Hot!' and the bandit crept up and touched—or tapped—the upturned hands. If the blindfolded one could guess who the bandit was then he must take his place, and the game began again.

It was a very good-natured affair, with much giggling and whispering. Then Alice, tiptoeing up behind her uncle, was named and so had to kneel to take her turn. She let Mary slip the dark mask around her eyes, then called, 'Hot Cockles! Hot!' and waited for the touch, sure that she would never be able to guess who it was unless it would be Chris—she was sure that she could recognise his hand on hers in any situation.

Henry, who had taken no part in the game so far, chose at this moment to do so. He came up behind Alice and dealt her a stinging blow with his clenched fist. She winced and withdrew her hands. Chris, who had also decided that he was better employed enjoying the wine and the sight of his love enjoying herself, moved out of the shadows. He confronted Henry.

'God damn you! How dare you?' He bent and helped Alice to her feet, turning her hands over and pressing his lips to the reddening palms. He removed the covering and looked reassuringly into her eyes. Henry closed in.

'You speak blasphemy in my house! How dare *you*?'

Walter hurried forward. 'Now, boys! 'Tis but a game, you know. A little boisterous, Henry!' He frowned at his nephew. 'But no harm done, I'm sure. Alice?'

'No, indeed,' Alice got out. 'I was just a little. . . surprised, is all.'

Walter looked at Chris. 'There. So let us leave it now. Damn fool game anyway. Hunt the Slipper now. 'Tis already hidden and a good prize for the winner. Alice, you come with me, and we'll get a good start.' He put his arm around Alice and led her away. The others followed uncertainly, leaving the two young men where they stood.

'A nice display,' Henry said.

'You think so?'

'To attack me so in my own home, yes, I do.' He turned away, but Chris laid a light hand on his arm. 'What?' He tried to stare the other man down, but Chris had too much personal dignity to be set aside.

Chris withdrew his hand and met Henry's eyes. 'You must answer for what you have just done,' he said softly.

'In what way?'

'In any way you choose.' There was a silence; one of Walter's giant hunting hounds lying before the fire discovered an itch and scratched himself noisily.

'I think you should be careful,' Henry said at length.

'I am being very careful,' Chris returned. 'But once before I allowed you to treat Alice so—this time I cannot let it pass. I may appear to you to have found a. . .respectable skin of late, but you know me from the old country. Am I clear? My friend?'

'Friend?' Henry muttered. 'We used to be that, each to the other, but you have let this. . .woman come between us. Have you thought about that, Chris?'

'I have. But no man is my friend who treats any woman so. I said to you at Gull's Nest that we have both come a long way, Hal. We have, and it is a different way. *That* I can come to terms with, and hope you may in time do the same. But over Alice there is no negotiation.'

'What do you suggest, then? Pistols at dawn?'

Margaret Rokesby, who had missed most of the games to supervise the activity in the kitchens, now entered the hall. She came to them.

'Chris! I'm glad you are down here, I have so wanted

to have a little talk with you. But if you are in private conversation with Henry, I can——'

Henry said quickly, 'Do have your talk with Chris, Margaret. I will join the others.' He glanced at Chris. 'Another time, then?'

'Definitely,' Chris agreed.

When Alice came down a little later she found Margaret and Chris sitting before the fire chatting, and Henry nowhere to be seen. Thank God, she thought as Chris rose to give her his chair. The three stayed talking of this and that until the others came streaming down the stairs for nightcaps and a last bite of something to eat before retiring.

'Tired?' Chris asked Alice when he took her to her room two hours later.

'A little. But happy. Come in with me and talk a little?'

He opened the door, but did not enter. 'No, sweetheart. I am almost totally reformed now, but to be alone with you—in your bedchamber—that might try my new respectability too far.'

'Nothing happened between Henry and you? After the. . .game, I mean?'

'What should have happened?' he asked. 'Perhaps I took your good advice and remembered my. . . position.'

'I'm glad.' She reached up to kiss him and she saw that his eyes were a hot, bright blue. 'Are you going to bed now?'

'Where else?' He pushed her gently into her room and closed the door.

She undressed slowly. In two days she would be gone from here, and Chris too. Then she would be back at Ashley and would plan her marriage. A marriage she had not been able to believe in truly, but now she could. She went to the window and looked out. A frozen world, she thought, but I am warm—warmed in the knowledge that the man I love loves me also. She hugged herself in anticipation of the rest of her life with that man, but something was nagging at her mind. She turned away from the quiet view from the window and sat down on the bed.

I cannot sleep just yet, she decided, and will read awhile. Upon this thought her candle sank in its liquid wax and died. She exclaimed in annoyance. She could rouse one of the maids and ask her for a replacement, but it was so late. . . She would just go down to the hall and take one of the many tapers still alight there.

On the stairs she could hear voices, and identified them immediately as belonging to Chris and Henry. She stopped, her heart pounding, then heard the door to the gardens open and close. She hurried on down and peered out of the window.

Two figures were etched black against the snowy landscape. Henry and Chris in violent argument. As she watched, Henry raised his arm and her mind slipped a cog and she could see, as clearly as the dark figures, her grandmother's writing in her journal. Her heart, racing already, seemed to beat in her throat. No! she thought desperately. Such things cannot happen! But then one of the figures moved and came towards the house. Henry opened the door and came in, slamming it behind him.

He would have passed her without a word but she said to him, 'What has happened, Henry?'

He turned to her, his eyes blank. She looked back out of the window and saw that Chris had disappeared.

'Where is Chris?' she asked. 'Where has he gone?'

'Straight to hell, I hope,' Henry said politely. 'Excuse me please, Alice.' He climbed the stairs and disappeared around the bend.

The snow had frozen hard underfoot that day, but

Alice heard the sound of delicate hooves upon it. She looked out again and saw Chris pass the window, spurring his mount to a speed which did not take account of the bitter conditions.

CHAPTER TWELVE

MINUTES passed and Alice remained as if frozen at the window. Fox Hall, beneath its blanket of snow, was cradled in a great silence. At last she became aware of the sound of the uneven beating of her heart, and her mind began to function again. Impossibly, what she had so dreaded had come about. History was about to repeat itself. Henry and Chris had quarrelled in exactly the same way as two other men had, all those years ago. One or other of them had called for a duel, and Chris had gone home, just as his great-uncle had, and tomorrow— Oh, but it could not be true! It was too fantastic! But. . . Her life had been fantastic in its parallel with the old story so far, had it not? Surely the tragic finale would be the same.

In her agitation she had been wandering in circles around the room. She stopped and stood perfectly still, summoning self-control and courage. Surely the girl who had undertaken to take help to a soldier on a battlefield many miles from her home, who had protected that soldier from the surgeon's knife and then half dragged him another hundred miles to safety, could now do something about this situation. She thought of all the other trials she had had at Ashley over the past years. She had solved them, had she not? But what to do? Talk to Henry? Beg him to reconsider? But, no, what would he care for that? If he should wound or kill Chris, that would please him very well—or, should it be the other way around, Chris would be equally finished. Henry's comrades had shown themselves prepared to accept a Royalist into their ranks on sufferance, but if that man should attack one of their number——

276

No, she must talk to Chris. Plead with him. He *loved* her; surely he could put away his pride rather than cause her the utter misery she would be in if he threw everything away. But pride was such an inherent part of his nature, it was hard to imagine him compromising it. But she must try, and at once. How to go about it? He would have gone to Oaks, a short enough ride in normal conditions, but hazardous in this weather. She went to the window and looked out. Perhaps it would be possible—there was a full, bright moon—if she could only ask someone for help. Jack Madesley was the ideal person, of course, but where was he quartered? She could hardly go searching in the men's accommodation for him. Betty? Oh, no, she would raise so many objections that it would be morning before she was done arguing. No, she must go alone to the stables, find and saddle Julia. She looked down at her lovely dress—quite unsuitable for this enterprise, but she dared not go up to change for fear someone would stop her. Quietly she let herself out of the house and, lifting her skirts, took the path to the stable-yard. The Carrington servants had cleared all the paths in the vicinity of the manor and she had no difficulty taking Julia from her warm stall and finding a saddle.

Beyond the boundaries of Fox Hall it was a different story. The lanes had been partially cleared by farm traffic, but were treacherously icy and, when she left Carrington land and pursued her way to Oaks, the going was slow indeed. The snow reached her feet in their thin satin slippers, dragged at her trailing skirts. Julia's breath came in smoky streamers as she laboured on, and it was so cold. Cold. Within a quarter-hour she was soaked to the knees, and chilled to the bone.

Gaining the short drive to Oaks Manor, sheltered by the trees which gave the manor its name, she saw that the house was in darkness. But no, as she drew nearer she could just make out the flicker of candle and firelight in the hall. She got stiffly off her horse, and stumbled like an old woman to the door and raised the knocker. For several minutes there was no movement from within, then the door opened and Chris stood there. He raised the candle he held and its light shone on her face.

'What——? Alice! What on earth——?' He set the candle down and picked her up and carried her in.

'Julia,' she got out between chattering teeth.

'In a moment.' He put her down on a settle before the newly lit fire and, seizing the poker, thrust it into the flames. The damp logs sputtered and smoked, but a brighter blaze appeared. Turning back to her, he knelt and removed her sodden shoes. 'Now your dress?' He half lifted her and fumbled with the buttons. She should protest, she thought, but it all seemed so natural somehow. She was cold and wet and had come to Chris and he was caring for her, in his casual capable way, with no particular awareness in his gentle hands.

When she was in her shift he took a lap-robe from another chair and tucked it around her. He scooped up her discarded clothing. 'What extraordinary armour you women wear,' he remarked, without a trace of embarrassment. 'I marvel how you get through a day of eating and drinking and even dancing. Your dress is ruined, I fear, and also——' he grinned '—probably your reputation. I am alone here—even old Madge is visiting her cronies in the village. Why have you come? No, don't say anything yet. I must see to poor Julia.'

Alice stretched out her hands and feet to the fire; the feeling was coming most painfully back now. When Chris returned she was warm and oddly drowsy. He went to a cupboard for mugs and, brushing off the poker and heating it, scalded wine.

'Drink this.'

The liquid burned her mouth but completed the cure. She looked at him over the rim of the mug. How had she expected him to look and act? She did not know, but certainly not like this. He had taken a chair outside of the circle of light from the fire and she could not see his face when he asked her again.

'Why have you come?'

The best way was the straightforward way, she decided. 'I saw you arguing with Henry earlier, I guessed that it was about me, and I have come to. . .beg you not to go through with what you have arranged.'

'What is it you think we have arranged?'

'Why—to fight. . .a duel.'

He gave a shout of laughter. 'A duel? With Henry? My dear Alice, why should I wish to do that?' His voice was teasing, but there was a note in it she did not recognise.

She flushed, and her voice was not steady as she said, 'I am wrong, then? Well, I'm glad. . .'

'You don't sound it. You thought I was so enraged that Henry should mistreat you again that I would challenge him?'

'I don't know what I thought. . .' The shock of seeing him and Henry apparently reliving an old nightmare, of her feverish imaginings, of her horrible journey here and her present humiliation in finding out that she had reacted in such a melodramatic way, was too much for her. She burst into tears.

Still he did not move from his seat, but said mildly, 'Well, don't cry for joy, my dear. If it makes you feel any better, I did indeed ask Henry to account for himself, and he took such exception to my words that he forgot his Puritan ethics and challenged *me*. But don't worry, I refused him.'

'You. . .refused him?'

'Certainly. I have no intention of risking the faint possibility that his aim might be in for once.'

She lifted a corner of the robe and dabbed at her eyes. 'I see. You must think me a fool coming here like this.'

'I am always glad to see you, Alice, you should know

that. How you will explain it to your aunt and uncle—let alone the Carringtons—I have no idea.'

'Oh, don't tease me! Just call me a romantic fool, and I will agree with you!'

'What has any of this to do with romance? The word implies love. Do you actually know anything about love, Alice?'

'You can ask me *that*? When you know what I feel.'

'I'm not sure I do know what you feel,' he said in a considering way. 'You fell in love with me very suddenly, after all.'

'As you did with me! How is it different?'

He reached for the bottle which he had set on the hearth. 'How different? In this way: it is not, and I quote, "an old remembered love", Alice. It is something completely new and unique. I don't love you because we share history together—either our own or our ancestors'. I love you for what and who you are now.' She could not see his face, but hers was clear to him in the leaping flames. He watched her consider his words, frown as she tried to understand them, then went on, 'You read that ancient journal, and so did I, but we received different messages from it. I, for instance, did not *like* the personalities contained therein. Not my great-uncle, for realising his love for a married lady, but continuing to play her friend. For that is what he did, is it not? Continued to come to her home, in the absence of her husband—his friend—and act in some martyred way? I did not care for her behaviour either. To receive him, to allow him to know that she returned his affection with no hope of the situation ever being resolved. You and I are not like that. You are not like the first Alice Ashley, for your loyalty—once given—is absolute. When you discovered that you had made a mistake with Henry you told him as immediately as you could. And I did the same this night. I told Henry that I loved you, that our. . .arrangement, made for practical purposes on my part in the first instance, was now renewed for the reason of my love for you. A love which will never change, never die.' He saw her doubtful face change as he said this, but he had not finished yet. 'Also, I did not much sympathise with Edward Ashley. I feel, instead of calling out his best friend, he would have done better to turn his wife over his knee and give her a sound spanking.'

Alice sat up. The robe slipped from her bare shoulders and her arms gleamed in the firelight. Her extreme slenderness, the strong and determined bones of face and jaw, blurred in the soft light, gave her an appearance of vulnerability.

Chris turned his beaker in his hands. Perhaps he had said enough. His instinct was to go to her, to take her in his arms and go no further with this discussion. But it was too important to him for that. Alice was too important to him to deny her the chance of understanding. He said, 'I'm sorry if this is not what you want to hear.'

'I want to hear it,' she said, lifting her chin.

'Very well, then. Yes, I could have accepted Henry's challenge. God knows I wanted to. . . Probably I would have killed him, but it might have been the other way around. If so, then maybe I would have been content in those last moments. I would gladly die for you, Alice, but would much rather *live* for you. And that is why I asked you if you knew anything about love. For, to me, love is all kinds of different emotions, making up the whole. Living at Oaks—I love my home, Alice, I realised how much when it was no longer mine—with the woman I love more than even these blessed sticks and stones, could be a kind of paradise for me. I want to spend the rest of my life here with you, making strong children, sitting across the table at meals with you, probably in dispute over some matter or other—for we will not change overnight, you and I—growing old with

you. I want to see our sons and daughters going out into
the world from the porch of Oaks, knowing that they
have your sweet blood in them as well as mine. But you
are crying again, darling——'

'Take no notice of that,' she said. 'But go on with
what you are telling me.'

'Very good, if that is what you want. . . Do you
remember what that poor tutor we had a long time ago
during the time of sickness used to say? He used to insist
that the past makes us what we are. We agreed with
him—for not to do so resulted in a crack across the
knuckles with his cane. But I didn't believe that then,
and I don't now. I believe that each man—and woman—
is moulded by the circumstances they find themselves in
in their particular moment in time. We cannot be
forever looking back. I suppose many people thought
that I was doing just that when I enlisted on the side of
the King during the war. Looking back. To time after
time when Rokesbys had stood up for, and with, their
monarchs. But I went to war simply because I dislike
having my life ordered. Once there, I discovered
another cause for fighting, but it had no relation to the
high-flown ideals of many of my comrades. I fought
each battle, did the best I could in every engagement,
because I knew that in so doing I could in some way
protect those comrades. . . You accused me of spending
two years fighting an enemy I hated and despised, but
that was not so. I did not hate and despise them,
because I did not *know* them.'

He paused to refill his glass yet again, and she said,
'You are always so good to your friends.'

'Hmm. I have tried to be. You also accused me of
turning you away because of my greatest friend—
Henry. Perhaps at first this was so. I tried, really *tried* to
like the man I loved when he came back from the war,
Alice. I tried to understand that his convictions were
genuine, that he had changed, but that beneath the

veneer he was still the same. All that reasoning worked quite well until he molested you. Then I discovered a strange thing: it is possible to love someone and yet dislike them intensely. For that is how I felt on viewing your bruises, Alice. Dislike. For whatever reasons he had attacked you I still loved him. Then I rode over to Fox and talked with him and found that I didn't like him. And one should like one's friends, you know.' The young Chris showed itself in his voice just then, and Alice could have wept again, but stifled her tears and let him go on. 'So I did that outrageous thing—I told him that I intended marrying you myself and he could take the situation or leave it. Later Henry and I came into conflict again. He fought me over the release of my men, Oaks men, who had gone to war and were now confined in prison. That was a mean thing to do, and I disliked him afresh. But there still were the old remembered seeds of friendship in my soul. I found I could forgive him for that. But tonight. Tonight, I relinquished that friendship forever. When he struck you during that ridiculous game I thought, How dare he do so? But I also thought, He loves her and 'tis the frustration of that emotion making him act so. Even so, I had to tax him with it. When the rest of the company had gone to their beds I invited from him an explanation. At first he would not answer. He found my attitude so intimidating that he left the hall and went out into the snow. There he told me. . . He told me that, far from loving you, his greatest wish was to marry you in order that he might show you your place.' Chris looked into his glass. 'I have heard many strange reasons for marriage, but never that one before. . . Anyway, then I lost my temper, and there followed recriminations on both sides. With him recalling incidents from our childhood long-forgotten by me. . . With me daring him to say again that he wanted you to wife just to. . .to—— It was a desperate scene, Alice, and ended in the way I

have described to you earlier. Now I suppose you will
be truly amazed that I did not agree to meet him in the
coming dawn.'

'No, I am not amazed,' she said composedly. 'For
what has he to do with us?'

'He is. . .not to do with us?' he repeated.

'No indeed,' she said briskly. 'For we have moved on
from such things. Have you not just been telling me
that? The past, Chris, that is where Henry and all such
memories belong. We are different people now, is that
not so? Those we still love—and there are some, you
know—must understand that, or become memories too.'

He thought about what she had said, then, 'I agree,
so there is little more to say, except that earlier I said
that I would rather live for you than the alternative. I
meant that. But will we start our life together with you
wondering why I chose not to fight for you? Why I have
come tamely home this night?'

'No, for I think that it was harder for you to come. . .
tamely home than the reverse. You might have taken
Henry on with pistol or sword, but the real battle you
engaged in was with your own self in not doing so, and
that is the one which counts with me.'

She laughed. Oh, that laugh, he thought. That joyous
laugh. I would know it anywhere and will be hearing it
for the rest of my days. . . He said, 'I'm still a beginner
in the new games I shall have to play. I might fail.'

'Not so. Failure is not in your nature, once you have
made up your mind. That is the hard part for you.
No——' She raised a hand and again the firelight
shimmered on her body. 'I take back that comment for
fear you will say that I am remembering the old Chris,
and I have set my mind to regarding you in a totally
different way. Once I hated that thought—that those I
thought I knew might change—now I see it is the natural
and right order of things. One question I must ask,
though.'

'Do so.'

'Where will I sleep for the rest of this night? With old Madge not in residence as chaperon?'

'Where would you think? Bearing in mind that this is the house of a poor Royalist soldier, who consequently has no means to employ servants to do his bidding as to domestic chores. My own bed is the only one at this time free from damp and mould.' Chris might have changed in many ways, but certain priorities were still in place.

Alice laughed again. 'Am I supposed to believe that? When I know that every able woman within twenty miles has been here scrubbing and cleaning for you?'

At last he felt he could move from his neutral place. He came to her and knelt by her chair. 'You may believe it,' he said, putting his arms around her. 'Have I *ever* lied to you?'

LEGACY *of* LOVE

Coming next month

THE GOLDEN LURE
Juliet Landon
Airedale and York, 1350

Two years after the ravages of the Black Death life was hard,
but Ginevra Mallard's life at the priory was unaffected—until
the prioress sent her home. Her brother Alan had not paid
fees for two years and, once home, her skills as an
embroiderer were not needed. What was she to do?

Alan's liege lord offered a solution—but Sir Jais de la Roche
was altogether too powerful and disturbing physically for
Ginny to countenance marriage to him! Like a trapped bird,
Ginny fought for her freedom, but the lures Jais offered were
hard to resist…

A LADY OF INDEPENDENT MEANS
Sarah Westleigh
Regency 1815

In accompanying her aunt Amelia, the Dowager Countess of
Nazeby, to Paris, Miss Louisa Finsham had no idea what
would be revealed of her aunt's life. A visit to the battlefields
of Waterloo opened the floodgates, but the visit did not
please Lord Hugh Deverill. Nor did he like Louisa's apparent
encouragement of certain gentlemen, when it was clear she
had no intention, or need, of marriage. Such strictures did not
sit well with Louisa, who set out to teach Hugh a
lesson—one that backfired on them both.

LEGACY of LOVE

Coming next month

THE YANKEE
Kristin James
Texas 1868

Margaret Carlisle was 'on the shelf', having spent the better part of her twenty-two years looking after her siblings, and forced to live off the charity of her carping aunt. But all that changed when the Yankee walked into her life… Ex-Union colonel Andrew Stone had had his fill of grudging 'southern hospitality'. His marriage to respectable Miss Carlisle would make life a lot easier for his young daughter, and love would never complicate *this* union—no matter how bewitching Margaret's eyes began to look!

THE RAVEN AND THE SWAN
Laurie Grant
Northumberland 1536

Kyloe Priory was to be dissolved, by order of King Henry VIII—and its new owner, Sir Miles Raven, was expected any day.

The Prioress was dying, and novice Gillian Mallory wouldn't leave her, even though this meant she would be left alone shortly, with nowhere to go. Unexpectedly, Miles proved a tower of strength, and helped her to return to her home, Mallory Hall. But even here, the intrigues of the Tudor court reached out to snare them.

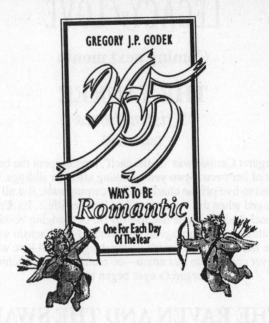